NO JUSTICE
NO PEACE

K Noct 06

NO JUSTICE
NO PEACE

"The return of Kiley Jacoby Abrams in *How Can I Be Down?*"

by
Brenda M. Hampton

Published by Voices Books & Publishing
P.O. Box 3007
Bridgeton, MO 63044
www.voicesbooks.homestead.com

Printed in the United States of America
First Printing March 2005

Library of Congress Catalog Cord No: Pending

ISBN 0-9761410-8-6

ACKNOWLEDGEMENTS

I can't believe this is novel number seven! Thank you Lord for opening my eyes so that I could find my talents. I give all praises to you for making me the gifted and successful writer that I've become.

As always, to my family, I appreciate your continued support through this journey I take. I am blessed for you all and I know that I could not make it without each of you extending your love and generosity.

To my dedicated readers who I promised a shout out in this novel: Michelle Armistad, Toni McDaniel (girl you are off the chain), Nicole Mickens and the wonderful Tina Price. Thank you so much for talking my novels up to many of your friends. I am grateful and your kindness will stay with me forever.

Finally, to the VOICES family of authors. Thank you for allowing the Voices Team to assist with your literary works. I wish you all much success and I enjoy working with each and every one of you.

D.S. Bailey
Up In Flames
www.middlepassage.homestead.com

Nikki Loyd
Memoirs of Sin
www.nikkiloyd.homestead.com

Lesley Nowlin
Dirt Ball Bad

W.S. Burkett
The Pleasure Seeker

INTRODUCTION

It's crazy how life is; one minute you're here and the next minute you're gone. Being locked down in prison for damn near ten years, I might as well have been dead. It was pure deep hell and definitely wasn't no place for a man like me to be. Yes, I killed those who murdered my daddy, and yes, I'd for surely done away with the fool who killed my brother, Kareem. But, I wasn't a threat to society. I didn't just kill people for nothing. If anything, I knew I couldn't depend on the judicial system, and if I had to take matters into my own hands, so be it. To this day, I have no regrets for what I'd done. I do, however, regret being in a place where some motherfuckers just don't give a shit. Many have killed for the fun of it, or just because they didn't have shit else to do. But, who in their right mind would want to come to a place like this? Papa Abrams, my daddy, said prison was no picnic and he for damn sure didn't lie. He'd had many connections before he was killed and I was lucky that many of those brothas still remembered the legacy he'd left behind. I made friends easily, but for many of the other brothas, especially the younger ones, that simply wasn't the case.

I'd listened to them many of nights, as they cried for their Mama's to save them. No doubt, they were turned into instant bitches, and there wasn't a damn thing they could say or do about it. There were many brothas locked up for stupid shit like: car jackings, robberies, and minor drug possessions. They hadn't a clue the price they'd have to pay after being put behind bars. It was more than anyone could imagine, and in a place like this, even their mamas couldn't save them now.

For me, the only good thing about being in here was seeing my boy, Quincy. We saw each other on occasion. The guards were sure to keep us far apart as much as possible, but the times we saw each other, that's what kept me sane. He'd gained his respect before I got here, and for a white boy, who still considered himself a colored man, having so much respect on the inside was rare. Either way, we still had each other. Our bond was like no other. I'd always known how strong our bond was, but when he took the wrap for what I'd done, I looked at him in a different way. He was blood to me, and if anyone ever crossed him, they'd have to answer to me.

I guess being so down on myself for being in here was my own damn fault. It wasn't like I didn't have love on the outside because I did.

1

My son Desmon's mother, Ginger, begged to come visit me, but I refused to let her do so. I never wanted Desmon to see me like this and all I had were pictures from when he was five years old, up until now. I'll be damned if he didn't grow up to look like Kareem. And even though Kareem had been gunned down right in front of me, I knew having Desmon in my life again would be like having my brother once again.

Not only that, but my ex-girlfriend Jada wrote me from time to time. Lord knows I didn't expect to hear from her, but her letters were just a little something else I could hang on to. Eventually, she made arrangements to visit me and seeing her sometimes was like a breath of fresh air. After all the hurt she'd caused me in the past, she was there for me once again. We'd reminisce about how crazy our relationship was and about how much Kareem hated her. I knew he was probably in Heaven upset with me for keeping in touch with her, but again, she was something to keep me going. From time to time, she'd put money on Quincy and my books and made sure we had just about everything we needed.

Recently, though, her latest letter informed me that she'd gotten married. She mentioned her dope-slanging fiancé every once in a while and I told her not to have any regrets. Why wait on a motherfucker behind bars anyway?

At first, my appeals appeared to be hopeless. And even if I were released, there was no guarantee I'd even trust Jada again. Ya see, my trust for women had definitely come to an end. After Officer Candi Campbell pretended to be someone she wasn't, not only did I have little respect for women, but for the police as well. Years ago, Candi worked her pussy on me for months to get a confession. But after all is said and done, I'm going to have the last and final laugh. Revenge is so sweet and I've tasted it each and every day I've been in here. Bottom line, my lawyer insisted there were too many FBI fuck-ups. He continued to pursue my case for years, and since there was never any evidence found against me, and I continued to proclaim my innocence, there was no way to keep me behind bars. My man Quincy was in the same predicament. Yes, he'd confessed, and he'd been convicted. Money had a way, though, of working shit out for a brotha. According to our attorney, Mr. Bradshaw, the police scared both Quincy and me into confessing. All they had was bags full of money, and according to us, we didn't know

2

who it belonged to. There were no drugs, certainly no weapons that connected Quincy or me to the murders, and when the time came for Candi to testify, she broke down on the stand and pleaded the fifth. That itself, wasn't enough to keep me behind bars for the rest of my life.

I'm sure she knows I'm on my way out. The police probably got her and that bitch Veronica under police protection, while at the same time, plans to keep a close eye on me. Honestly, Quincy and I want those bitches bad for how they played us. I've dreamed about snapping Candi's neck plenty of nights, and all I think about was the smirk on Veronica's face when the officers cuffed me and escorted me to the police car. Even though Candi had fallen in love with me, she fucked herself by not testifying. Had she done that, maybe things would be different. Who knows? But, I know I'm delighted to be getting out of this motherfucking place. I can't wait to see my son, and to have sex with Ginger again. In her letters, she talked about what my release day would be like. How much sex we would have. Moreso, how desperate she is to feel me again. She's definitely no desperate than I am. Just the thought of fucking her makes me come, and when I have her in my arms again, it for damn sure will be on.

So, one more night and I'm out of this hellhole. Bradshaw is in the works of tying up Quincy's case and said it would be just a matter of months before he'll be released. He's just as anxious as I am, and I'd promised him I'd have things in order by the time he made it out. I wasn't sure what I would do, but selling drugs again was not an option. Rufus had gotten out of jail a few years back and started to run his game in L.A again. He sent money to Bradshaw, Ginger and Desmon, and always sent a little extra-extra for me as well.

According to Ginger, though, her and Desmon were barely making it. She complained that the money Rufus sent wasn't enough, but I suggested she find a fucking job and stop sucking up the welfare system. She claimed she'd been kicked off welfare and said she'd been getting a disability check because of her injured back, along with food stamps. When I accused her of being lazy, she stopped writing me. Several months later, she said that she took my advice and got a job as a waitress at a nightclub. She insisted every bit helped and said she had no choice because Desmon was a hand full to raise. She claimed she'd been to hell and back with him. Said he was hardheaded, disrespectful, and was headed down the wrong path. When I asked her to have him write me, he never did. I'd send him thinking of you cards and cards on his birthday, but never got a response. I'd made many more attempts to reach out to him, but I guess he wasn't having it. Now, though, this was our time. It was time for me to make things right and to make sure my son didn't wound up like me. I didn't have much to be proud of, but I stood by my name. The Abrams men were known for sticking together through thick and thin, and whether Desmon liked it or not, he'd have to soon adjust.

FREEDOM RINGS

I didn't sleep a wink throughout the entire night. Of course, getting the fuck out of here weighed heavy on my mind. When the buzzer sounded off for breakfast, I was on the floor doing my morning sit-ups. I'd become overly obsessed with working out and had taken my body to a whole new level. It was solid as a rock, smooth as a baby's bottom and tight. Even my thighs, I couldn't believe how thick they'd gotten, and my waistline was a perfect thirty-four inches wide.

Frank, my roomy, hopped down from the top bunk and placed his foot on my chest. He grabbed the towel I used to wipe my sweat and snapped it in my face.

"You think you bad cause you gettin out of here, don't you nigga?" he laughed.

I snatched the towel and rose up on my elbows. "Believe it or not my stomach feeling kind of queasy. I think I'm glad, but I know everything ain't gone be all gravy on the outside either."

"It might not be," Frank said, removing his foot. He took a seat on the bottom bunk. "But anythang beats being up in here."

"You got that right."

The guard yelled in at us. "Come on, ladies, stop messing around and move it!"

We looked at each other and shook our heads. Any other day, I would cuss Joe's ass out for mouthing at us like that, but today, I refused to let him steal my joy. Instead, I gathered my things for my shower, and afterwards, Frank and me headed for the Dining Hall. Nobody told me what time I'd be released, so after I ate, and had a chance to see Quincy, hopefully I'd be on my way out.

My eyes searched the noisy hall for Quincy. Sometimes he'd show and sometimes he wouldn't. It depended on if the guards found something else for him to do. They knew I'd be anxious to say goodbye, so it wouldn't surprise me if they came up with some shit to keep him occupied.

The clock ticked away. I'd finished breakfast and gave my last goodbyes to several fellas who stopped by the table to chat and wish me well. When I saw Quincy's roomy, Pedro, I eased my way over to him.

5

I dropped my almost empty tray on the table and sat next to him. "Say, man, where's Quincy?"

"He's in the laundry room," he answered with a mouth full of food. "You know they don't wanna let you see him today."

"Shit!" I yelled and then looked around. I patted Pedro on his back and told him good luck.

"Don't do it, Kiley," he nodded. "If they catch yo ass sneaking around they'll put you in the hole, mon."

"Well, I'm not sneaking around. I'm going to look for Quincy."

"Be careful. And tell yo girlfriend, when you see huh, I said to let you suck those titties." He put his hands in front of his chest. "Mon, she got great looking titties." He referred to the pictures of Ginger taped to the wall beside my bed.

I laughed with Pedro and got up to find Quincy.

After I dumped my tray, I eased my way to the door. Nobody seemed to notice, as the room was still packed with loud talking men. Shortly, a fight broke out and since the guards were occupied with that, I walked abruptly to the laundry room to find Quincy. Both guards who stood nearby the laundry room were pretty cool, so I politely asked them if I could talk to Quincy for a minute. They yelled Quincy's name, and when he turned around, he saw me. He pimped out of the door with a dark blue and white bandana tied around his head. His black spiked hair showed at the top and he grinned from ear to ear. We both looked each other up and down in our light blue button down shirts and dark blue pants. I'm sure Quincy was thinking this was the last time he'd see me dressed in this bullshit.

"What's up, man?" he said. He tightly grabbed my hand and bumped his chest against mine.

"You know what's up, fool. I came to tell you I'd see you in a minute."

"A minute it is…and hopefully, not too much longer."

"It shouldn't be. Bradshaw said maybe a few more months."

"Yeah, that's what he told me. But, I'm truly hurt that you're leaving, damn! I can't believe you're hours away from being a free man."

"Me either. I feel as if I'm dreaming and I can't wait to see my son."

"Is Ginger picking you up?"

6

"Yeah. Nobody told me what time I'd be leaving, but I told her to be outside no later than eight o'clock this morning."

Quincy looked at the clock on the wall. "It's almost nine o'clock already."

"I know. And they'd better hurry it the fuck up before I change my mind."

We laughed.

Quincy punched my chest. "So, what you got planned? With how big you've gotten, you might want to train for boxing."

I punched him back. "Look at you, nigga. I see that the exercise yard did you some favors too. When I used to punch you like that, you'd fall backwards."

"Bullshit, Kiley. You ain't never punched me and I almost fell backwards. You thinking about that weak ass brother of yours, Kareem."

I snickered. "Yeah, he does come to mind quite often. I can't believe how much him and Desmon have in common. Ginger say I got my work cut out for me."

"I'm sure you do, especially if he's anything like Kareem was." Quincy looked at the ground and cleared his throat. "So, uh, like I said…you got plans or what?"

"Yeah. I plan on getting my son together, fucking the shit out of my gal, and finding a job. You know I'm gonna chill at her place, right?"

"Yep," Quincy said, as we looked at Joe coming our way. Quincy opened his arms up for a hug. "Take care, Kiley. And please, please, please don't bust nobody's damn head open until I get out."

"I promise you I won't. As long as you promise to keep yo ass out of the hole until you get out of this place."

"Will do, my brotha. Certainly, will do."

Quincy and me exchanged the love and before Joe could even open his mouth, Quincy went back into the laundry room.

"I've been looking for you, Mr. Lee," Joe said.

"It's Kiley, Joe. And there's no doubt that you knew where to find me."

"Don't get smart with me, boy! You'd better watch your mouth or I'll make sure you spend a few more days here chatting with the ladies." He shoved my arm and nudged me back towards my cell.

7

"Hurry up and gather your things before I decide to tell the warden you snuck off to give your girlee a goodbye kiss."

I didn't even respond to Joe. He'd caused me many of days in the hole, but today was not going to be the day.

Gathering my things was just the beginning. They fucked around so long that by the time I even made it to the gates, it was almost three o'clock in the afternoon. Ginger told me she'd be in a white Ford Escort, and as the gates opened, I could see the car from a distance. As soon as she saw me, she got out and hurried towards me. I hoped to see Desmon follow, but he was nowhere in sight. I smiled at her and when she reached me, she jumped up and straddled my hips.

"I am so damn glad to see you," she said staring into my light brown eyes. I held her tightly around her waist, and without saying a word, I sucked her lips into mine.

We kissed for a while, and after Ginger slid off my hips, she stood in front of me with her arms resting on my shoulders. She moved her head from side to side. "You look so, so good. I can't believe how handsome you've gotten."

"I must say ten years has done nothing but enhance your booty too, girl." I laughed. "I mean, your beauty."

She smiled and playfully pushed my shoulder. "So, I see you've picked up a sense of humor?"

"Something like that." I took her hand and we walked towards her car. "So, you know what I'm about to ask, don't you?"

"And based on my letters, you should know what I'm about to tell you. I haven't a clue where Desmon is. Yesterday, I asked him if he wanted to come with me and he didn't answer."

I nodded and opened the car door for Ginger. I then went to the passenger's side and got in. Ginger leaned over and gave me another kiss. She wiped her lipstick off my thick lips and traced my goatee with her finger.

"Are you as happy to see me as I am to see you?"

"Yes."

"Then why doesn't it seem like it?"

"Ginger, you know I'm not a man who show his emotions. Never have been and never will be. Just know I'm happy to see you."

"And what about me makes you happy?"

8

"I'm happy that you look good for a thirty-eight year old woman, I'm happy that your round beautiful eyes still light up when you see me, I'm happy that your hair is still braided how I like it, and I'm delighted that your body has not changed one bit."

She winked and rubbed my cleanly shaven baldhead. "I'm happy too. Now, let's hurry home so I can get you out of your clothes and hold your body in my arms. You know, those pictures you sent had me playing with myself many of nights."

I laughed and reached over to rub Ginger's carmel brown legs. As she drove, I eased my hand between them, and placed my fingers where I'd dreamed many of nights they would go. She squirmed around in her seat and widened her legs as I quickly brought her juices down. She grabbed my wrist and looked over at me.

"Why'd you do that?" she whispered. "Couldn't you wait?"

"I just wanted to feel it. Haven't felt it in a long time and I wanted to make sure it was exactly how I left it."

"I don't know about all that, but whoever's been there lately, don't stand a chance now that you're back."

In broad daylight, Ginger pulled over to the curb and reached to unzip my pants. She pulled my goods out and covered it with her mouth. After feeling the warmth and her tightening up on my head, I quickly came.

"Now that we've gotten that out of the way," she said, zipping my pants. "I have a surprise waiting for you."

"I can't wait."

Ginger's surprise was to show me the new place she'd gotten. She still lived in East St. Louis, but this townhouse was slightly bigger. As we walked through the door, she had black and silver balloons all over the living room with a banner that said welcome home. I was truly touched, but since Desmon was still nowhere in sight, I was a bit disappointed. I reached for Ginger's hand and kissed the back of it.

"You are so sweet, and thank you for making me feel at home."

"Anything for you, Mr. Kiley Jacoby Abrams. Now, what would you like for dinner?"

"Whatever you feel up to cooking is fine with me. Anything...except red meat. Chicken is fine, but I don't eat red meat anymore. Besides, whatever you cook, I'm sure it'll beat what I've been served."

9

"Well, baby, that's over and done with. You don't ever have to worry about going back to that place again."

Ginger smiled and gave me a quick tour of her new place. It was cool, but with all the money Rufus said he'd sent, I thought it would be a lot better. She still had some of the old furniture from her previous place and the only difference was the townhouse had a basement. What pissed me off more than anything, though, was how cluttered it was. Ginger had never been a good housekeeper and for a woman who barely worked, she knew better. As for the basement, she said that Desmon's room took up most of that. When I asked if I could go see it, she told me to feel free. Before I went downstairs to check out his room, I stayed in the kitchen and watched her cook dinner for us. She rambled on and on about her friends and family, but I couldn't get my mind off what I felt between her legs today. She'd definitely been fucking somebody, but it wasn't like I expected her to be celibate since I'd been gone. Then again, maybe I wished she had. We never talked much about her seeing other people, but by the way her insides felt, it was obvious somebody had tapped into it. She was still as sexy as the day I left, and proving that to me, she wore a tight blue jean ruffled skirt that hugged her fat ass and clung well to her curvy hips. The tiny red tank shirt she had on showed her midriff and squeezed her breasts closely together. She had long micro braids that hung down her back and since they were clearly away from her face, anybody could see how beautiful she really was.

When she snapped her fingers in my face, I was in another world.

"Kiley, what is wrong with you? You've been so quiet."

"I'm just thinking, baby, that's all."

"Thinking about what?" she said, and then walked back over by the stove to check on the grilled chicken.

I removed my shirt and laid it on the kitchen table. I stood shirtless and undid the top button on the pair of 501 wide-legged Levis' I wore. Ginger turned around and looked at me. She could tell what was on my mind.

"Don't you want to eat something first? I figured you'd be awfully hungry."

"You guessed right, because I am hungry." I walked over and turned the knob on the stove off. Then I eased Ginger's skirt above her hips and pulled her panties down. She stepped out of them and quickly turned around. She placed her hands on top of the counter next to the

10

stove and bent slightly over. I stood close behind and unzipped my pants. After I pulled my throbbing manhood out, I pressed it against her ass. I held her hips tightly and closed my eyes.

"I don't know whether to stick my dick in you right now, or taste you first."

"Just fuck me," she moaned and reached for my goods. After I helped her insert it, my legs instantly weakened.

"Baby, I…I'm about to come," I said taking deep stokes inside of her. "I can't help it!"

She leaned over further and damn near touched her toes. I widened her ass cheeks, and quickly filled up her insides with my juices. I took deep breaths while still holding her ass.

"I hope you're not upset with me," I said.

"No, Kiley," she rose up and turned to face me. "I know you'll make it up to me—soon. If anything, we're just preparing ourselves, right?"

I nodded, gave Ginger a kiss on the cheek, and zipped my pants. After we wiped up, she started on dinner again and I headed downstairs to check out Desmon's room.

The basement had one small window, so it was hard for me to see. When I reached for the light switch, it didn't even work. I saw a lamp next to his twin sized waterbed, so I reached for it and turned the light on. I figured by looking around his room, I could learn something about him. Long hanging black beads covered the doorway, and posters of Bob Marley hung on damn near every wall. Along side of them, were pictures of naked women and ashtrays with smoked blunts in them were on the floor. Since he played football, he had trophy's everywhere and a plaque that named him last year's most valuable player. I saw a few framed pictures on his entertainment center, but none of them was of me. He had one of Ginger, and the other had to be of his friends, and possibly a girlfriend. She was rather attractive and since the Abrams men pretty much had good taste in women, I was sure there was some type of connection with her. Lastly, I opened his closet and finally knew where all the money Rufus sent had been spent. He had all kinds of name brand clothes and shoes that filled the closet to its capacity. I couldn't believe it, and as I reached for one of his leather jackets, a letter fell out. When I opened the letter, so I thought, it was actually his report card from last quarter. He had three D's and three F's. Days missed showed

28 and GPA wasn't worth a damn. It was obvious that neither was the school for allowing him to play football.

After I folded the report card to put it back into his pocket, another light came on. I turned my head and Desmon stood at the bottom stair. He stared at me with his hazel eyes and I stared back. My heart raced at a fast pace as I felt Kareem looking in my direction. Desmon slowly walked over by me, and without saying a word, he closed his closet.

I stood shirtless and held my arms out. "Can I get a hug, a hello or something?"

"Can I get you to stay the fuck out of my room?"

I moved back. "Well, damn. I was just trying to check you out, that's all."

"Yeah, well, I don't need to be checked out." He took his blue jean cap and jacket off and tossed it on the bed. He then picked up his basketball, lay on the bed and twirled the ball on his finger.

"So, I see you like basketball too, huh?" I said. He looked at me, rolled his eyes and continued to twirl the ball. "What's your beef, Desmon? I'm not gonna kiss your ass to find out, but I'm curious to know. I've tried to contact—

"I ain't got no motherfucking beef—so there. Now, if you don't mind, I'd like some privacy."

"Well, I do mind. We need to get a few things straight—right here and right now. Whether you like it or not, I am your father. You will respect me and—

"Man, please," he said getting off the bed. "Gone on out of here with that bullshit! You need to—

"I need to what!" I yelled in his face and then pushed him back on the bed. He quickly hopped back up and stood in front of me. A tad bit shorter, he touched his thick chest against mine.

"You need to get out of my room like I asked you to!"

Just then, Ginger came rushing down the steps. She ran over and grabbed my arm. "Baby, please don't. Not now, okay?"

"Not never," Desmon yelled and stepped away from in front of me.

"What is wrong with this fool, Ginger?"

"Nigga, what's wrong with you?"

I bald up my fist, and before I could punch him, Ginger held me back. "Kiley, please don't! You're only going to make matters worse."

"I will not be talked to like that Ginger! What are you raising...a fucking animal or something?"

"On that note," he said reaching for the gun underneath his pillow. He placed it behind his back, and down inside his pants. "Mama, I'll see you a little later. This animal you raised needs to go search for his prey." He walked away and hurried up the steps.

"You do that, motherfucker!" I yelled. "And next time..."

I heard the door slam. I took a deep breath and slammed my fist against my hand.

"I can't believe that shit just happened," I said, looking at Ginger.

"Baby, I told you...he is out of control. I don't know what is wrong with Desmon."

I got angry. "What do you mean by you don't know what is wrong with him?"

"I mean, I haven't a clue why he talks like he does, why he doesn't come home—

"Why he smokes marijuana, gets bad grades in school, skips school on a regular basis, and has unprotected sex quite often. I've been in his room for ten fucking minutes and I can tell what kind of damn fool you're raising and why! Don't stand there and give me that lame ass excuse that you haven't a clue as to why he acts the way he does! You know damn well why!"

"And don't you dare stand there and yell at me like I haven't tried to do nothing about it! I've tried, Kiley, but Desmon will not listen to—

"Then make him listen, goddamn it! Put your foot in his ass and make him listen!"

"Fine," she said, turning to walk away. "Since you're here now, why don't you do it! I don't know about you, but I want to keep my life! Desmon gets so angry sometimes—

"Are you telling me you're afraid of him? Is that what you're saying?"

"All I'm saying—

"You're more pathetic than I thought! How in the hell can a mother be afraid of her own damn son! I can't believe you, Ginger." I shook my head and walked by her. "Damn, I can't believe you."

I went upstairs and walked right past the food on the table that she'd cooked for me. I went into the bathroom and closed the door. In deep thought, I sat on the edge of the tub and ran my bath water. Ginger knocked, but I asked her to leave me in peace.

After taking a lengthy bath, I wrapped a towel around my waist and carried my clothes into the bedroom. Ginger sat naked in bed with her knees pressed against her chest. She looked at me and wiped the tear that had fallen from her face.

"I did not expect for our first day back together to end up like this. Desmon needs you Kiley, but you can't expect to come here and change things overnight. Please don't fully blame me for the way he is. Your not being here contributed to his actions as well, and I did the best I knew how without you."

I tossed my clothes in the chair and sat on the edge of the bed. Hurt by my own son's words, I rubbed my face with my hands. Ginger came up from behind and massaged her hands deeply into my shoulders.

"I'm sorry," I softly said. "I shouldn't have come to you like that, but I was hurt by his rejection."

"Don't worry about it. Let's just get some rest and deal with it tomorrow."

Ginger scooted back on the bed. After I took the towel from around me, I crawled in between her legs and wrapped my arms around her thighs. Her legs fell far apart and she rubbed my baldhead and neck with her hands. I gave her much pleasure, and unable to remain in the same position, she laid back and tightly gripped the sheets.

"You certainly haven't lost your touch doing this, have you?" she softly moaned.

I continued and after Ginger let her juices flow into my mouth, I placed her legs high on my shoulders and couldn't help myself from fucking her so well.

We'd been at it for hours. I'd only come one time and that wasn't shit compared to Ginger's four times. She tried every position to get me to come again, and the only one that worked was when she straddled me backwards in the chair and touched the floor with her hands. I dug deep into her and stretched her legs apart so I could observe my entries. When she glazed me up with her last come, I quickly returned the favor.

Afterwards, I lay naked on my back with Ginger lying naked between my legs. The ceiling fan turned in circles and blew cool air on us, as we were both out of breath. I rubbed up and down her back to comfort her.

"Baby, I'm beat," she mumbled. "My insides are killing me."

"I had no intentions on hurting your insides. My job is to only make it feel good."

"Oh, I'm feeling good. I feel like a million dollars lying between the legs of this big hunk of a man I got. I don't know what to say about your body, but its...its got it going on! I just can't believe how much I still can't handle you, though."

"You will," I said, continuing to rub her back. "Now that I dropped that heavy load, I promise next time I'll be more gentle."

Ginger gave off a soft snicker, and shortly after, fell off to sleep. As usual, I couldn't sleep a wink. I continued in deep thought about Desmon, and by the time I heard him come through the door, it was almost five o'clock in the morning. I wanted to go fuck him up, but instead, I thought hard about how to handle my situation with him going forward.

LIKE FATHER, LIKE SON

By six o'clock in the morning, I was out of bed. I moved Ginger over to the side and went to the living room to do my morning sit-ups. After I finished those, I slid into my gray sweat pants and white t-shirt that was in my duffle bag. I didn't have many clothes to wear, but I did have something to workout in. I opened the front door and headed outside for a quick jog around the neighborhood.

For the most part, it was pretty quiet. The area had gone down a lot and there were more vacant houses since the last time I'd been around. Liquor stores were all over the place and I must have jogged by at least seven new churches that were on nearly every corner. In addition to that, I'd passed a few prostitutes that hung out early as well. One approached me as I walked into a convenience store to get some bottled water. I gave her a looked that could kill and she walked away. While in the store, I opened up the freezer and grabbed a 20 oz. bottle of cold ice mountain water. I could see the Arab who worked at the counter, eyes search me as I walked through the store and looked for nothing else. I was just fucking with him because it pissed me off how they insisted on watching a Black mans every move. As I made my way to the counter, a Latina woman: pretty face, smooth light skin, wavy long hair, and fairly decent body, quickly caught my attention. She held two gallons of milk in her hand and a box of cereal. I walked up to her as she struggled to hold everything.

"Would you like some help with that?" I asked.

She looked me up and down. "Sure. Thank you."

I took both gallons of milk from her and carried them to the counter. She placed the cereal on the counter and the clerk rang up her stuff. After she paid him, she turned around and thanked me again.

"Hey, no problem."

She smiled and removed the heavy bag from the counter. After she walked out, I paid for my water and left.

I gulped down the water in no time and headed back for home. On my way, I saw the Latina woman again, as she walked with the heavy groceries in her hand. Wanting to offer my help again, I quickly jogged up next to her. She turned and looked frightened.

"I didn't mean to scare you, but ain't that bag kind of heavy?"

"No, it's okay. I got it." She smiled and continued to walk. The cool breeze blew her wavy curls in front of her face and she reached up to move them away. Awfully cute, I thought, and then I turned around and walked backwards in front of her.

"So, if you don't mind me asking, what's your name?"

"But, I do mind you asking." She smiled again.

"Okay. My name is Kiley. Kiley Abrams to be exact."

She didn't say anything and continued to walk. As the bag seemed to get heavier for her, she stopped and handed it to me. I reached for it and held it in my arms.

"So, you want me to carry your bag, but you're not going to tell me your name?"

"Yep," she said. We continued to walk side by side. When we reached her apartment complex, she dug in her purse for her keys. After she pulled them out, she looked at me with her dark brown slanted eyes.

"Thank you, Mr. Kiley."

"Anytime." I gave the bag to her, grinned and turned to walk away.

I'd barely made it to the end of the street before she loudly yelled my name. I quickly turned and looked at her still by the doorway.

"Yes," I yelled from a short distance.

"It's, Onna Lopez."

"What?" I said, and then walked closer to hear her.

"I said...my name is Onna."

"Do you mean Anna?"

"Yes. However you'd like to pronounce it. But, it's Onna."

I winked. "Okay, Anna. Thanks for telling me your name and have a good day."

"You too." She opened the door and I ran off to continue my jog.

By seven thirty, I was back at home. Ginger was still in bed asleep and I knew Desmon was still resting after coming in at five in the morning.

I showered, and afterwards, I sat in the living room and searched the newspaper for a job. That task took up less than fifteen minutes of my time. Everybody wanted experience and since I didn't have any, so it seemed to be a waste of time. Not only that, but most companies wanted a drug test and said a background check was needed too. Bullshit, I thought, so I placed the paper on the floor. I picked up the remote, turned the television on, and lit the unfinished joint that was in the astray in front of me. I took a few hits and leaned back on the couch. My thoughts were on Desmon, money and some mo pussy. I'd thought about how good Ginger was to me last night, how I knew once Jada found out I was out we'd soon make up for lost time, and Anna. What a sight for early morning eyes she was. Always being very observant to my surroundings, I could tell she didn't have much money by the Plain-Jane ass sundress she wore, her worn down sandals, and the apartment complex said the rest. Kid or Kids? Yes, I was sure that's who all the milk was for. And a soon to be sex partner? Without a doubt. I could tell she was interested by the way she gazed at me. Her eyes said that she wanted me, and wanted me bad.

I took a few more hits from the joint, and before I knew it, I was out like a light. Shortly after, I was awakened by Ginger. She straddled my lap and put bite marks on my neck.

"Now, you can not be laid up here looking this sexy on a Saturday morning, Kiley." She nibbled on my ear.

No doubt, I was horny so I rolled on top and kneeled between her legs. Getting into position, I put one of my legs on the floor and scooted myself right into her.

Within seconds we were at it again. We couldn't help ourselves and there was much lost time to be made up for. I had no problem with the way she put it out there and enjoyed every moment of her satisfying my manly needs.

She moaned and I moaned. When she talked dirty, I talked dirty. But when she lay on her stomach and I inserted myself from behind, I'll be damned if Desmon didn't come upstairs to confront us. Embarrassed, I leaned forward to cover Ginger's naked body with mine. She shamefully turned her head away from Desmon and closed her eyes. I didn't have much to say my damn self.

"Look, I'm trying to sleep. I got a game today and I'm tired. Please have some fucking respect, au-ight?" he demanded.

"If you want respect, you got to give it," I said casually. "Now, if you don't mind, I'd like to finish up."

Desmon gave me a cold stare. "You do that. Finish up with your leftovers. I'm sure Moms—

"Desmon!" Ginger yelled. "Watch your fucking…!"

I covered Ginger's mouth with my hand and looked at Desmon. "You are treading on extremely thin ice. Man, I'm seconds away from kicking your ass and calling it a day. Before I do, please!" I yelled, "get the hell away from me before I get off this couch and bust a cap in yo ass!"

I couldn't believe he stepped further into the room. "I ain't afraid of you, Nigga! Bring it on, motherfucker!"

Before I knew it, I hopped up and charged at Desmon. I grabbed him by his upper neck and pushed him up against the wall. His head hit the wall hard, as I stood in front of him full of anger.

"Are you ready to die, Desmon?" I yelled with a tight grip on his neck. "DO NOT FUCK WITH ME, MAN! At this point I don't give a shit what your problem is, but the disrespect stops here and right now! Do you understand?"

He didn't say a word. He gritted his teeth and the look of raging anger covered his entire face. "Do you understand!" I yelled louder and tightened up on my grip. He held his neck tight so he wouldn't feel so much pain. Ginger ran over and begged me to let him go.

"Stop this, please! Kiley, let him go!"

I eased up on his neck and got no response. After letting him go, I took a deep breath and walked away. Desmon spoke calmly to me, as I headed to the bedroom.

"You die, blood. Your ass is dead."

I turned and grinned at him. "I'm not afraid of dying. You need to prepare yourself, though." I walked into the bedroom and slammed the door.

Shortly after, Ginger came into the bedroom and closed the door. She reached for her robe on the bed to cover up. I stood with my hands on the dresser and looked down at the ground.

"What am I gonna do with him, Ginger?"

"For starters, you need not to put your hands on him. Kiley, you will hurt him."

"I'm not going to hurt him, Ginger. But, I've never had anybody talk to me like that. And if they did...

"And if they did, I'm sure they paid for it."

I turned around, folded my arms and looked at Ginger as she sat on the bed. "What did he mean by leftovers? I hope to God you haven't been putting yourself out there like that."

"Kiley, Desmon is full of shit. Since you've been away, I've been with maybe two men…three at the most. He's the one downstairs fucking all the time. Ask him how many times I've walked in on him, or I've heard his action going on."

"You mean, you allow a fifteen year old to have sex in your house and don't say nothing about it?"

"What do you want me to say? Should I tell him not to, even if he's going to do it anyway? Or, should I be glad he's not out in the streets having sex with these young girls?"

I looked at Ginger in disbelief. "I know I don't have the best morals and values, but what in the hell is wrong with this picture? Do you have any control over what he say and do?"

"Look, don't start with me. If I can recall, you once told me you and Jada had sex at your parents' house all the time. What in the hell is the difference?"

"The difference is, stupid ass, I didn't want my son brought up like me. You see where it got me, don't you? Can you put forth a little effort and take on your role as a parent?"

"It's too late for that shit. And I've played out my role as the only parent for many, many years. You need to face the fact that Desmon ain't gonna change, and throwing him up against a wall and making threats for damn sure ain't gonna prove nothing."

"Talking to you about this is hopeless. I would tell you how I really feel, Ginger, but your feelings might get deeply hurt. He mentioned a game today, right?"

"Yeah, so what?"

"I'm making plans to go. Are you going with me, or are you going to sit on your ass and wait for the next man to come along and fuck you?"

Ginger reached up and smacked me. "I'm not going to be disrespected by you, Kiley! You can take your few rags you came here with and leave!"

Tempted, I glared at Ginger, and shortly after, changed my clothes to go to Desmon's game. I didn't tell him I'd be there, and I was sure my presence didn't matter to him either way.

Around noon, I interrupted Ginger on the telephone and told her I'd be back. She didn't respond, so I headed out of the door. Before I walked to the game, I stopped by the convenience mart and bought a pack of cigarettes. My nerves had gotten bad, and the feeling of having little money in my pockets drove me crazy. Later, when I got back to the house, I planned to call Rufus to see if he'd help a brotha out. If not, it was certainly time to hook up with Jada to see what she could do for me.

By the time I made it to the game, it was standing room only. The bleachers on both sides were filled to capacity. To watch the game, I leaned against the fence that was several feet away from Desmon. At first, he didn't see me. But, when he came off the field hyped up after he sacked the quarterback, he then noticed me. He took his helmet off and rolled his eyes at me. When he threw it on the ground, the coach ran up to him. The coach said something to him, and whatever it was, it seemed to calm Desmon down.

I continued to watch Desmon play and observed many things about him. He was a hell of a defensive tackle, and basically, played better than anyone on the team. Not only that, but he was a leader. He was a sophomore who played on varsity and the other players listened to him. When they made bad plays, he'd be sure to let them know about it. His haters were definitely here too, as I listened to them talk their shit and make remarks about him. And as for the young ladies, he could certainly have his choice. His name was screamed out loudly, quite often, and many made their way close to him to say hello. His assumed girlfriend had to be the cheerleader who he couldn't keep his eyes off of, and her the same. They smiled at each other during the game, and when he made a good play, the other cheerleaders would look in her direction. The picture of her in his room pretty much confirmed my assumption. If it wasn't her, then it was definitely the one in the bleachers who wore his jersey. Both were pretty decent: brown skinned, neatly layered short hair, groomed well and had a preppy look about them. The difference was height and figure. The cheerleader was tall and slender, whereas the other young lady was shorter and a bit on the thick side.

During half time, I managed to snatch a seat on the bleachers. Even with the red wife-beater I wore the sun cooked my body even more and my forehead sweated. I wiped it and took a few more puffs from the cigarette I'd gotten earlier. I wanted a joint, but I definitely had to wait until I got home for that. After I put the cigarette out, I was surprised when I looked up and saw Anna standing next to me.

"Do you mind if I sit?" she asked.

I shook my head and leaned back on my elbows. Anna took a seat next to me. She had on number 23's jersey, and wore a pair of tight blue jean shorts with it. Her hair was in a bouncing ponytail and she had two bottled waters in her hand.

"Here," she said, reaching over to give it to me.

"Thanks."

I took the bottle and opened it. After I took a few sips, I put the bottle next to me. "So, I guess you got a son who plays football, huh?"

"No, I have a nephew that plays football. He's like my son, though. I've been his guardian for many years."

"I see. Number 23, right?"

She nodded. "Yep. How about you? Why are you here? It's funny I've seen you two times in one day and I've never seen you before."

"That's because I'm following you." Her smile faded. "I'm just kidding. I'm here because a friend of mine asked me to come. His son plays for the other team."

"Oh, I see. Then, maybe you should go on the other side to look for him."

"There's no where to sit. I'm fine right where I'm at."

Anna was quiet. And when the game started again, Desmon got another Quarterback sack, and the crowd went crazy. I silently kept my happy emotions to myself. After he walked back to the bench, I saw him look to where I stood before. He continued to look throughout the game, and when it was over, the final score was 41 to 7, with Desmon being on the winning team. I thanked Anna for the water and stood up to leave.

"Kiley, before you go, maybe I can—

A voice interrupted. "Excuse me, but don't I know you from somewhere?"

"Who, me?" I asked, as I looked at the woman I didn't know.

"Yes, you. I can't remember your name, but I never forget a face."

"You must think I'm someone—

Anna interrupted, "Kiley, I'll see you around. It was good seeing you again."

I said goodbye to Anna and turned to face the other woman. "Seriously, you must think I'm someone else. I've never seen you before."

She smiled. "Well, good. Then you won't have a problem calling me if I give you my phone number. I hoped that wasn't your girlfriend, because I saw you over there standing by yourself." She reached out and gave me a piece of paper.

"That was pretty smooth. And your efforts has definitely earned you a call."

"I hope so," she said, and then stepped down. She waved goodbye and walked off with her friends.

I put the number in the pocket of my blue jean shorts and looked around for Desmon. I could see the team heading back to the locker room, so I made my way over to the door so I could congratulate him on his way out.

I stood for a long while and waited. A few fans from the other side were close by and talked shit as the players came out in bunches. Finally, when Desmon and his crew came out, somebody threw a rock that hit him on the side of his face. I didn't do shit but back away. Motherfuckers swarmed like bees and went at it. There wasn't a cop, or nobody in sight to stop the action. I kept my eyes on Desmon, as he seemed to have everything under control. That was until I saw this grown-ass fool pull a knife out of his pocket. Foolishly, Desmon challenged him and that's when I intervened. I grabbed Desmon by the back of his shirt and pulled him backwards. Not knowing who I was, until I stood between them, Desmon had his fist bald up, about to punch me. The fool with the knife lounged out at me, and the tip of his blade slit my arm. I raised my shirt and pulled out my piece from down inside my pants. I aimed it at him, and with no hesitation, I pulled the trigger. It caught his shoulder and he fell backwards. After that, the place scattered with people. Motherfuckers ran to their cars in fear. I followed Desmon to his car, and after he unlocked the doors, we both got in. He slammed the door and looked over at me.

"What in the fuck did you do that for? I don't need your damn help."

"I wasn't helping you. That son of a bitch cut me, nigga. Now, shut the fuck up and get me the hell out of here."

He leaned back in the seat. "I ain't going nowhere. Going back to jail might be good for you."

I pulled the gun from my pants again and aimed it at Desmon. "By the time I count to three, this piece of shit ass car better be heading off this lot like all the rest. If not, just remember that I loved you. TWO!"

"But, you skipped one."

"Three!" I turned my head away from Desmon and pulled the trigger again. His driver's side window shattered and then he started the car.

"Well, damn! You don't be bullshitting, do you?" He said, driving off.

I ignored him and watched as more cars scattered. The police quickly made their way through and raced by us on the way out.

"Do you see all the ruckus you've caused?" He said, looking at the police cars. "And what about my window? I want my window fixed—soon!"

I looked at my arm as blood dripped from it. It wasn't a deep cut, but it was deep enough where it needed to be wrapped in bandages. When we got to the stoplight, Desmon continued to ramble on and on about his broken window. I calmly asked him to pull over.

"For what?" he asked and then pulled over.

I opened the door and got out. I then leaned down and looked at him, "Good game. Next time, though, control your attitude. It's liable to cause you a serious loss."

"Man, fuck you," he said and then sped off.

I walked to the convenience mart again, and picked up a bandage for my arm. The Arab who worked there became very familiar with my face and gave me a smile this time around.

When I got back home, Ginger was in the kitchen cooking dinner. She had the phone pressed up against her ear, and talked to one of her girlfriends. I sat at the kitchen table and placed my hands behind my head. She saw the disgruntled look on my face and quickly ended the call.

"What happened to your arm?" she asked as I'd already started to wrap it.

"I got cut by a piece of glass that was on the bleachers."

She took a seat in front of me and held my arm. "Let me see it. I'll wrap it for you."

I held my arm up while Ginger wiped the blood off with a towel and wrapped it. I stared at her and waited for her to ask me how the

24

game went. She never did. After she wrapped my arm, she opened the refrigerator and pulled out a head of lettuce.

"Do you want a salad with your baked chicken?"

"Do you even give a fuck anymore?"

She slammed the lettuce on the counter and looked at me in anger. "Kiley, what do you want from me? What are you talking about now?"

Since I refused to argue with her, I got up and walked into the living room. I turned the television on and plopped down on the couch. There was no doubt I was disgusted with Ginger, and with myself for what had happened today. What example had I set for my son? I'd only been out of prison for two days and already had to drop somebody. I didn't know if the brotha was dead or alive, and frankly, didn't give a damn. Today proved to me I was a walking time bomb. So much anger was inside of me and I didn't know how to get it out without hurting somebody. What was I mad at, though? As I thought more about it, it all flashed back to Desmon. He had so much control over my mind, and my thoughts, and didn't even know it. He could trigger my mind off in a minute by saying or doing the wrong things. Just like Kareem did. The only way to deal with him was to fuck with his mind as well. He wanted me to argue with him in the car, but when I got out and told him what a good game he'd had, I'm sure that messed him up. He tried hard to push my buttons and there was no way I could continue to let him do so.

A DIFFERENT KIND OF LOVE

Desmon didn't make it home until almost four-thirty in the morning. And when he did, he brought company with him. Within moments after his arrival, I could hear the action from downstairs coming through the vents in the bedroom.

As I eased out of bed, Ginger lay naked beside me. We'd worked through our previous argument by fucking, and afterwards, she was fast asleep in my arms.

Making Desmon aware that I was up, I walked hard on the floor, flushed the toilet and ran water in the sink. I then put on my robe and headed downstairs to confront him. The basement was pitch black and when I reached to screw in the light at the bottom of the steps, the light came on. I couldn't see much, but I could tell they were naked. I could also see it was the cheerleader from the game who was on top of him.

"Say, man," I said. "I'm trying to get some sleep. I got a busy day ahead of me, so have a little respect, au-ight?"

Desmon patted whoever her name was on her ass. "Gabrielle, get up for a minute." She pulled the cover over her and moved next to him in bed. After he reached for his shorts and slid them on, he walked over by the steps and confronted me.

"Daddy, father, poppy, or whoever the hell you wanna be, don't try to play daddy now. Now ain't the time because I'm busy! So, go back upstairs and continue to plow my mother like the rest of her boyfriends, au-ight?"

"I plan to. And in the meantime, you go back over there and continue to plow Gabrielle, and the young lady who was here the night before, and the one who had your jersey on at the game, along with the ones who can't stop calling this damn house."

Gabrielle cleared her throat, "Desmon, I'm ready to go."

"In a minute," he replied.

"I'm ready to go now!"

He looked at me. "You don't want me to make you my enemy."

I laughed. "What's the difference? I thought I already was. Look, the young lady said she's ready to go, so take her home."

"Please," Gabrielle added with attitude.

26

"See, she's begging." I leaned forward and whispered in his ear. "It's obvious she's in control of things. It would be a shame if she started to cuss you out in front of me. Don't embarrass yourself. Just take the young lady home like she asked."

As I turned and walked away, I could already see Gabrielle putting her clothes on. Surprisingly, Desmon had more damn respect for her than he did for Ginger and me. I listened at the top of the stairs as he tried to explain my accusations and begged her to stay. She started to cry and refused to listen to him. After I heard a smack, I just knew things would get heated, but they didn't. I listened, as they walked upstairs together, and I hurried over to the kitchen table and took a seat. I pretended to be occupied with the newspaper in front of me.

She opened the door and wiped the tears from her eyes. She rolled her eyes at me and walked by without saying a word. Desmon gave me a hard stare and continued to follow her to the door. After he gave me one last look, he slammed the door on his way out.

Ginger slept until almost noon. I'd already taken my morning jog, and had done my sit-ups for the day. I was on the couch cleaning my gun.

"You keep that thing like it's your bible or something."

"It doesn't compare, but I appreciate you keeping it in a safe place for me while I was gone."

She yawned. "You know I gotta work at the club tonight, don't you?"

"No, I didn't know. I thought partying was on Saturday nights, not Sunday."

"Please, these folks around here party seven days a week. Sunday's be off the chain. That's when I make the most money."

"What time you leaving?"

"Around nine. Would you like to come with me?"

"I guess. I don't have much to wear, but hopefully I'll find something."

Ginger got her purse and reached inside. She pulled out two one hundred dollar bills and gave them to me. "Here, go find you something to wear. I remember when all you did was give, give and give to me, so don't let your pride stand in the way of you taking this money."

"Thanks," I said, reaching for it. I'd always had my own and it didn't feel right taking the money from Ginger. Even though I used to kick her out tough, for some reason, I felt less than a man.

Ginger gave me the keys to her car, and before I left, I called Rufus on his cell phone. He didn't answer, but I left a message and told him to get back with me as soon as possible.

Not knowing the latest fashions, I hurried to the mall to find something to wear. I found a pair of black linen pants and a short sleeve linen shirt to match. Having a little cash left over, I purchased the cheapest bottle of good smelling cologne I could find.

I got back to Ginger's place around a quarter to six. We ate dinner, fucked, and then prepared ourselves to be gone by nine. After I got out of the shower, Ginger got in. I went to the bedroom and dried myself off. Shortly after, the phone rang. I picked it up, but no one was there. I said hello again, and they hung up on me. This continued on a few more times, and finally, I recognized the voice on the other end. It was Rufus.

"Sorry about that, man. My cell phone be trippin," he said. "Anyway, what's going on, my nigga."

"What ain't going on, Killer?"

"How does it feel to be a free man?"

"I can't complain."

Rufus laughed. "Not one bit. But, uh, I thought you were going to holla at me as soon as you got out."

"As soon as I got out, calling you was the last thing on my mind. Man, I was anxious to dive into some pussy. And been diving ever since."

"I hear ya. And I hope you're heading this way soon. I told the ladies to expect you soon. Shit down here has been off the chain."

"Well, I ain't trying to go that route. Actually, I called to see if you'd do me a favor."

"Shoot."

"I'm broke, man. I need some jack. I don't want to work, nor do I intend to, but a nigga gotta have some money—soon."

"Then come back to L.A., Kiley. Man, we setting this shit off. You'd be proud of me and I'd be happy to hook a brotha up. It's just like when Papa Abrams ran the show. The only thing missing is you. Think about it, au-ight?"

"I will, but in the meantime, help a nigga out."

"Say the word. Tell me how much and it's on the way. I got a few fellas shaking and moving through the Lou in a few days. I'd be happy to have them make a special delivery for me."

"I need two hundred g's. I don't have transportation, I don't have—"

"Done deal. No need to explain. I'll call you in a couple of days and tell you where to meet them."

"Thanks. You know I owe you one for taking care of the family while I was away too."

"That was chump change. Besides, I didn't always send what you asked because I really didn't trust Ginger. Something with her didn't sit right with me."

"Yeah, I know. And again, thanks. I'll talk to you soon."

"Adios Amigo. In a few days, baby, you'll be set."

I hung up, and soon after, the phone rang again. I thought it was Rufus calling back, but instead, it was a brotha asking for Ginger.

"She's taking a shower. Who is this?" I asked.

"Craig. Is this Desmon?"

"Uh-huh."

"Then, tell yo Mama to call me back. I was gonna stop by but I wanna make sure it's cool."

"It's cool."

"Then, tell her I'm on my way."

"Okay."

I hung up and went to the bathroom to trim my goatee. My head was already cleanly shaven, so I hurried to put on my clothes. Finally, Ginger came out of the bathroom and walked into the bedroom to find me. When she didn't find me there, she came into the living room where I sat on the couch.

"Damn, baby, you look good," she said standing in front of me. She leaned down and gave me a kiss.

"Gone ahead and get dressed so we can go."

She dropped the towel from around her and squatted down in front of me. "Can I taste you before we go. I told you how much seeing you at your best turns me on."

I leaned back on the couch and reached for the button on my pants. After I unzipped them, Ginger pulled my dick out. She stroked it a few times with her hands, and then placed it in her mouth. I closed my eyes and tilted my head to the side. Definitely to my satisfaction, I moaned and let it be known loudly that the feeling was too good to me.

Shortly, there was a knock at the door. Since I'd already unlocked it for Craig to come in, I yelled for him to do just that. Ginger didn't even have time enough to rise up. And when she did, she looked over at him with my dick in her hand.

He slowly walked in and closed the door behind him. Ginger stood up and I reached down to zip up my pants.

"What's up with you?" he said angrily.

She reached for the towel and covered herself with it. "I told you to call before you came over here, didn't I?"

"I did call...but, what the fuck up with you sucking this nigga's dick."

"Hey, look, leave me out of it," I said. "I thought Ginger told you what was going down between her and me."

"She ain't told me shit!" He looked at Ginger. "So, that's how it is? You gone play me like that?"

"Look, I told you to call, Craig."

"Bitch, I did call! Just answer the fucking question!"

"Craig, please leave. Don't be coming over here calling me out of my motherfucking name."

"I'll call you what the fuck I wanna call you!" He opened the door. "And tell your bitch ass son don't be playing games with me! He knew damn well you had company!"

Now, that sparked a nerve. I hopped up and grabbed his shirt to pull him back inside. I slammed the door, and tightly grabbed the back of his neck. I pressed his face hard against the door and dug my elbow deep into his back.

"That's my fucking son you talking about, nigga! She ain't gotta tell him shit! If you ever bring your ass around here again, disrespecting him or his mama, you gone have to answer to me!"

After I slammed his face into the back of the door a few times, I opened it and pushed his ass outside. He mouthed a bunch of bullshit to me, and as I was about to reach for my gun, Desmon pulled up in his car with another companion. They got out and walked towards the door. He looked at Craig, and then brushed up against me as he walked inside. Ginger pulled me away from the door and closed it.

"You need to calm down," she said. "He's only a friend of mine who—

"I don't give a fuck who he is! Just go put your damn clothes on so we can go!"

She rolled her eyes at me, said hello to Samantha and left the room. Desmon smirked at me, as they sat on the couch and rolled up a joint. I watched as he lit it up and placed it between his lips. He took a few hits and passed it to her. She shook her head and he reached out to give it to me. I walked over and smacked it out of his hand.

"This place ain't big enough for the two of us. Something's got to give, or somebody's got to go," I said.

He picked the joint up off the floor. He then put it back into his mouth and lit it again. After he sucked in the smoke, he spoke calmly, "You're right. For the first time, we agree. You really should go. Especially since you and Moms boyfriends can't seem to get along. Now that you've messed up her money, she's bound to kick you out. And from what I hear, sex doesn't keep a woman in this day and age. Ten years ago, maybe. But, time moved on without you. And as soon as you realize that, I think you'll be okay."

"Maybe time has moved on without me, but it's never too late to make things right. If you give me a chance, I promise you won't regret it."

Desmon looked at Samantha, "Let's go downstairs for some privacy." She stood up and they both headed downstairs.

I felt as if I was fighting a battle that couldn't be won. As I replayed the previous last three days in my mind, Desmon had been raised in chaos. It was obvious Ginger and her men kept up drama. She didn't support him in anything he'd attempted to do, and as long as we smoked weed and had sex in front of him, what else could he know? My irate behavior wasn't helping either. I'd damn near killed two people in the three days I'd been out. Three long days that made me feel as if I were better off in prison. Maybe leaving wasn't a bad idea. Maybe I was better off in L.A. with Rufus and his boys. I didn't see any light at the end of this tunnel, but I knew I had to make some serious plans and make them soon.

I waited and waited for Ginger to get ready. When she came out, she was dressed in a short black skirt that hugged her hips and a white silk shirt. The buttons were undone and her cleavage was enough to

31

invite any man to her. She looked nice, though, and I couldn't complain. Besides, she was out to make money, so it wasn't shit I could say even if I wanted to.

We didn't have much conversation in the car, and it was a short ride from her place to the club. After we went inside, Ginger introduced me to a few people and seated me at a table near the dance floor.

"So, what can I get you to drink," she said, and then placed a napkin on the table.

"Shit, I haven't had nothing hard to drink in a long time. Just give me a beer for now."

She smiled and walked away. Shortly after, she came back with two ice-cold beers. She placed them on the table. "I'll see you later about my tip, okay?"

I nodded and picked up the bottle to take a sip. Ginger walked away and served another table close by.

At first, the place wasn't packed at all. But by eleven o'clock, everybody started making their way in. Two of Ginger's friends sat at the table with me and bugged the shit out of me with all the questions they had. I said very little to anyone because after what happened to me in the past, I learned to keep my mouth shut. They were cool company, though, and cracked me up with how much they talked about people and dissed the brothas who asked them to dance.

As for the ladies, several caught my attention. I didn't know if being locked up for so long had me checking out everything that walked by, or if there were simply just some badass gals in the room. Either way, I had my eyes on plenty, they had their eyes on me, and so did Ginger. When one came over to ask me to dance, I saw Ginger from a distance shake her head from side to side. When I stood up, she headed my way.

"Uh, no, no, no," she said, looking at the chick who asked me to dance. "He's busy right now."

The chick looked at me. "Are we gonna dance or not?"

"Ginger, it's just a dance. It ain't like she came over here to ask for some sex."

"Tell me about it," the chick said, and then rolled her eyes.

Ginger pointed at me and smiled. "Go ahead and have your fun, Kiley. And don't be all up on her either."

We walked to the dance floor, and the whole time we danced, I could see Ginger and her girlfriends scoping me out. I wanted to get close to the chick, but I didn't. And when the DJ kicked down a slow song, Ginger stood close by and cleared her throat.

"I'm gonna let you get back to her because she is working my damn nerves," the chick said.

"Mine too. Sorry about that." I leaned forward and gave her a hug. She grinned and got off the floor.

"What was the hug for?" Ginger asked as she followed me back to my seat.

"Do you want me to have fun tonight or not? I thought I was here to enjoy myself. So, cool out, au-ight?"

She pouted. "But I can't stand the way some of these bitches looking at you. And you the same. Just have fun and don't disrespect me up in here tonight."

"Never."

I walked back to the table and took a seat. The place got even more packed, and after a while, I barely even saw Ginger. The last time I'd seen her, she had racked up on the dollars from some brothas who seemed to want more than her to take their order. I didn't trip and continued to check out the ladies.

Sitting near the dance floor was the best place to be. Surprisingly, when I looked up, I saw Anna again. Her curly long hair was down and a few stands dangled in her face as she danced. Her outfit was simple: a white short dress with silver buttons down the front. It had a huge pocket on the front and a belt that tied neatly around her waist. She showed her silky smooth legs, and from where I sat, I had a good view of what was between them. No doubt, she had my attention, but when somebody tapped my shoulder, it quickly startled me. I turned to see who it was. It was the chick from the football game.

"I thought you were going to call me," she asked.

"And I am. I just hadn't gotten around to it."

She looked me up and down. "You look even better dressed up."

"And let me pay you the same compliment."

"Would you like to dance?"

"Not right now. A little later, okay?"

She nodded and told me she'd see me later. She wasn't bad looking, but she reminded me too much of Jada. Big boned and a fat ass

33

to go with it. I'd planned to call her, but after what happened at the game, I kind of forgot.

Ginger made her way back over to me and brought me another drink. I'd stepped up to Cognac and felt a bit woozy. I closed my eyes to syke myself out of the headache that was coming, and when I opened them, Anna stood on the dance floor in front of me. She motioned with her hand for me to come dance with her. No hesitation, I got up and went to the dance floor. I wrapped one arm around her waist and held my other hand with hers. Barely meeting up with my chin, she laid her head against my chest and slowly moved from side to side with me.

At first, we didn't say much at all, but our body movement said we enjoyed being in each other's arms. Anna moved her head back and looked up at me. She stared into my eyes and then looked at my lips. I looked at her thin glossy lips and wanted badly to touch hers with mine. Having the same thought as I did, she reached for the back of my head to pull me to her. I nodded and softly whispered. "Not now."

She looked disappointed and looked away. Letting it be known to her that I did want her, I loosened my one hand from hers and wrapped both of my arms tightly around her waist. I lowered my face and rubbed it against her soft curly hair. You'd of thought we'd known each other for years, but it was something about Anna that gave me a different feeling. Being this close to her I heard no music, I saw no one, and it was as if we were in a place all by ourselves. Breaking my concentration, she leaned back again and looked at me.

"Your eyes say a lot, Kiley. You certainly have something on your mind." I continued to look at her and didn't say a word. "You don't have to talk to me, but in the meantime, can I tell you what I'm thinking?"

"I...I already know because your eyes say a lot too," I said.

She smiled. "Then, what are they saying?"

"How about you tell me."

"Yo quero tú a jodes mi."

"Okay, that was cute. But, I don't understand your language."

She laughed and then whispered. "I said, I want you to fuck me."

"When? Right now?"

"No, not right here, silly. Soon, real soon."

I couldn't help but have a hard on while talking and dancing with her. And thinking about taking her up on her offer, I backed away and told her I needed to go to the restroom. After we separated, I left the dance floor to find Ginger. When I couldn't find her, I went to the restroom to take a leak. On my exit out, the night had gotten even better. To my surprise, the lady I'd been dying to see came into the club with a Baller by her side. It was Candi. She damn sure still had it going on and clung closely to the brotha. I watched as they went to the VIP section and took a seat. Her body was still in tact and the black strapless jumpsuit she had on proved that it was. Her straight black long hair was parted through the middle and hung down her back. And sexy, sexy, sexy, was written all over her face. I'd thought for a moment about how I fucked her so well, and the memory of her holding a gun in my face and reading me my rights flashed before me.

Ginger came over and twirled her fingers in my face. "Wake up, baby. I know you ain't that bored."

"As a matter of fact, I am. Let me get the keys to your car so I can take my butt home. This alcohol got me kind of sluggish and I got a banging ass headache."

She reached in her pocket for the keys. "Here. I'll get a ride home from Deborah. Don't expect me until at least six o'clock and try to get some rest. You haven't had much sleep at all, have you?"

"Not at all. I'll see you when you get home." I kissed Ginger on the cheek and walked away.

I looked around for Anna, while at the same time, I hoped Candi wouldn't see me. I'd questioned one brotha about the Baller she was with and he told me his name was Dominique. Said he was big time on the east side and joked about him being the next president. When I asked him about Candi, he said that he didn't know much about her. Said Dominique always had a new flavah by his side and he'd only seen her with him a few times. I thanked him for the info, and when Anna caught my eye, as I stood by the door, I slightly motioned my head towards the exit. After she walked out, I waited a few minutes and then left. She was leaned against the exit door with her arms folded in front of her. I walked up to her and took her hand.

"Come with me," I said. We walked to Ginger's car and got inside. Shortly after, I pulled in front of Anna's apartment and we both got out. Saying nothing to each other, she unlocked the door, and we went inside. The apartment was dark, and after she closed the door, I backed her against it. I removed her belt from around her waist and ripped her dress apart with my hands. I felt for her panties and tore those off as well. Her heart beat fast as I placed her breasts in my mouth and started to suck them. I massaged them together, and as I worked on those, she undid the buttons on my shirt and removed it. Her body trembled, and when I took my hands off her breasts, I placed my hands on the sides of her face and held her cheeks. She removed her hands from my pants, and held my face in her hands as well. I licked around her buttery soft lips and then stuck my tongue deeply into her mouth. Our lips worked well together and we smack them together for a long while. As our kissing came to an end, Anna took my hand and walked me through the small living room. The kitchen was adjacent to it, and she stopped at the bottom of the steps. She looked up, to what I assumed was her bedroom. For me, that was a long way up. She started up the stairs, and as I scoped her ass in front of me, I couldn't wait to taste her. I pulled her down on the steps and kneeled on the step in front of her. She held herself up by using the rails and I placed her thighs on my shoulders. Now, taking my time, I pressed my lips against her inner thighs. I made my way to her pussy and licked between it to separate her lips. Her clitoris was juicy and hard, so I circled my tongue around it and then went deep inside.

Anna's body jerked several times, as she couldn't keep still. She trembled all over and took lengthy deep breaths in and out. She came quickly, and backed away from me as if she were in fear. When she reached the top of the stairs, I stood in front of her and unzipped my pants. I stepped out of them and lay between her legs. She wrapped them around my back and I reached down to insert myself.

It was a slippery slope, as Anna backed away from the feeling again. She held my upper hips and moved them slightly back.

I leaned forward and pecked my lips with hers. "I'll be gentle," I whispered. She moved her hands away from my hips and I rose up. I placed her legs against my chest and rubbed them. Still inside of her, I parted her legs and maneuvered slowly in and out of her. On occasion, she'd tense up and hold my hips to make me stop. When I did, she'd eventually move again and that was my cue to stroke again.

Sex between us went on for a while, and a bit uncomfortable at the top of the stairs, I suggested going to her bed. I eased myself out of her and when we made it to her bedroom, I lay on my back and put her on top of me. She straddled my lap and when I went back inside of her,

36

she didn't move. I held her ass in my hands and lifted her slightly off my dick.

"Just take your time, okay?" I said.

She nodded and I helped her work up and down on me so it wouldn't hurt. As she seemed to get the hang of it, I removed my hands from her ass and let her work it on her own.

Anna's insides felt good. She was tighter than I'd ever expected, but she worked fairly well with me. I kicked up a serious sweat, and as I reached for her ass to massage it, my grip kept slipping away from the wetness of her behind. As I felt myself about to release, I laid flat on my back and took deep breaths. Anna sat up straight and quickly bounced up and down on me. Her titties were in motion, as well as her pussy that was soak and wet. She ran her fingers through her curly long hair, and after we came together, she fell forward on my chest. I softly rubbed her back with the tips of my fingers.

"Are you okay?" I asked. She nodded her head and wouldn't look up at me. I rolled her over in bed next to me and she placed her head on my muscular arm. She twirled her finger around my chest and placed her leg across mine. I rubbed up and down her leg, and before I knew it, she was sound asleep. Tired, I dozed off too.

By the time I woke up, it was almost nine o'clock in the morning. I sat up on my elbows and squeezed my eyes tightly together. I hadn't slept that well since I'd gotten out of prison and it was one damn sleep that was well deserved and long over due.

Anna was in the shower. I heard her Spanish music playing and pulled the white sheets back to get dressed and go. When I looked down, though, I saw blood on the sheets. I looked at myself and there was a little on me as well. I then went to the bathroom door and knocked. The music was so loud that she didn't hear me. I turned the knob and entered. I moved the shower curtain to the side, and Anna had her eyes closed as she let the water stream out on her face. She sung the Spanish lyrics to the song, and to get her attention, I stepped in the shower behind her. Startled, she opened her eyes and turned her head. She smiled at me and I wrapped my arm around her waist. I took my other arm and wrapped it around her neck. She kissed my arm and I kissed the back of her head.

"Did I hurt you," I whispered. "I'm sorry if I hurt you."

"No, you didn't."

"Were you a virgin? I mean…you were really tight and—

"No. But, I haven't had sex for a very long time."

"Why not and why me?"

She took my arm from around her neck and turned to face me. "Because I like you. I'll tell you about my past another day, okay."

I nodded and Anna lathered up soap in her hands. She touched my chest and moved her hands throughout my entire front side. When I turned around, and pressed my hands against the wall, she worked my backside. I, of course, returned the favor. And after we rinsed ourselves off, we went back into the bedroom and fucked again.

I messed around at Anna's place until damn near one o'clock in the afternoon. I knew I'd get cussed out, if not, put out by Ginger, but my time with Anna was well worth it. She walked down the steps in front of me, and when we made it to the kitchen, she offered me something to drink. In shock, on front of the refrigerator was a picture of Desmon with her nephew. I pretended not to know who he was and asked her about him.

"That's Antonio's best friend, Desmon. Antonio's been at his place since last night." She smiled and pulled the picture off the refrigerator. "They've been through so much together. I can't even begin to tell you."

I definitely wanted to know more but I didn't want Anna to know I was Desmon's father. There wasn't no telling what she'd heard about me, so I left well enough alone.

"So, do you have any kids of your own?" I asked.

"No, I don't have any children. Antonio is like my child because he's been with me forever."

"I see." I took a sip from the glass of Kool Aid she'd poured and sat it on the counter. "Listen, I'd better get going."

"Yes, you'd better."

She walked me to the door and I leaned in for a goodbye kiss. Before I knew it, things started to get hot and heated again. This time, she backed me against the wall and held my face with her soft hands. I raised her short silk gown from the back and rubbed her ass. After she asked me to stay, I reached my hands up and rubbed her hair backwards.

"I'll be back. You have my word I'll be back."

"What about your phone number? Can I call you?"

"Not right now, but soon, okay?"

She backed away from me and opened the door. I stepped out and told her goodbye again.

Ginger's place wasn't too far away, so I drove slowly to it. I knew all hell was about to break loose, and surely after I pulled up, it did. She busted out of the front door and yelled for the keys to her car. They weren't mine, so I didn't hesitate to turn them over. I dropped them in her hands and walked into the house.

"What happened to this supposed to be headache you had, Kiley! I thought you were coming home last night!"

"I was," I said, walking casually into the bedroom. I removed my shirt. "Something else came up, though."

"Something else like what! Some pussy? It's obvious you've been with somebody! Your clothes all wrinkled and her perfume is lighting up the fucking place!"

"If you say it is, then I guess it is. I told you something urgent came up, and that's all there is to it."

She sat on the edge of the bed furious. "One damn day, Kiley. You and me haven't had one damn day of peace since you've been out of jail. Everyday it's something with you. I don't know how much more of this shit I can take."

I walked up to her and placed my hand on the side of her face. "It won't be too much longer, okay. Hopefully, we'll all be able to move on and soon."

I opened the front door and sat on the steps to the upper level townhouses. I massaged my temples and thought about my fourth day out of prison. Things weren't getting better for me, as I'd hoped they would. Desmon was nowhere to be found, and Antonio hadn't for damn sure spent the night here. I didn't know what the hell was going on, but I knew my respect for Ginger was gone the day I got home. Honestly, I hated her for raising Desmon the way she did. I know damn well I could have done a better job than she did, but there was no way for me to go back in time.

SOME THINGS NEVER CHANGE

For the next few days, things were on the down-low. Rufus called and we made plans for my package to be delivered. Of course, it came with instructions. Apparently, one of the fools who was coming to deliver my package had been stealing money from Rufus. He explained the situation to me and asked if I would take care of it for him. He'd even offered to throw in an extra fifty grand and told me the other brotha, Marc, had instructions to get rid of the body once I was finished. What the hell? I thought. Rufus had taken care of my family while I was away, and if it wasn't for him, I wouldn't have ever known about Donovan having Papa Abrams set up to be killed. Either way, I agreed to it and prepared myself to take care of it upon their arrival.

Ginger and I had only seen Desmon twice this week. He came in with Antonio one time, and another time with Gabrielle. I guessed she'd forgiven him because shit seemed to pop off in the basement as it had done before. For the time being, I kept my distance. Not only from him, but from Ginger as well. She'd talked her shit, but when I gave her what she wanted, she shut the fuck up. Actually, I'd gotten kind of tired of fucking her. Anna was on my mind, but I wasn't going back her way anytime soon. When I felt that strongly about a woman, I knew it only meant trouble, so the further away I stayed, the better.

Late Friday night, I asked Ginger if I could use her car. Before she handed over the keys, she asked where I was going.

"I talked to Al earlier this week about finding me a car. He's supposed to hook a brotha up, so I'm going to see what's up."

She dropped the keys in my hand. "Please don't do what you did last time. Everything's been going cool between us and I'm not up for a bunch of drama tonight."

"Just give me a couple of hours. Besides, once I have my car, I won't have to ask you for yours."

I pecked Ginger on the lips and stepped outside. I lit a cigarette and took a few puffs, then got into the car. On the drive to South St. Louis where I was supposed to meet Marc and Cortez, I thought about how I would put my money to good use. A car? Definitely. Some clothes? Without a doubt. A decent place to live? Yes. Things for Desmon? Maybe. Quincy? Of course.

I turned off Grand Ave and pulled into an alley. I saw Marc and Cortez parked exactly where I told them to meet me. I pulled Ginger's car next to theirs and we all got out. I remembered Marc from back in the day, so he and I gave each other a slamming handshake. Cortez didn't say much.

"Damn, man," Marc said. "Yo shit is tight. The pen buffed you out like that?"

I nodded and took a few more puffs from the cigarette. Marc opened the trunk and pulled out a huge black suitcase. He sat it on the ground.

"Ain't no need for me to count it, is there?" I asked.

"Naw, man," Marc said. "It's all there."

"Are you sure?" I took another puff of the cigarette.

"Yeah, I'm positive."

I kneeled down on one knee and started to unzip the suitcase. Before I did, I looked at Cortez. "How about you, Cortez? Are you positive my shit is all here?"

"Definitely...most definitely."

Marc slowly backed up. Cortez turned his head to look at Marc and that's when two bullets from my gun blew right into his chest. His body jerked backwards and hit the ground. Blood splattered everywhere and I wiped a few drips of it off my face. I then put the gun inside of my pants and picked up the suitcase.

"Tell Rufus I said thanks," I said. I dropped the cigarette to the ground and stomped it out with my foot.

"I will," Marc said panicking. "But, help me put this nigga in the trunk, man."

"I ain't got nothing to do with that. That's your job."

"Come on, Kiley. Don't leave me standing out here next to no dead body."

I looked at Marc's scary ass and quickly got pissed. One thing I hated more than anything was a wannabe gangsta who didn't have guts to follow through with a plan. "Look, I've done my job—now, you do yours! Put him in the fucking trunk, take his ass to another city, and dump him!"

I opened the back door to Ginger's car, tossed the suitcase inside, and afterwards, I left.

41

Before I went home, I stopped at Al's place on Natural Bridge Ave. and gave him a little somethin-somethin to get me a car. I knew he'd get me something nice and he told me he'd bring it to me by noon tomorrow. After I cleaned myself up a bit from the incident in the alley, I shot the breeze with him for an hour or so and left.

When I got back to the crib, Ginger and one of her girlfriends were in the living room talking. I strolled in with the suitcase and hurried into the bedroom. After I slid the suitcase underneath the bed, I went back out to join them.

"Baby, you remember Allison from the other night, don't you?"

"Yep," I said. I sat on the couch next to Ginger and she passed me a joint.

"What's that on your face?"

"Where?"

She rubbed my face as a dab of dried up blood was on it. I'd forgotten to wash some of the specks off my face.

"Is this blood or something?"

"Yeah, baby. Some fellas got to fighting at Al's place and I tried to break the shit up."

"You need to be careful. Let them niggas bust each other damn heads."

I took a hit from the joint and passed it back to Ginger. I then got up and went to the bathroom. I thoroughly washed my face and ran cold water on my hands. I'd wanted to take a shower, but I decided to wait until later. Since Ginger was occupied with her girlfriend, I went back into the bedroom and locked the door. I pulled the suitcase out and tightly held the money in my hands. It had been a long time since I'd seen this kind of money and it surely felt good. Soon, I started to count it. After getting mid-way there, I reached for the phone to call Rufus. He quickly answered.

"All I have to say is, you are one psycho motherfucker, Kiley!"

I laughed. "What in the hell are you talking about?"

"That nigga Marc called me whining like a bitch. He told me what you said and I couldn't do nothing but crack the fuck up. Cause, you still my nigga. That's why I need you here with me."

"No can do, Rufus. I got plans, man. Plans that do not include moving back to L.A."

"So, it's like that, huh?"

42

"I'm afraid so. Quincy will be out in a few and we gone get ourselves a nice place to chill, find us some everyday-pussy-giving-ass women, possibly have some more babies, and live until I'm a hundred years old."

"What a boring life? But, it's yours. I ain't mad at cha, but the Kiley Jacoby Abrams I know, can't have a simple life like that."

"That's the one you used to know. I'm trying to change Rufus. In a few more months, you'll see how much I've changed."

"Nigga, tell that to the fool you just blew away a few hours ago. You don't have it in you, man. And as soon as you realize that, I hope you'll make your way back to me."

"Whatever you say, dog. I'll chat with you in a few days, alright?"

"Thanks for handling my bitness. I'll check with you in a minute."

Rufus hung up and I put a several hundred dollars in my wallet. I placed the suitcase back underneath the bed and felt like a new man. When I came out of the room, Ginger said that her and Allison were going over to Allison's house to play cards. She asked if I wanted to come along, but I declined.

After they left, I got comfortable in my boxers and stretched out on the couch. I placed a thick pillow on my lap and slowly faded.

I was in a deep sleep, when Desmon and Antonio came busting through the door. I'd already reached for my piece and when I saw that it was them, I laid the gun back down on the floor.

"Say, man," Desmon said to me. "You got any mojo on ya?"

Immediately, I could tell him and Antonio were fucked up. Trying to have one peaceful night, I realized that I couldn't. I slowly got up and tripped his ass to the floor. He fell hard and hit his head. I kneeled over him and grabbed him by his collar.

"Didn't I tell you I was gone fuck you up if you keep disrespecting me?" I yelled. He gathered spit in his mouth and let it out in my face. I took my fist and slammed it hard in his face. The tough lil motherfucker hit me back, and I'll be damned if I didn't grab his ass off the floor and throw him into the wall in front of me. Ginger's whole entertainment center came crashing down and the glass cracked as it hit the floor. Blood dripped from Desmon's mouth and he angrily stood up and charged at me again. With all my strength, I pushed him back again.

He fell hard, and soon after, the stupid fool got up again. This time, I made it clear I wasn't playing. I caught him with another right in his face that instantly floored him. He rolled over on his back and spit blood out of his mouth. Antonio, being the damn fool that he was, looked at my gun on the floor and reached for it. He cocked the trigger and aimed it at me.

I held my arms out and smiled. "Shoot me, you lil punk motherfucker."

"Dez," he yelled. "All you gotta do is say the word and this fool is history."

Now, this really fucked me up. I kneeled down next to Desmon and pulled him up by his collar. "Did you hear him! Your boy said all you gotta do is say the word! So, say the word, nigga, so we can get this over with!"

He looked at me with hostility in his eyes. "I hate you, Kiley! Lord knows I hate you!"

"Then tell your fucking friend to pull the trigger!"

"You—

"Tell him! Shut the hell up and tell him!"

Desmon didn't say shit. I shoved him backwards and karate kicked Antonio in his stomach. He flipped over the couch and the gun dropped out of his hand. I picked it up and looked at both of the pathetic fools.

"Yeah, that's what I thought. You niggas ain't about shit!" I grabbed my blue jean shorts and shoes off the floor. I then opened the door and slammed it on my way out.

After I slid my shorts and shoes on, I walked around and waited for things to cool down. I wanted to go to Anna's place, but I didn't want to run to her when there was trouble. Instead, I walked to the nearest payphone. I called Jada on her cell phone and she quickly called back.

"Kiley, is that you?"

"That's what I said, didn't I?"

"I've been waiting and waiting to hear from you. Where are you?"

"In front of Jay's liquor store on State St."

"I need directions. I have no idea—"

44

I told Jada where it was and she said that she was on her way. Shirtless, I sat on the curb and waited for Jada to come. Within the hour, she pulled up in her spanking brand new Lexus. She unlocked the doors and I hopped in. She looked over at me.

"I don't want no drama, Kiley. If you and your woman been fighting—

I took a deep breath. "Good to see you too, Jada."

She rolled her eyes and drove off.

There was no conversation between us. Jada looked straight ahead and drove and I looked out of the window. I did, however, look over at her a few times. I'd noticed the huge wedding ring that damn near weighed down her finger, the clothes she had on were named brand shit, and several hundred-dollar bills were stuffed in the Gucci purse that sat close by her side. She'd thickened up a bit more, and her sandy brown hair was still in a ponytail. Some things just never change, I thought. Pertaining to her and me as well.

She drove to the *Holiday Inn* and parked the car. It was obvious what was on her mind, but as angry as I was about what had happened, I really wasn't in the mood.

"Do you remember this place?" she asked. I nodded and leaned back in the seat. "Do you want to go inside or not?"

I reached for the door handle and opened the door. Jada grabbed her purse, and after she locked the doors, we went inside. I stood closely behind her because I didn't have a shirt on. She got a room and I followed her to it.

When we got inside, Jada sat on the edge of the bed and I leaned against the dresser with my arms folded.

"Jada, I don't feel like having sex tonight."

She gave me a stare. "Did I ask you for any sex tonight?"

"I assumed—

"Well, you assumed wrong. If you must know, I just wanted to see you. I missed you and I wanted to be sure you were okay. By the looks of things, it's obvious you're not."

"No, I'm not. But you know I ain't never been one to talk about my problems, right?"

"You need to stop with the secrets. There are some people who you can trust."

"Very few."

"Yeah, well, that's just how it is. I hope that after all we'd been through, you feel as if you can trust me."

"Trust you to do what, Jada? To call the police on me when shit don't go right like you did in the past? To fuck my partner cause things ain't right with you and me?"

"Kiley, that was a long time ago. I admit I made some stupid mistakes, but so did you."

"You got that right. Mistakes that I don't want to make again."

"You know, you didn't say all that when you were in jail. It was all good then, so what happened baby? Have you had a change of heart since you've been out?"

"Maybe."

"Whatever. It don't even matter."

Jada turned away and looked down at the ground. I walked over and sat next to her on the bed. "This hotel was the last place you and me had sex," I said. "You didn't think I remembered, did you?"

She moved her head from side to side, implying no.

"Why'd you come here, though?" I said. "If you didn't want to have sex with me then why'd you come here?"

"I don't know. I've thought a lot about you...about us over the last few years and we shouldn't had never broken up. We'd been through thick and thin together and I never got over you. To this day, I can't stop thinking about your punk ass." She smiled.

"It's nice to know I was thought about because I'd for damn sure thought you'd moved on with your life. Especially, since you're married now and everythang."

She looked at me and pointed her finger. "You know damn well I don't love him. I was looking for a replacement for your Black ass."

"Big mistake."

"You're damn right it was. But...but what about you? Do you have any feelings left for me?" I was silent. "Kiley, tell me. And don't lie either."

I closed my eyes and rubbed them with the tip of my fingers, as I was in deep thought. I looked at Jada.

"Along time ago, baby, I would have given you the world. Again, that was a long time ago. I have nothing left for no one, but Quincy and my son."

"But, I'm talking about me or any other females. You can't tell me you ain't got no feelings for anybody."

"Jada, I got love for Quincy and Desmon. Baby, other than that, that's it. I stopped giving my love to women after what happened to me. I promised myself I would never love again."

"Were you in love with that bitch Candi?"

"No, but it's just the trust I gave her. I trusted the shit out of her and opened up to her in many ways I shouldn't had."

"Have you seen her since you've been out?"

"Believe it or not, yes."

Jada looked shocked. "Seriously?"

"Yep. I saw her at a nightclub. She didn't see me but I definitely saw her."

"Kiley, you ain't up to nothing, are you?"

"I'd rather not say."

"Whatever it is, I don't want to know. Please be careful though. I'd hate for something to happen to you."

I lay back on the bed and looked up at the ceiling. "Would you rub my back like you used to do? Your fingernails used to feel so good scrolling up and down on my back."

"Now, you know for a fact, when it comes to me, in order to get something, you've got to give something."

I snickered. "Then take your damn clothes off, girl."

"I thought you'd see it my way."

Jada and me got down to business. One moment I was there and the next minute I wasn't. Desmon was on my mind so I kind of rushed Jada so we could go.

It was way after two o'clock in the morning when she dropped me off. I asked her to drop me off at the corner to cut down on the tension between Ginger and me.

"Until next time," Jada said, leaning over to give me a kiss.

I rubbed her thick legs. "Yeah, baby, until next time." I got out and closed the door.

On my way to Ginger's place, I lit a cigarette and smoked it. I put it out by the front door and entered. It was kind of quiet, so I went into the kitchen to find something to eat. There wasn't much, so I grabbed a box of cereal and poured it into a bowl. I added milk and sat down to eat.

I was on scoop number three when Ginger walked in and stood angrily before me. She smacked my face and tossed the cereal on the floor.

She spoke calmly. "What in the hell did you do to my son?"

"I ain't do shit to *our* son. We talked, he didn't like my conversation and that was it," I looked up at her. "Now, don't put your hands on me again."

Her eyes watered. "Have you even seen his face? How could you do that to him! I don't know whether to call the police on you or not. You are an animal, Kiley! You should have stayed locked up if you think I'm going to let you come in here and beat on my son like that!"

"Our son needs some discipline! Had you put your foot in his ass along time ago, I wouldn't have to do it now! But you were too busy, though. Too busy lying on your damn back and giving out your lousy ass pussy. You ain't been about shit, Ginger! Tell me what the fuck is your purpose? Desmon comes in here when he wants to, he doesn't go to school, he gets high out of his damn mind, he fucks his bitches in your shitty house, and what do you do? Not a damn thing. You pat him on the back by buying him expensive clothes to look good, and buy him a car when he ain't even old enough to drive! So, I don't give a rats ass how you feel about me hitting him. It wasn't the first and it won't be the last! He's gonna fear me! And every time he thinks about disrespecting me, I'm gonna make sure he thinks twice! Every time he think he can come in here when he get good and ready to, I got something for that ass! And if he even think about sharing a joint with me again, I'm gonna show him who the real weed wacker is around here! And, you know why Ginger?" She turned her head and looked away. I stood up and grabbed her face tightly in my hands. "Because my father kicked my ass when I disrespected him. All it took was one time, and it was an ass kicking I will never forget. To this day, dead or not, I respect him and worship the ground he walked on. Someday, Desmon is going to feel the same way about me. I'm gonna make sure of that."

She smacked my hand away from her face. "If your daddy was all that, then how in the hell did you to turn out to be the ignorant motherfucker that you are today?"

"Because it was a bitch like you who helped raise me!"

Ginger reached out to smack me again and I quickly grabbed her wrist and twisted it. I pushed her away and walked into the bedroom.

Feeling the pressure, I plopped down on the bed. I sat back against the pillows and my eyes watered from the thought of Desmon. I hoped like hell I hadn't hurt him too badly. Moreso, I needed confirmation I was going about this the right way. I surely didn't have all the answers, but it was the only way I knew how to get him to straighten up. The last thing I wanted was for him to be like me. There had to be a better life for him...it just had to be.

TELL ME IT'S JUST A DREAM

Saturday, by noon, Al was right on time with my new set-the-fuck-out ass Cadillac. It was black, had all the right trimmings, and had soft black leather interior. Before he left, I told him to hook Quincy up with a little somethin-somethin as well. He said he would and jetted.

Immediately following Al's departure, I went straight to the malls and hooked myself up. Wasn't no need to ride like I was, and look like a bum.

By nearly days end, the trunk was filled and could barely close. I had mega shit and had even picked up Desmon a few things. Now, I know what I said to Ginger for doing the same, but a part of me knew after what happened yesterday, he would start to see things my way. In addition to buying him something, I'd even stopped at the jewelry store and picked out a diamond necklace for Anna. I wasn't sure why, but I just felt like doing it.

After my shopping spree, I stopped to get a cell phone because I needed one badly. Ginger always had the line tied up, and if it wasn't her, it was Desmon staying on it all night long. Besides, since I'd picked up a few numbers at the mall today, I had to have something to use if I even intended to call the ladies I'd met back.

Before going home, I stopped at the corner and hollered at a few fellas who stood nearby looking up to no good. It was obvious what they were up to, and after I pulled over to the curb, they came up to the car. I lowered the window and they looked into the car.

"Yo, man, what's up?" one of them said.

"Any of you brothas know a Dominique?" They looked at each other and humped their shoulders. I rose up and reached into my back pocket for my wallet. I pulled out a hundred dollar bill and looked at them again. "Again...any of you brothas know Dominique?" One reached for the money, and the other pulled his hand back.

"Naw, bro, we don't know no Dominique?"

I nodded and looked straight ahead. "So, tell me...what's it gonna cost me?"

"Nothing. I told you we don't know nobody named Dominique?"

"A thousand...two. All I want is for you fellas to tell him to call me, that's all."

They looked at each other. "Fool, how you know we won't just take yo money and run. You don't trust us to really tell him to call you, do you?"

"If I give you one grand a piece, and Dominique doesn't call me by the end of the day, you won't even have time to spend the money. Now, do we have a deal or not? If not, I'll go make my deal elsewhere."

They turned to each other again, and then looked at me. "You got a deal. Give us your damn number."

I unlocked the door and they got in. After they did, I watched in my rearview mirror as a police car was headed our way. He rolled slowly by and looked over at us. After he nodded, I nodded back and he drove off.

I wrote my name and number on a piece of paper and marked it urgent. I gave it to one of the fellas, along with the agreed upon two grand. I reminded them that if they didn't deliver, they wouldn't live to see the next day. They assured me Dominique would call and I jetted.

Ginger was in the bedroom folding the laundry when I came in. I hung my clothes in the closet and didn't say anything to her. When I went back outside to get more bags, she came to the door and watched me. She looked at the car, and then returned to the bedroom.

"What's all this?" she said.

"I needed a few things. A friend of mine hooked me up."

"That's good. Is he gonna hook up a place for you to stay?"

"Maybe, or maybe not. But, is that your way of asking me to leave?"

"Kiley, you know we can't go on like this. You've said some really hurtful things to me and I am more than angry with you."

"And, you've also said some hurtful things to me. Just get over it. I have. Today is a new day, baby, ain't no need to trip."

"Sorry, but it's not that easy for me. I would like for this to work out for all of us. You need to stop pointing the finger at me, and take a look at yourself. If you—

"Ginger! It's over, baby. You don't say nothing to me, and I won't say nothing to you. I got business here. And until my business is finished, I'm not leaving."

The phone rang and she reached for it. She held it in her hand and looked at me.

"I think it's Quincy. Do you want me to accept his call?"

51

"Please."

She accepted and handed the phone over to me.

"What up, playa?" I said, and then sat on the edge of the bed.

"I got good news, man."

"Oh, yeah. What's up?"

"Bradshaw said I am out of here! I got one more week. After that, this hellhole is history!"

"Well, I'll be damn. Things are certainly starting to look up."

"You're damn right they are. I am hyped, man! And, I can't wait until Friday."

"Me and Ginger will come pick you up. I don't want to come by myself cause I don't want no shit."

"Fool, you can send a dog to come pick me up. I don't care. As long as yo ass is here no later than...let's say, nine o'clock."

"Now, you know they gone fuck around. They probably mad as hell, ain't they?"

"Haters! All over the place. And that motherfucker Joe, he can't stand to look at me. Him and me been at it all damn week."

"Don't trip with him, Q. Ignore that punk. He just mad cause we out smarted that ass. Whatever you do, avoid his ass until you get out of there."

"Oh, I am. But, listen...my time is up. I'll see you Friday, and please, please, please don't be late. And do a brotha one last favor, au-ight?"

"What's that?"

"Get me a nice quiet room, with a Jacuzzi tub, some champagne, and of course, some pussy. Not just any pussy, but some good pussy."

I laughed. "What the hell you want me to do, sample it or something? Now, I'll make arrangements to get you some, but I can't promise you how good it'll be."

"Then, do your best. I know your best is always good enough."

"It always is, ain't it? Love ya, dog. See ya in a bit."

"Right back at ya. Deuces."

Quincy hung up and the biggest smile I hadn't seen in a long time covered my face. Ginger cleared her throat to get my attention, as she could see how thrilled I was.

"Did you say something?" I asked.

"I said, who are you to make plans for me on next Friday?"

"Aw, baby, please. This is real important to me. I just don't want to go alone."

"Ain't no big deal. Just because I'm mad at you doesn't mean I don't still love you."

I smiled and gave the phone to her as it started to ring. It was one of her girlfriends, so I left out of the room not wanting to hear her yakking.

As I walked into the kitchen, Desmon sat at the kitchen table. His head hung low and he talked to someone on his cell phone. I opened the fridge and reached for the orange juice. After I closed it, I turned the carton up to my lips and he looked over at me. My heart dropped and I spilt some orange juice on my shirt. I turned away and blinked my eyes at the sight of his face. I sat the carton of orange juice on the counter and leaned against it. After I maintained my composure, I turned back around and watched as he continued his conversation.

His face was fucked up. His right eye was fiery red and the other was swollen and closed. The right side of his face was badly bruised and one side of his upper lip hung over his bottom lip. It hurt me like hell to see what I'd done and I couldn't even come up with anything that justified that kind of beating.

I grabbed a bag of Doritos from the shelf and sat at a chair across the table from him. He continued on with his conversation and when he stood up to walk away, I interrupted him.

"Do you mind if I talk to you for a minute?"

He gave me an angry look and sat back down. Shortly after, he ended his useless conversation. I was sure the person over the phone couldn't understand a damn thing he said as he mumbled the entire time. He put his baseball cap on backwards, opened his legs and placed his elbows on his knees. Avoiding me, he looked down at the ground.

"What?" he mumbled.

"I…I just wanted to apologize for yesterday. I did not intend to hurt you the way I did, but I can't let you continue to do and say the things you do. You've got to know you be out of line. I had a bad day yesterday and I snapped."

He rubbed his hands together and closed his eyes, as I talked.

"Is there anything else?" he said.

"Yes," I hesitated and took a hard swallow. "I love you more than anything in this world. You have no reason to believe that, but if you

53

give me the opportunity, I'll prove it to you. Believe it or not, you're why I have the desire to live. Before I leave this earth, I am determined to make you a better man. You've got to help me, though. I can't do it alone, Desmon. And as much as I love my father, my brother, Quincy, Rufus, and myself, I don't want you to be like us. It was rough…too rough, and in the end, we've all had a costly price to pay."

He continued to stare at the ground and there was silence. I saw a few tears hit the floor in front of him. He sniffed, "Is there anything else?" he mumbled, again.

I paused. "Didn't you have a game today?" He nodded.

"Did you go?" I asked.

"Not like this. Coach told me to sit this one out."

"Maybe next week, then."

"Maybe so." He stood up, opened the door to the basement and went downstairs.

It wasn't the best conversation between us, but it was a start. I couldn't complain and was on a serious high after talking to Quincy and finally getting some where with my son.

Before it got too late, I drove to Wal-Mart and bought Ginger another entertainment center. It was way better than the one she had, and as I was in the living room putting it together, my cell phone rang. I rushed to answer it.

"Who is this?" he asked.

"Who is this?" I replied back with attitude.

"Fool, I heard you were looking for me. Is this Kiley?"

"Yes. Is this Dominique?"

"State your business and stop wasting my time."

"It's imperative that I meet with you."

"Yeah, well, take a number. I'll call you back when I got time."

"I suggest you make time. Now, I got some important information for you. Somebody I know is out to get you. If you don't want to know who it is, then pretend this call never happened."

"Man, there's plenty of niggas out to get me. I fear no one."

"No doubt, but I ain't talking about no niggas. I'm talking about one of your female companions. Now, I'm not gone say shit else over the phone. If you want to know more, I need to hear what day and time."

"Next Saturday. I'll call you Saturday and tell you where to meet me."

I didn't say nothing else and just hung up.

The week dragged on. Desmon didn't say much to me, but he did ask about my car. He even asked if he could drive it and after I told him no, he got an attitude and left. I'd noticed he hadn't been to school all week, but I assumed it was because of his face. It had started to heal, but for a pretty boy, every mark had to be gone before he'd show his face to anybody.

I damn near had to drag Ginger out of bed on Friday. It was almost nine o'clock and I promised Quincy I wouldn't be late. It wasn't like he would be standing outside waiting because I knew they'd bullshit around with him, like they bullshitted around with me.

Earlier in the week, I'd made arrangements for him liked he'd asked. I had two badass gals all hooked up and waiting for him at a hotel with his champagne and Jacuzzi tub. As fine as the ladies were, I wanted to join them, but I didn't want to take the excitement away from Quincy since I knew how anxious he would be.

In addition to that, Al hooked up another Cadillac for me. This one was white, with soft white leather interior. It was off the chain and I was sure Quincy would love it.

Ginger and me didn't say much in the car. I think she was still a bit upset with me about Desmon, but after I laid it on the line for her, I didn't think she'd want to hear my mouth again.

She pulled into the same spot she was in when she picked me up. I hopped in the back seat of her car and she pulled out a magazine.

"We gone be a while, so you might as well get comfortable," she said.

I leaned back on the seat and closed my eyes. I must have dozed off because by the time I opened them, it was a little after eleven o'clock. Ginger looked at me and rolled her eyes.

"You be snoring too loud. I'm glad you don't sleep as much at home. Lord knows I'll never get any sleep."

"Whatever," I said, looking out of the window for Quincy. "Have they even opened the gates?"

"No. I haven't seen anybody."

"Well, keep looking."

Ginger smacked me on the leg with the magazine. "Don't you take your butt back to sleep. Talk to me or something. I'm getting bored."

I sat up. "What do you want to talk about?"

"About Desmon. And...about why you haven't had sex with me all week."

"Desmon and me gone work things out. And, I haven't had sex with you all week because you're the one who's been acting all funny and shit."

"Of course. You shouldn't have called my pussy lousy."

"If it were lousy, then I wouldn't be in it."

"Then why did you say it?"

"Out of anger, Ginger. Nothing more and nothing less. Besides," I said, placing my hand over my dick, "I planned on making up tonight anyway."

"Did you?"

"Uh-huh. You ain't got a problem with that, do you?"

"I might. But, you know you always got the solutions to my problems, don't you?"

"Always," I said, and then looked out for Quincy again.

Time had moved on. I'd nodded off again and even Ginger had dozed as well. By now, it was almost three o'clock and I figured Quincy had to be making his way out soon.

Feeling cramped in the back seat, I got out to stretch. Ginger did the same and started to complain.

"He should be out in a minute. This around the same time they let me out."

"This is ridiculous, baby. I'm tired. I didn't mind waiting for you, but..."

"Just cool out, au-ight? It shouldn't be much longer."

Ginger leaned against the car and I stood in front of her. I pressed myself against her and she smiled.

"Don't play, Kiley. You can't smooth me over with your so called charm."

I pulled her to me and wrapped my arms around her waist. "Give me a kiss."

"No."

"Come on, now, give me a kiss."

56

She held her lips tightly together. I placed my lips on hers, and soon after, hers loosened. We smacked lips and Ginger backed away. She played with the top button on my button down *Sean Jeans* shirt.

"Why'd you go buy yourself all these nice clothes and didn't think about me?"

"I did. I bought you an entertainment center, didn't I?"

"That's because you broke it."

"I didn't break it. Desmon broke it."

"With your help."

"I'll buy you something later, okay."

She nodded and hopped on the hood of the car. I stood between her legs and inched my hands up her shirt to play with her nipples.

"Would you stop playing? You haven't been this excited since the day I picked you up. I hope Quincy's presence keeps your attitude this way."

I laughed because Ginger was certainly right.

By six o'clock, I started to get worried. Ginger was tired of waiting and so was I. We'd gotten in and out of the car several times and tried to keep our conversation going to pass by the time.

When eight o'clock came, I'd given up. I called Bradshaw on his phone, but his answering machine said the office was closed. I told Ginger let's go home and I hoped Quincy called me from somewhere if he'd gotten out.

Slightly worried, I hung around the house for the rest of the night. Ginger went out with one of her girlfriends, and Desmon was in the basement with several of his friends.

Every time the phone rang, I ran to it. It was for Ginger or Desmon, but never for me.

By midnight, I knew something was wrong. I lay in bed, in the dark, and stared at the ceiling. My heart ached and all kinds of shit ran through my head. The only thing that could have gone wrong is maybe he got put in the hole. That for damn sure would have delayed his time, but I knew he wouldn't do nothing stupid since he was so close to getting out.

About four in the morning, Ginger strolled in blasted. She took her clothes off at the door, and crawled up to me in bed. I was wide-awake and for damn sure wasn't in no mood for fucking.

She did what she knew best and placed my dick in her mouth. It took forever for me to rise and when I did, it slowly but surely went back down.

"Not tonight, baby, I got something heavy on my mind," I said, and then moved her over to the side.

She glared at me in the partially dark room. "Come on, Kiley. You said that we—

"I know what I said earlier, but I'm not in the mood, okay."

"Just five minutes," she said, reaching for my hand. She placed it between her legs. "Can't you feel how horny I am?"

Ginger's insides were drenched. I tickled her with my fingers and dug them deep inside of her. She moaned for me to fuck her. I quickly turned her on her stomach and hurried on top of her. I pecked my lips down her back and then made my way to the end of the bed. I stood up and then grabbed her feet and pulled her towards me. When she backed her ass up against me, I slammed myself inside of her. I pounded her hard because I was mad. Mad because Quincy hadn't called, Mad because Desmon and his friends were downstairs smoking weed, and definitely mad because I told Ginger's ass I didn't feel like fucking. If she had to be the one to pay for it, then so be it. I continued to fuck her hard and the headboard slammed hard against the wall. She tried to move away, but I squeezed her hips tightly to keep them in place.

"Ki...Kiley," she moaned and lowered her head. "You're hurting me. Baby, slow down...that shit hurts."

"You told me to fuck you, didn't you? I'm just doing what you asked." I continued on doing my thang and after Ginger came, I pulled out and released my juices on her ass. She fell on her stomach and let out a deep sigh. I massaged her butt and rubbed my juices all over her butt. I then smacked it hard and told her I'd see her in mid morning.

I went into the living room and laid on the couch. After I flipped through a few channels, I then rolled up a joint and smoked it. Soon, I was high as hell. I could barely keep my eyes opened and finally fell off to sleep.

I was awakened by Desmon's tap on my shoulder. He told me the phone in the kitchen was for me and I quickly raised up to get it. Anxious to see if it was Quincy, I didn't have time to put on any clothes, so I followed Desmon to the kitchen to get the phone. He looked at me and shook his head.

"Do you need a towel or something?" he said, and then picked up a bag of Doritos.

I ignored him and picked the phone up that laid on the table.

"Hello."

"Kiley."

"Who is this?"

"Pedro," he said in a low voice. "Quincy's roomy."

"Man, I know who you are…what's up?"

"I got bad news, mon."

My heart dropped. "Wha…what's up?"

"Quincy dead, man. They killed him."

A cold chill came over me. "What the fuck you just say?"

"Listen, I can't say much, but he told me if anything happened to him to call you."

I dropped to one knee, lowered my head, and spoke softly. "Pedro, please tell me this is a joke. If it is, don't play with me like this."

"Kiley, I'm sorry, it's no joke, mon. They say he killed himself, but you and I know better. I gotta go, I'll call you soon."

He hung up and the phone dropped out of my hand. I covered my eyes with my hand and the tears started to fall. Angry, I stood up and slammed the phone against the receiver on the wall.

"No! No! No! No! Hell fucking naw!" I yelled. The phone broke off into pieces as I continued to slam it against the receiver. In a rage, I dropped the phone pieces in my hand and pounded the kitchen's table.

"This shit is not happening! What in the fuck is going on! Somebody tell me what the fuck happened!"

Ginger ran into the kitchen and stood in the doorway.

"What's the matter!" she yelled. "What happened?"

I sobbed as tears continued to pour down my face. Spit dripped from my mouth and my entire body was numb. I took deep breaths and looked at Ginger. "I don't believe this shit. My…my boy is gone!"

I stood up and pressed my hands on the table. Ginger came over and wrapped her arms around me. She told Desmon to get me a glass of water.

"Baby, I…I'm sorry," she said. "I don't know—

I moved Ginger away from me and wiped my hand down my face to clear it. I hurried off into the bedroom and slid into my jeans. Ginger stood in the doorway with her arms folded.

"What are you getting ready to do?"

I ignored her and continued to put on my clothes. After I did, I reached for my gun and slid it down inside my pants. She blocked me from leaving the room.

"Kiley, don't. Please don't. How many people are gonna have to die, huh? I don't know much about the bible but I do know God said vengeance is his, baby. Not yours."

"Move!" I yelled in her face. "Today, it's mine!" Seeing how angry I was, she moved aside and I hurried to the front door. I opened it and pushed the screen door away. I rushed to my car and after I got inside, I slammed the door shut. I squeezed my chest as it ached so badly. Then I rubbed my body to ease the pain. I felt as if I were losing my mind and when the pain wouldn't go away, I reached for my gun. I laid it next to me and squeezed my eyes tightly together. When I opened them, I looked up at Desmon as he stood in the doorway. He munched on the Doritos and slowly walked up to the car with the glass of water in his hand. After he opened the passenger's side door, he got in and took a seat. I hated for him to see me like this, so I leaned my head back on the headrest and closed my eyes again.

"Say," he said, smacking on the chips. "I really don't know what just happened, but I'm sorry to hear about your friend. I gotta a close friend too, and if anything happened to him, I don't know what I'd do."

I hesitated then responded. "You'd go kill the motherfuckers who were responsible, wouldn't you?"

"I probably would. But then again, that would make me like you. I ain't trying to be like you, though."

"Good," I turned and looked at him. "Now get out of my car so I can go."

"I got a game at three. You...you gone make it, right?"

"I...I'll try."

"Try hard. You've already missed nearly ten years of them, don't make it anymore."

"Would you get out of my car, please?"

Desmon opened the door and got out. I drove off and hadn't a clue where I was driving to. My intentions were to go kill up as many guards as I could at the prison, but I knew for sure who was responsible. Joe was definitely my man and I didn't care what Ginger, Desmon, or anybody else said, he would surely pay for what he'd done.

I drove around for a few hours doing nothing. Dominique called, but I had to put our appointment off for another day. He wasn't too happy about it and accused me of playing games with him. I assured him it wasn't no game because it wasn't. If it wasn't for Candi and that slick ass bitch Veronica, maybe all this shit wouldn't have happened. I was beyond angry and many people were gonna have to pay for Quincy's death.

Around four o'clock I stopped driving around and headed to Desmon's game. My eyes were swollen and were a blood shot red. I'd smoked several blunts in the car and had stopped at the liquor store to get something strong to drink.

By the time I got to his game, I was pretty messed up and only stayed around long enough for Desmon to see me. He looked over at me several times as I stood by the gate and watched him play. As I turned to walk away, somebody called my name. I didn't turn to see who it was because I knew it was Anna. I kept on walking and soon her voice got further away. When I reached my car, I looked to where she was, and she turned her head the other way.

I simply wasn't in the mood. Yes, I dug the hell out of her, but I didn't have time for her. Moreso, I didn't want to put her into this mess I was about to get myself into. I'd been putting my feelings aside, and avoiding them because I was afraid to face the fact that a woman's love was creeping it's way into my heart once again.

A TIME TO KILL

Going home last night was out of the question. I didn't want Desmon to see the agony I was in, and I wasn't up for a bunch of questions from Ginger. I got a room for the night and couldn't stop thinking about Quincy for nothing in the world. The last time we talked flashed before me throughout the night. I saw his smile, I visualized us slamming our hands together, and I imagined his death. I'd visualized what had taken place in my mind, and the more I thought about it, the angrier I got.

For me, there was no need for Pedro to call me back. I wasn't going to wait another minute to do what had to be done. I knew Joes's check out time was at six o'clock so I prepared myself to pay him a visit. I'd found out where he lived months ago because of all the trouble he'd caused me while in prison, I'd made plans for him anyway. Better sooner than never, I thought, and today was not going to be his lucky day.

Not only for him, but it was time to get down to business with Dominique. I called him back and made arrangements to come to his place at ten o'clock tonight.

Either way, I had a busy day ahead of me. I stayed at the hotel until five o'clock and then headed out. By the time I got near Joe's place on Page Avenue it was almost five-thirty. I parked my car around the corner and walked to where he lived. He lived in some crappy high-rise apartments, so I took the black metal stairs up to his back door. I knocked a few times to make sure he wasn't there, and then I picked the lock and made my entry. His place was in a mess. It didn't surprise me that the fat white motherfucker lived like a pig. He had food and shit lying around and the whole damn place smelled like piss. To make matters even worse, he had a slu of magazines that showed naked women. Had the nerve to be Black women and that really pissed me the fuck off.

I continued to look around his place for a while and when I looked out and saw him getting out of his car, I hurried into a sliding closet in his living room. I peeked through the door crack and watched as he came in with a brown grocery bag in his hand. Another guard, Big Bo, who was pretty cool with me, came in after him. Bo took a seat on the couch and Joe walked over to the TV and slid in a tape. They both munched on some chips, as they sat and watched what seemed to be porn. They went back and forth about the women pussies, and when I heard Quincy's name, I was all ears.

"That fucking cock sucker, Bo," Joe said. "He had it coming. I swear to God that son of a bitch had it coming."

Bo nodded. "Ya damn right he did. I can't believe that motherfucker thought he'd get off without having to pay a price. Didn't he know there was a price to pay for wanting to be a nigger?"

"Yeah, if he didn't know, he for damn sure knows it now." They both laughed.

"I'd give anything to see the look on that fucker Abrams face when he finds out his girlee's dead." Bo nodded and Joe looked back at the TV. "Suck it, baby," he said gazing at the TV. "Look at the lips on that Black bitch."

I was just about to let him see the look on my face when he turned to look at Bo again. "Bo, I hated that fucker Abrams. Sometimes, I knew you had love for them niggers, but I wanted his ass so badly."

I slid the door over. "Then take me motherfucker." I fired two shots directly into his chest. Him and the chair he sat in flew into the wall behind him. He held his chest as his hands trembled in front of it. Soon, his eyes faded. I aimed the gun at Bo.

"Kiley, you don't want to do this," he said slowly getting up off the couch.

"Oh, yes I do." With no hesitation, I pulled the trigger twice again. I fired one in Bo's head and the other into his chest. After that, I hurried to the door. Since I knew the assholes were on their way to hell, I wanted to make sure they went past it. I turned and took one more shot at Joe, and another shot at Bo. This way, they'd be damn sure to say hello to the devil for me.

Ready to finish my business for the day, I stopped at *Taco Bell* on Delmar to get a bite to eat. Normally, when I had to do shit like that, a part of me felt guilty. This time, I had no regrets.

After I got my grub on, I drove around for a bit. When it neared time to meet Dominique, I headed for his place.

I couldn't believe he gave me the correct address to where he lived. That proved to me he was dumber than I thought. I really didn't like his ass, nor did I care if he went to jail. I wanted Candi so badly that I didn't even give a fuck what I thought of Dominique. I wasn't going to kill her because that would have been too easy. With her being a detective, they'd for damn sure come after me. So, I hoped this fool Dominique had a little balls about him. If not, I'd have to make plans to do something different.

When I got to his house, which was on the north side of St. Louis, one of his boys answered the door. I walked in and he told me to have a seat. The crib was laid the fuck out and in the living room where I sat, he had a black leather s-shaped sofa with glass round tables beside it. The carpet was white as snow and exquisite, black, white and red humongous artwork covered the white walls. Dominique stood above the t-staircase and looked down into the living room at me. He tied his silk robe together and walked slowly down the stairs. He stopped to mumble something to his partner who'd opened the door, and then walked over to the bar and poured himself a drink. Afterwards, he took a seat in one of the red leather round chairs.

"I would offer you something to drink, but I don't know you like that."

I looked at his midnight black ass and smiled. "Listen, like I said before, I'm here to do you a favor. If you wanna keep up with the smart ass talking, then you'd better talk that shit to somebody else. I don't play like that."

"Mr. Kiley, what's on your mind? You sought me out, playa, so speak."

"You and me got something in common. Her name is Candi and I don't think you know what she's after."

"Man, you came over here with some beef about one of my bitches? Besides, I don't even know no gal named Candi."

"I'm sure that wasn't the name she gave you. It was the chick you were at the club with the other night."

"I've been to the club with many ladies. Which one…"

I got frustrated. "The dark chocolate one with the long black hair. She had on a black strapless jumpsuit and got a body out of this world."

"Cassandra? That was Cassandra."

"Candi, or Cassandra…whatever she calls herself these days. Whatever it is, she's a detective. Several years back, she along with one of her partners, plotted on my boys and me. I did ten years in prison because of that bitch and I'm here to give you a heads-up to watch your back."

"Man, you gotta be bullshitting. Not Cassandra. And what does her partner look like."

I described Veronica to Dominique and he yelled for his partna Chris. Chris came into the room.

"Hey, man, this Kiley. Kiley this Chris."

"What up?" Chris said.

I nodded.

Dominique looked at him. "You got a picture of Teco and his gal?"

"Maybe, I don't know. I can go check, though."

"You do that. If you find one, bring it to me."

Chris left the room. Dominique looked back at me.

"So tell me about how all this went down, Kiley."

"It ain't much to say. I met her through one of my partnas, she pretended to be digging on me, got real close to me, and made me reveal some things to her I hadn't revealed to anyone."

"How long did you know her?"

"For a good lil while. At first, I knew something was up, but then I gave in. I was going through some shit, and she pretended to be there for me."

"Did you fuck her?"

"All the time. Pussy made me weak, man."

"Hmm...interesting."

"Why? Cause you feeling me?"

"Naw, man. I've only known her for two months. She hasn't attempted to give me no booty. I mean, I've tried, but she keeps coming up with excuses. Saying, it's too soon. And let's wait. The more and more I think about the shit, the more I know something is up."

Chris came back into the room. He handed Dominique the picture and he then gave it to me. I looked at it. "That's her. That's Veronica. She was on my boy Quincy."

"Her name is Valencia to us." Dominique stood up and walked over to the bar. "So, what you aiming for Kiley? I'm gonna handle my business soon, but is there anything else you want from me."

"Nope. All I want is one thing."

"What's that?"

"I wanna see her before she dies."

"That's it?"

"Yeah, that's it."

"I can arrange that. She's always running to me when I'm under pressure so what if I call her tonight."

"Sounds like a good idea to me."

Dominique poured me a drink aside of his and brought it over to me. He placed it in my hand. "Information like what you gave me is worth something, Kiley. I appreciate it and I'm damn sure gone hook you up, alright?"

We slammed hands together and Dominique left the room to call Candi. When he came back, he said that she was on her way.

"If you don't mind," I said. "I need to go make a run. I'll be back in a few hours. Just make sure she's still here."

"Will do," he said, and then walked me to the door.

I really didn't have nothing to do, but to go clear my head. Shit was getting pretty deep and I needed to take a moment for myself. Since I hadn't given Ginger my cell phone number, I pulled my phone out to call her.

"I swear to you I…I'm about to lose my mind," she said. "Between you and Desmon not coming home, I'm going crazy."

"I just called to let you know I'm okay. I'll be home tomorrow."

"Am I supposed to thank you for calling? I've been up all night thinking about how upset you were when you left. You haven't done anything stupid, have you?"

"No, Ginger. Understand that I just need some time alone, okay! You know how I am when I'm going through something."

"Yes, I know. But, please hurry home. I'm sorry about Quincy, but nothing can bring him back. You still gotta live baby. Especially for that hardheaded son of yours. At least you called. I never hear from him."

"I'm sure he's okay. Just hit me on my phone if and when he gets there."

"Okay. I love you."

"I know you do," I said and then hung up.

A part of me knew Ginger really did love me…in her own special way. I cared for her too, in my own little way as well. Love, though? Never. My connection with her was my son and if it wasn't for that, our relationship would have never made it this far.

After I chilled in my car for a while, I headed back to Dominique's place. It was well over two hours later, and I walked up to the door and lightly tapped on it. Chris came to the door and told me to have a seat in the living room. He told me Dominique would be out shortly to get me.

I waited and waited for Dominique to show, and he didn't come down to see me until damn near an hour later. He walked up to me and I stood up.

He pointed upstairs. "She up there sleep. Go handle your business."

I slowly walked up the steps and looked at the double white doors that led to his bedroom. I walked up to the doors, placed my hand on the knob and turned it. When I stepped in, Candi lay on her side as she faced the wall. The room was lit with candles, but I could see her very well. She had on a red short silk robe that must have slid over as she slept. Her dark chocolate ass showed and her hair was spread out on the black silky sheets.

I tipped toed over to her and eased next to her in bed. I placed my hand on the side of her hip and rubbed it. When she smiled, I could see her dimples. She slowly opened her eyes, and when she saw me, her eyes opened wider. I quickly covered her mouth and squeezed her face tightly.

"Hello, Officer Campbell. What a surprise?" I whispered.

She nodded and her eyes slowly filled with water. "Shh...no need to get upset. I'm not gonna hurt you, okay?"

She nodded again.

I kept my hand over her mouth and reached my other hand down to untie her robe. She placed her hands on top of mine.

"Move your hands," I whispered in her ear. "If you don't move them, I'm gonna have to hurt you."

She moved her hands and I pulled her robe back. I moved it to the side and made her lay on her stomach.

"You remember how we used to do this, don't you?" I said, pressing my body weight on top of her.

She nodded.

"And, I know you haven't forgotten about me, have you?"

She moved her head from side to side. "Then as long as you still love me—and you do still love, right?" She nodded. "Then, let's catch up on old times."

She tried to move her mouth away from my hands.

"Do you got something you wanna say to me?"

She nodded and I slowly removed my hand.

She cleared her throat and spoke softly. "You don't have to believe me right now, but I regret everything I did to you. That's why I couldn't testify, Kiley, you've got to believe me. I was just in so deep, that I...I couldn't tell you the truth. And even though I wanted out, they—"

I placed my hand over her mouth to shush her. I then continued to whisper in her ear. "I believe you. You're damn right I believe you. But, that is no excuse for what you did to me. You made a fool of me, and I can't be made a fool of. You took years away from my son, and me, and I can't forgive you. I can, however, make shit right between us again."

I reached down and unzipped my pants. I rolled my dick between Candi's ass and forced her legs opened with mine. Tears streamed down her face, and she wiggled around to try and stop me. My hand still covered her mouth so I pulled her head back hard.

"I swear...I'll break your fucking neck!" I yelled. "Now, be still."

She calmed herself and I teased her with my dick. I placed my fingers inside of her and the bitch had the nerve to get wet.

"You like this, don't you?" I whispered. "You know damn well that you want my dick inside of you." She moved her head from side to side. "Yes, you do. I see you're still a good liar. But, I couldn't help it baby. You see, I had to get one last feel of this good powerful ass pussy before it goes to waste. By all means, this the pussy that fucked my whole life up. Now, I couldn't let it go without saying goodbye, could I?"

Candi started to cry harder. And the harder she cried, the more I teased her with my fingers.

"Do you remember how we use to come together?" She didn't respond. "Well, I do. Unfortunately, I can't come with you today, but I want you to come by yourself." She moved her head from side to side again. "Come on, baby. I need your cooperation. And the longer you take, the more painful this is going to get. So, give me what you got. I don't want no fake shit either."

I removed my hand from Candi's mouth and placed my finger on her clitoris. After giving it several strokes, I opened her wider with my other hand and rubbed gently against her walls. She dropped her face into the pillow and squirmed around to stop me.

"Now, that's what the fuck I'm talking about," I yelled as I felt her body jerk.

"Kiley, please," she sobbed. Her lips quivered as she spoke and tried to turn around. I wouldn't let her. "Don't do this to me, please! I said that I was sorry. You have no idea how sorry I am and I never ever meant to hurt you! For God's Sake I have nightmares about what I did to you."

I backed up and smacked Candi hard on her ass. "Now, that's ironic. I still have my nightmares too. I ain't gone tell you about mine because you might not like them."

Ready to wrap this up, I stood up and zipped my pants. She quickly turned around to look at me. "Please come to your senses. I will walk away from all of this, right now. I will leave St. Louis and you or Dominique will never see my face again. Kiley, I know you don't want to do this to me. You know how I truly felt about you."

"You're right. And I remember how you felt about me. That's why I'm not going to hurt you. I told you what I wanted. I couldn't let you leave without saying goodbye."

She wiped her tears and dropped her face into her hands. I turned to walk away.

"Kiley, help me," she pleaded. "Don't let nobody hurt—

I quickly turned. "Bitch! You want me to save you after you fucked me over the way you did? The day you walked your ass into my life is the day you fucked up! It's evident you didn't learn a lesson because you still out here using your *skills* to bring a nigga down. So, now, it's time to pay up! I would have the pleasure of dropping you myself, but I don't want your blood on my hands. After the night is over, I'm gonna wash them and never look back again."

"Don't. Please don't!" She continued to yell as I made my way to the door. I opened it and Chris entered. He dropped an envelope in my hand and walked inside. I snatched his arm.

"Make sure you give her one for me," I said. He nodded, and as he walked further into the room, I grabbed him again. "Naw, make that two."

He grinned and I walked out. No sooner had I made it to the bottom stair, I heard the shots loudly ring out. One for Dominique and two for me.

FIGHTING MY FEELINGS

I'd kind of kept things on the down-low. The police had been lurking around asking many questions about Candi's disappearance, and when Veronica came up missing, more hell broke loose. They'd even brought me in for questioning, but since there seemed to be no connection with me, they had to let me go. Even while I was there, they brought up Joe and Bo, but I pretended to be in complete shock, as if I didn't know nothing.

Ginger knew something was up, but I refused to talk to her about it. Especially since, I'd noticed some of my money missing. I didn't trip because I'd already known I couldn't trust the bitch. Now, all she had to do was ask for the money, but she had to be sneaky about the shit. Thing is, I had no problem giving it to her, but she was fucking herself up more and more when it came to me. If that wasn't enough, my suspicions of her doing drugs became a reality when I found some cocaine in her dresser drawer the other day. It fucked me up, but I should have known something else kept her from being the mother I thought she should be to our son.

I was mad about the money, especially if she was using it for her habit. But at the time, I didn't trip. In the envelope, Dominique had given me fifty thousand dollars. There was a note inside that instructed me to pick up another package, and when I did, he gave me an additional hundred thousand for keeping his ass out of jail. After that, we cut ties and I made it clear to him I didn't want any type of connection between us. He agreed.

I'd briefly spoken to Quincy's mother in L.A. and she said that his body was flown back to them. She asked if I would attend his funeral and I declined. The way I last seen him was the way I wanted to remember him. I had a thing for dead bodies anyway and funerals just weren't my cup of tea. Even though his mother never really liked me for moving her son to St. Louis, she told me she appreciated the love I had for Quincy and wished me well. That's all I could ask for and I told her to tell Quincy I loved him.

I got bored with hanging around the house, so I went for a quick drive through St. Louis. I stopped to wash my ride and then I stopped at

Al's shop to holla at him about the car he'd gotten for Quincy. We made arrangements for him to sell it to someone else and split the profits. After finishing up my business with him, I headed back to Ginger's place.

I saw Anna walking down the street while carrying a few bags of groceries, so I pulled up next to her and blew the horn. She looked at me, and then turned her head and kept on walking. I lowered the window and drove slowly next to her.

"So, you can't even say hello," I said, trying to keep my eyes on the road. She ignored me. I continued to try and make conversation with her, but she wouldn't say a word. By the time she reached her apartment, she went inside and closed the door. I parked my car and got out. I knocked on the door, but she wouldn't answer.

"Open the door, Anna," I said. The kids outside laughed at me as I must have looked like a desperate fool. "Please. These kids out here talking bad about me." She still didn't respond. I stopped knocking for a moment and then knocked again. "Would you please open the door?"

She cracked the door. "Go back to wherever you've been, Kiley. Just leave me alone."

"Can I tell you where I've been? Just open the door, okay?"

She closed the door and removed the chain. When I walked inside, she stood by the door with her arms folded. I leaned down to kiss her but she moved away.

"Please don't," she said.

I walked over to the couch and took a seat. I rubbed my hands together. "Look, I'm sorry for not calling or coming to see you. I've been kind of busy."

She remained by the door. "That's fine. I didn't expect to hear from you anyway. You got what you wanted and so did I."

"So, that's all you wanted?"

She rolled her eyes and looked away. I stood up and walked over to her. I turned her head so she could look at me. "Is that all you wanted?"

She nodded and then covered her face with her hands. She started to cry. "I feel so used, Kiley. I hadn't given myself to any man since I'd been raped and the only reason I did that was because I felt something special with you."

I pulled her to me and held her in my arms. "I'm sorry. I wasn't trying to play you, Anna. Really, I wasn't. I just had some other things to take care of, that's all."

She backed away and looked at me with her pretty brown watery eyes. I placed my hand on her smooth and silky rosy red cheek. "Just go," she said. "Please, just go."

Without any delay, I reached for the door and opened it. I could see all the hurt I'd caused and didn't want to hang around to see anymore. I got in my car and left.

When I got home, I couldn't stop thinking about Anna. Ginger and me ate dinner together, and afterwards, she left with a friend of hers to go to the *Casino Queen*. Desmon and Antonio were in the basement with the music blasted, so I went downstairs to see if they wouldn't mind turning it down.

"Can I just take a little nap, please," I said.

Desmon hesitated, but turned the music down a little. Since they were playing cards, I asked if I could join in. They claimed they were in the middle of a game and said I'd be an interference. So instead, I stayed downstairs and watched.

It started to get pretty late, and they were still at it. I'd dazed in and out as the thought of Anna was still heavy on my mind. Thinking, my eyes searched for Antonio's keys. I saw them on Desmon's bed and tried to make my way over to them. When I got busted with them in my hand, I came up with a good lie.

"Man, ain't your car blocking mine in? I was gone make a run, so I need to move your car."

Antonio nodded his head and I quickly went upstairs. I searched through his key ring and pulled off two keys that looked to be house keys. After I walked outside and came back in, I yelled downstairs.

"Antonio!"

He stood at the bottom step and I tossed the keys to him. "You cool! Desmon, I'll holla at you later, au-ight!"

"Whatever," he yelled back.

I closed the door and went into the bedroom. I took the necklace I'd bought for Anna out of my shirt pocket and left. When I got to her place, there was a light on downstairs. The light to her bedroom, on the upper level was out.

73

I tried both keys. The first one wouldn't turn the knob, but the other one surely did. I opened the door and quietly closed it. The lower level was clear, so I made my way upstairs. The stairs creaked a bit, and when I got to the top stair, she called for Antonio. I walked to her bedroom door, and opened it. She was lying down in the dark.

"It's not Antonio, it's me."

"Who is me?" she quickly reached for the lamp and turned it on. "Kiley, how did you get in here?"

"You forgot to lock the door."

"No I didn't. I never forget to lock my doors."

"I'm telling you that you did. Tonight, you forgot to lock it."

She pulled her long hair away from her face. "Why are you here this late?"

I walked up to her bed and sat down. "Because I couldn't stop thinking about you. There's so much I want to tell you, but I can't tell you right now. Just be patient with me, au-ight?"

"I'm sorry, but I can't. It was a big mistake having sex with you and it should have never happened."

"You don't believe that and neither do I."

"Kiley, please go. I'm not prepared for the kind of relationship you want. You want to see me whenever you want to and I can't allow that. I cried for three days after you left. I waited for you to come see me again and you never did. And when I saw you at the game, it hurt so badly that you didn't even have the decency to speak. You didn't have to play me like you did." Anna's eyes watered again. "Like I said, just go. I don't need this in my life."

I rose up off her bed and stood up. "It is something about you, Anna, that I can't seem to shake from my mind. This feeling I have I...I'm afraid of it."

"It's nothing. Trust me, it's nothing you're feeling. If you were, you wouldn't have made this a one night stand."

Maybe she was right. I placed my hands in my pockets and walked towards the door. I reached in my pocket for the necklace and tossed it to her. "During one of my moments with you on my mind, I got that for you. I can't use it, so you might as well keep it."

I walked out and by the time I reached the second stair, Anna softly called my name. I turned around and headed back towards her room.

She held the necklace in her hand. "I don't like to be hurt. I've hurt enough in my lifetime."

"I've been hurt too. So, what are you saying," I said, still standing in the doorway.

"It's a bad feeling, isn't it? Especially, when you meet somebody and you know there's something there, but—

I got loud. "So, what are you saying, Anna!"

She pulled the cover off of her and slightly opened her legs. She said something in Spanish that I couldn't understand.

"What did you say?" I yelled.

She said the same thing louder in Spanish again.

"Speak English, damn it! I can't understand that shit!"

She smiled. "I said...would you lick between my legs like you did before? Will you show me again how to please you? And, will you hold me in your arms until I fall asleep?"

"Na, you didn't just say all that in Spanish."

She laughed again. "Yes, I did. Honestly, I did."

I removed my clothes and kneeled on the bed. I made my way up to Anna until we were face to face. She held my face in her hands and I leaned forward to kiss her. I sucked in her top lip first and then went for the bottom lip. Our tongues floated in each other's mouth and made a loud smacking sound.

"Umm, that was good," I said. "If you only knew what I'm feeling."

"Be sure to tell me later," she whispered.

Anna scooted down and I lay on top of her. I took small pecks on her neck and made my way down to her breasts. After I worked those, I pecked her stomach and inched down between her legs. She trembled the same way she did the last time I licked her insides and she quickly came in my mouth. Wanting to be gentler than I was before, I parted her legs and slowly worked inside of her. She was still tight, but had opened up just enough for me not to hurt her as much. When I placed her legs on my shoulder, that's when she pushed my hips back and wouldn't move with me. Her eyes watered.

I looked at her. "No need to cry. If it hurts that much, I'll stop."

She didn't say anything so I dropped her legs. When I did, she started to move around on me again. I was anxious to continue on, and even though we had a few setbacks, we managed to work through it.

Anna had gotten on top and rode me quite well. She'd even went down on me, and even though it wasn't the best blow job I'd had, the feelings I had for her made it feel right.

After we finished up, Anna lay in my arms and quickly went to sleep. I stayed up for awhile, thinking, and shortly after dozed off.

Around four in the morning, I moved my cramped neck around, and when I opened my eyes, Anna stared up at me. Feeling uncomfortable, I reached for the lamp and turned it on.

"What's up? Why are you looking at me like that?"

"What's the matter? I can't look at you now."

"Not when I'm asleep. Besides, it makes me think something's up when you look at me like that."

She smiled and rubbed my chest. "Well, nothing's up. I was just looking at how handsome you are. Also, I was thinking about how I don't really know who you are and I've taken to you so much."

"I feel the same way about you. You mentioned being raped and—"

"I asked for information about you first."

"Okay. I...I'm from L.A. I just moved here with my sister a few months ago, I have a son, and currently I work as a mechanic not too far from here."

"So, where does your sister live?"

"I'd rather not say."

"Why not?"

"Because it's not important."

"How about your son?"

"He still lives in L.A," I hesitated. "Now, that's enough about me. Tell me about you. I know Antonio is your nephew, but—"

"But, again, he's like my son. My sister was murdered several years ago and since she took care of me too, Antonio and me continued to stay together."

"I'm sorry to hear that. Do they know who killed her?"

Anna was quiet and then responded. "They don't know, but my family knows."

"Then why hasn't your family done anything about it?"

She moved around in my arms and then sat up. She looked at me and spoke softly. "Because my uncle, Ricky is the one who killed her. I'm only telling you this because I feel as if I can trust you, but he's the one who did it." She laid her head down on my chest. "He raped us for several years, and when my sister fought back, she paid for it."

"That's crazy. And you never said anything to anyone?"

"I told my mother, but she wanted to protect him. Protect the family from more hurt, she said. She told me if I didn't tell anyone, that she'd make the abuse stop. After that, it did. That's why when you and I—

"You don't have to explain. But, you don't think about that when I'm making love to you, do you?"

"No. All I think about is you being inside of me. How good you make me feel. How safe I feel in your arms. I've never felt that before. I was afraid to give myself to anyone, but I felt a new beginning the first time we got together. That's why, when you didn't call, I was so hurt. Maybe I'm wrong for feeling this way so soon, but—."

I kissed the back of her head. "No, you're not wrong. That's sort of like what I feel. I've been through a lot too, but now isn't the time for me to get into it." There was silence. "So, if you don't mind me asking…what's up with your nephew Antonio? I mean…he's never here. Does he ever come home?"

"Yes. He's real close with his best friend, though. Normally, Antonio spends the night at his place or at his girlfriend's house. When you hear the phone ring one time in the middle of the night, that's him calling to let me know he's okay."

I'd definitely heard the phone ring the few nights I'd been here. "That's cool. Is it hard raising him, though?"

"Extremely hard. Especially, since he and I have been through so much together. I try to be there for him, but sometimes I feel there's so little I can do. He's a good kid, but he doesn't do too well in school. He doesn't admit it, but I know he uses drugs."

"Maybe, it's the company he keeps. You mentioned something about his best friend the other day, didn't you?"

"Yeah, but Antonio had his issues long before he and Desmon met. They met a few years back when Desmon's mom put him out. He stayed with us for a few weeks and they've been good friends every since. I feel sorry for Desmon though. His father's in jail and his mother's a whore. She and I have had a few words from time to time, but we try hard to be friends because of the boys. Sadly, Desmon really doesn't have much of a family."

I tensed up at the things Anna said and couldn't stand to know more. My eyes even started to water as I thought about what Ginger and I both had done to our son.

Since I remained quiet, Anna looked up at me. I tightly squeezed my eyes together.

"Damn!" I said. "I think I got something in my eyes."

"Let me see," she said, as she touched my hand to move it away from my eyes.

"That's okay. Would you mind getting me a wet rag?"

Anna got out of bed and went into the bathroom. I quickly cleared my eyes. She walked over and handed the rag to me.

"Here. Are you okay now?"

"Yeah, I'm fine," I said, pulling the covers back. "But I need to get going."

"You're not going to stay?"

"I want to, but even though I'm a grown man, my sister still worries about me. I promised her when I moved here, I wouldn't become a burden to her. I at least like to show my face every night. She was upset with me when I didn't come home the other night."

Anna smiled. I could tell she didn't believe me. Hell, it was even hard for me to believe. Anyway, I got out of bed, kissed Anna goodbye and told her I'd see her soon.

I'd guessed Ginger was still at the Casino, so I went downstairs to see if Antonio and Desmon was still there. The thought of what went on while I was in jail frightened me, and I knew that when the truth came to light, all hell would break loose.

As I walked down the steps, I could smell the aroma of marijuana in the air. By the time I got downstairs, Antonio, Desmon and two more fellas, were passed out on the damn floor. I knew they were all fucked up as the empty beer cans proved to me that they were. Somewhat pissed, I quickly put Antonio's keys on his key ring and tapped Desmon on his shoulder to wake him. He stretched his arms and squinted his eyes.

"What?" he said in a grouchy voice.

"Come upstairs for a minute."

"Why? Can't it wait until tomorrow? I'm sleepy."

"Just for a minute, au-ight?"

Desmon followed me upstairs and I took a seat at the kitchen table. He stood by the fridge and folded his arms. I was silent for a while and he let it be known again that he was tired.

"What's up, Kiley? Man, I'm tired."

I hesitated. "Are you happy with your life?"

He gave me a funny look and hurried towards the steps to go back downstairs.

I put my arm in front of the door. "No, please wait. I'm serious," I said.

"You couldn't be," he said, backing away from the door. "Man, it is almost five o'clock in the morning. I just got to bed, and I'm tired. Right now, hell no I'm not happy. And, I ain't gonna be happy if you don't let me get no sleep."

"You can get all the sleep you want in a lil bit, okay? I...I just know your mother and I both have let you down and I wanna make sure things get better between us."

He shook his head. "Man, seriously, you got issues. I'm cool. I don't need nobody, and as a matter of fact, I ain't never needed nobody. Honestly, I don't know what else you want me to say."

I got frustrated and pounded my fist on the table. "Say that I fucked up. Tell me you would be different if I'd never gone to jail! Tell me you remember calling me Daddy and not no fucking Kiley! You gotta remember that Desmon. You have to remember how I was there for you before I went to jail. I'd come see you all the time and bring you your favorite ice cream. Chocolate."

I dropped my head and Desmon didn't say a word. He walked over to the chair and pulled it back. He sat down and leaned in close to me, as he rubbed his hands together. "I remember being with you when I was little. However, I do remember the day my uncle Kareem was killed, and after that, I remember you hanging the phone up on me when I wanted to talk. For years, I asked my Mama what happened to you, why you stopped coming around and...and she said because you went to jail. Okay, fine, I thought. Take me to him. I wanna see my Daddy. Even though he's in jail, I still wanna see him. She said no. Yo Daddy said no. After awhile, I said fuck it. You became a part of my past and that's where I want you to stay. Soon, Mama's other boyfriend's took on your role and I had plenty of Daddy's. Many of which didn't even compare to the Daddy I'd known, but I coped with it. So, man, I ain't trying to be a thorn in your side, but I'm just telling you like it is. I know you got issues—

"And you got issues too."

"Maybe. But I'm gone handle mine. You make sure you handle yours." Desmon stood up and walked back downstairs.

I took a deep breath, and after I sat in the kitchen thinking, I went to the bedroom. I took off my clothes, lay in bed, and stared at the wall. Things had to get better. There was no doubt in my mind that things definitely had to start looking up—and soon.

TIME TO COME CLEAN

For the next few weeks, things did get better. Desmon and me talked a bit more, I made it to his football games and I'd even let him drive my car when he'd asked. It was after the game and him and a few fellas wanted to parking-lot-pimp at a teenage club close by.

In addition to that, Anna and me continued to do our thang. I'd made love to her almost everyday and her pussy had accustomed itself to me. For the first time, I felt like something was mine and nobody else. And as for my feelings for her, they were now beyond my control. I hated to continue to lie to her, but there was no other way. It was obvious that she didn't have much respect for Desmon's mother or father and if she found out who I was, I knew she'd end it with me in a heartbeat.

The secrets and lies were killing me, though. Antonio had come home several times, and luckily, we were in her bedroom. She said that she wanted me to meet him, and I told her I just wasn't ready to do that yet. When she asked why, I told her the timing wasn't right and it would be inappropriate for her to introduce him to me so soon. She somewhat agreed, and for now, we were done with that issue.

My other problem was Ginger. She'd known I'd been seeing someone else and bugged the fuck out of me about it. She thought it was Jada, since Jada showed up the other day unannounced. Jada was pissed because she hadn't heard from me since our encounter and took it upon herself to come see me. I explained to Ginger that even if I were seeing somebody else, I would never disrespect her and allow Jada to come to her house. I did, however, give Jada my cell phone number so she could call me later, and she'd been blowing the damn phone up ever since. Her last message made it clear to me that if I didn't call her back, she'd never call my Black ass again. I purposely didn't call her back, just so she wouldn't.

Ginger was going through her normal routine for the week, walking around the house mad. I was laid back in the living room with my feet propped up on the couch. She came in and folded her arms in front of me.

"A white girl, Kiley? You have the nerve to play me off for a white bitch?"

"Ginger, what in the hell are you talking about?"

"I'm talking about these strands of long straight hair that I keep finding on your damn clothes. You've made it clear that whoever the hell she is, that you're not going to stop seeing her. If that's the case, why don't you go live with her so I can go back to what I did before you got here."

I ignored Ginger, got up, got dressed and left. I'd let Desmon use my car since he was going to Homecoming tonight, so I took a walk through the neighborhood. Desmon said he was going to the mall to pick up his tuxedo and promised to hurry back.

Instead of walking, I decided to jog. When somebody blew their horn at me, I turned and it was Desmon. I told him to go ahead on home and said I'd meet him there.

By the time I got there, it was a gang of young teenage girls close by Ginger's front door. I hurried over to see what was going down, but before I could get to them, a serious fight broke out. Motherfuckers were throwing punches, pulling hair and looking for any thing else they could find to bust each other's damn head. Since Desmon wasn't nowhere in sight, I continued to let the fools go at it. I'd even excused myself and walked by them to go into the house. Desmon and Ginger heard the ruckus and ran to the door. Ginger stood in the doorway and yelled that she was calling the police. And Desmon stood there and watched as I did. Soon, the place cleared and after at least thirty to forty minutes had gone by, the police never showed.

"I hate this damn neighborhood," Ginger yelled, as she continued to look out of the window for them. "Every time you call them bastards, they never show up."

"Then, don't waste your time," I said. "You know they don't give a fuck, so I don't know why you even called."

She looked at me as I sat on the couch. "Shut up talking to me. I'm still mad at your butt."

"Be mad all you like, baby. I could care less."

She rolled her eyes and walked away.

I went downstairs to see what Desmon's tuxedo looked like. He'd been so excited about going to Homecoming and I really wanted everything to turn out well for him.

I walked down the steps and he stood in front of the mirror with it on. I sat on the edge of his bed and he turned sideways in the mirror.

"So, what do you think? It look good, don't it?" he asked.

"I can't tell with the backwards baseball cap you got on. And the toothpick hanging out of your mouth don't help either."

He pulled his cap off and showed his waves. Then took the toothpick out of his mouth. I flashed back to Quincy, Kareem and me getting ready for our Homecoming dance in high school. I looked at Desmon and smiled.

"Now, that's better. You look nice…real nice."

Knowing how handsome he looked, he pimped over to his closet and opened it up. He reached for his wallet and looked inside. "Oops, I forgot. I ain't got no money. Do you think you can help a brotha out?"

"You knew damn well you didn't have no money. And, hell naw, I can't help a brotha out."

"Help your son out then. You don't want me to go out without no money, do you?"

"Aw, so you my son now, huh?"

"I'm always your son. And I'm always gone be your son. So, help a brotha…I mean, your son out."

I stood up and reached into my back pocket. I pulled out a fifty-dollar bill and reached out to give it to him. He looked at it, opened his mouth wide, and looked at me. "You kidding, right?"

"Hell, naw I ain't kidding,"

"Man, what in the hell is that supposed to do for me?"

"It's supposed to serve as an emergency. I assume you're taking my car, right?"

He smiled. "Yeah…I was going to ask you about that."

"I'm sure you were. But, uh, my car is on full, so you don't need gas. Make sure you eat before you leave, and if something urgent comes up, you got fifty whole dollars to work it out."

He walked up to me. "You're serious, aren't you?"

"Hell, yeah, I'm serious. If you knew you were going to Homecoming, then you should have prepared yourself for this day. You ain't old enough to get a job, but you could have cut some grass, cleaned some gutters or something."

"Ooo, Dad, now you know you ain't right?"

"Aw…so, I done stepped up to Dad now?"

"You've always been my dad and you're always gonna be my dad."

"You are so full of shit, Desmon," I said, reaching into my back pocket again. I pulled out four hundred dollars and gave it to him. He saw how much it was, and smiled after he took it from my hands.

"Now, that's much better. I can take my lady for a nice dinner and take her to an extravagant hotel so we can fu—

I stopped him. "Watch it. You need to cool out with all that."

"With what," he said walking back over to the mirror to check himself out again.

"With all the females. Who's the lucky girl tonight?"

He laughed and sat on the edge of the bed. "See, that's a long story. And if I had time, I'd tell you. But all you need to know is that it's not Gabrielle. You kind of messed that up for me."

"You messed that up for yourself."

"Maybe. But wait until you see Shannon." He shook his head. "She is…off the chain."

I stood up. "I'm sure she is. Just make sure you protect yourself, though." I reached into my back pocket and took two condoms out of my wallet. I dropped them on the bed in front of him. He looked at them and tooted his lips. Afterwards, he picked them up and laid them on his dresser.

"I'll see you in a minute," I said, heading upstairs.

I got all the way up the steps before I heard Desmon yell thanks. I yelled back at him and told him any time.

Surprisingly, Ginger ran around the house and tried to help Desmon get ready to go. She had her camera out and snapped many pictures of him and a few of me. For the first time, I felt proud. My son looked amazingly handsome and the smile on his face made me feel even better.

After he got ready, he left out and went to go get his date. Ginger and me waited patiently in the living room for him to return and said very little to each other. When he came back, he certainly didn't lie. His date was stunning. She wore a royal blue strapless silk long dress with slits on the side. Tiny diamonds lined the top of the dress and matched the diamonds she wore in her ears and on her bracelet. Her light brown skin was so smooth that she didn't need much makeup and her hair was neatly combed into a roll with a few strands that dangled on the sides of her face. As for her eyes, they showed the excitement on her face to be with Desmon and were the same hazel color as his.

Ginger continued to snap her pictures and when she told me to stand up with them, I could only smile. I stood up and after Ginger snapped the picture, we heard a bunch of yelling and cursing coming from outside. I walked over to the door to see who it was, and no sooner had I got there, shots fired quickly through the living room window. The glass shattered everywhere, and even though they'd already done so, I told everybody to get down on the floor. I crawled to my bedroom and got my gun from underneath the pillow. After I got it, I made sure everybody was okay and quickly opened the door. A burgundy car sped away with some of the chicks who'd been outside fighting earlier. One of them lay right in front of the doorway with bullet holes in her chest. She looked up at me with tears flowing down the sides of her eyes. I kneeled down next to her.

"Help me," she said, as the words could barely come out of her mouth.

"Ginger!" I yelled. "Call the police! Better yet, give me the motherfucking phone!"

Ginger rushed to give me the phone and Desmon and Shannon stood close by. She cried on Desmon's shoulder and he held her to comfort her.

When the dispatcher answered, I quickly tore into her. I told her what had happened, told her to have the paramedics hurry it the fuck up, and said if they didn't I was coming to get her ass for asking me so many questions over the phone.

Surprisingly, within minutes, the police and the paramedics arrived. By then, though, it was too late. The young lady that had been shot had already died. They covered her with a white sheet and the police asked if anybody had seen anything. Ginger stepped outside and spoke to them, and I went back inside to check on Desmon and Shannon. I didn't have much faith in the police doing a damn thing about it, so I wasn't going to waste my time talking to them.

Shannon sat at the table with her face in her hands, as she continued to cry. Desmon stood next to her and placed his hand on her back.

"I'm sick of this shit, man! They be fighting all the time. Over dumb shit too. It just don't make no sense."

"Why don't y'all head on out? Ginger and me will see what's up, but I don't want this to hold y'all up."

85

Shannon stood up and Desmon took her by the hand. After she went into the bathroom to clean herself up, they headed outside. Not able to look at the dead body, Shannon turned her head on Desmon's shoulder. They made their way through the police cars before making it to my car. Desmon honked the horn to let me know they were cool and then he left.

It was hours before shit started to settle down. When the young girl's mother came home from work, it was a mess. She went ballistic and so did the rest of the family who later showed up. Thing is, I knew exactly what they were feeling. It took me back to the day I found Papa Abrams body and to the day Kareem was killed. Unable to watch everything go down, I went back inside and closed the door.

After Ginger left for work, I stayed in bed and thought about where to go next. Not only was it time to get my son away from this place, but also, it was certainly time for our lives to make better sense. If anything, I knew if I was one unhappy motherfucker, then Desmon was as well. There wasn't too much positive shit going on and I knew it was up to me to change shit around. How could I be a better man when I was so accustomed to being who I was? I knew I had a heart, but I also knew my temper was one that couldn't be reckoned with.

After chilling in the dark for hours, I needed someone to talk to. I missed my boys like hell, and since Rufus was still the only one alive, I called his cell phone at damn near three o'clock in the morning. He answered and sounded wide-awake.

"Killer, it's me."

"What's up, man? Why you calling? Is everything cool?"

"Yeah, it's au-ight. I...I just feel so fucking lost since Quincy was killed."

"You know you my nigga, don't you? And you know damn well you don't have to feel lost, fool. Just move back to L.A. Shit is going magnifico, I'm telling you."

"All that, huh? I mean, it couldn't be no better than before. I don't want to live my life on the edge. I'd fosho have to bring Desmon with me and I can't stand to have him brought up like I was."

"Bro, a man gotta do what he gotta do. You know that my son and my daughter are both in the game. It's the only way I know how and I ain't mad about it either. Tomorrow ain't promised to nobody.

Whether you're a dope dealer, stockbroker, minister, teacher, whatever. When it's your time to go, it's just your time to go."

"I know. But going back to my previous lifestyle will be a setback for me. I'm not saying what you said doesn't make sense but..."

"But...but you need to come on back home, Kiley. If I got to come to St. Louis to get you myself, I will. Basically, we all we got. I got love for some of these fellas, but not how I got love for you. You'd be in control of this game right along with me. It's a low key operation and our chances of going back to jail are slim since I got some of the best working closely with me."

"What about killing people? You can't tell me all that shit has stopped."

"Hey, you know how that is. If it don't shake and it don't rattle, then we have definitely have had to roll. It comes with the territory and you know that."

"That's what I'm afraid of."

"Kiley, stop trying to be somethin that you ain't. I said it before and I'll say it again, you will never change who you've been or what you've been. You wanna know why?"

"Why?"

"Because you are what Pappa Abrams made you. It's in your blood. Just think about coming home and get back with me, okay."

"I will. And don't come for me until I ask you to."

Rufus promised me he wouldn't, and after he told me how sad Quincy's funeral was, I was even more hurt. So hurt, that I went into a deep sleep and didn't come out of it until I heard a voice that was all so familiar to me—Anna.

I hopped out of bed and when I pulled open the already cracked door, I peeked out at her standing in the living room while talking to Ginger. Before she saw me, I closed the door. Shortly after, I heard Ginger's voice come near the door. She opened it, as I'd already pulled the cover over my head like I was sleep.

"Kiley," she whispered. I didn't say nothing and her voice called for me again.

"What?"

"I want you to meet somebody. Get up."

"I'm tired, Ginger. I'll get up later."

"Come on, now. It's almost three o'clock in the evening and it's time for you to get your butt up. Besides, it's Antonio's aunt. She's been dying to meet you."

"I'll get up in a minute."

"Well, hurry up. She's joining us for dinner so make sure you put some clothes on."

I was silent and Ginger closed the door. Damn, I thought. How in the hell was I gonna get my ass out of this mess. I knew I should've been honest with Anna, but I couldn't.

I laid there for about another fifteen minutes trying to figure out what to do. The only thing that made sense was to get the shit out in the open. Now was the appropriate timing since Desmon wasn't here. He was still gone, but I figured he was okay.

A bit nervous, I pulled the covers back and eased my way to the bathroom since they'd already went into the kitchen. I took a quick shower and just as I tried to slip out of the bathroom to put on my clothes, Ginger saw me with a white towel around my waist and called for me.

"Come here for a second," she said.

"Wait," I said with my back turned. "I need to go put on some clothes."

"Just come here. The towel is covering you up, ain't it?"

Without another delay, I headed to the kitchen. I held the towel around my waist and stood in the doorway as Anna shockingly looked at me. Ginger stood with a wide grin on her face.

"Anna, this is my baby, Kiley. And Kiley, this is Anna. She's Antonio's aunt."

Anna couldn't get the words to come out of her mouth and neither could I. When I saw how startled she was, I finally spoke.

"Hi, Anna. Nice to meet you."

I walked up and reached my hand out to shake hers. Still not saying anything she stared at me and reached her hand out for mine. After we shook hands, I told her and Ginger I'd join them once I put some clothes on.

As I headed to the bedroom, my palms sweated and my heart pounded fast. By the look on Anna's face, I could tell she was either pissed or probably more confused by my lies.

After I put on my sweat pants and a wife-beater, I gathered my thoughts and headed back into the kitchen with Anna and Ginger. Ginger was by the stove putting some diced potatoes in a pot, while Anna sat at the table and listened to her go on and on about what went down at the club the other night. I took a seat at the kitchen table and quickly cut Ginger off to make conversation since Anna stared at me.

"Hey, Ginger, have you heard from Desmon yet?"

"No, he hasn't called. It is getting pretty late, so I guess I should call and check on him, huh?"

I looked over at Anna and quickly reached for my cell phone on the table to call Desmon. Surprisingly, he answered.

"I'll be there in a sec.," he said.

"Where are you? What in the hell kind of homecoming did you go to?"

"Man, I'm still at the hotel. I'll be there soon, au-ight?"

"Yesterday I was Dad. Now, today I'm back to being man, huh?"

"Okay, Dad. I'll be there in a few. After I drop Antonio and his date off, I got some unfinished business to take care of and I'll see you soon."

"That's better. Also, did you take your condoms?"

Ginger turned around and put her hands on her hips. Desmon laughed and then answered.

"Yes, I did. And I for damn sure used two of yours and two of mine. Now, I gotta go. She's breaking open number five and you're blocking over the phone."

He hung up.

Still trying to avoid Anna, I looked at Ginger still standing with her hands on her hips. "He'll be home shortly. He said after he drops Antonio and his date off, he'd be home," I said, knowing Anna was probably worried as well.

"Good," Ginger said. "And I'm so surprised you and Desmon are getting along better." She looked at Anna. "Girl, you should have been here when Kiley first came home. Him and Desmon were at it day end and day out." Anna didn't respond. She looked at me again and then looked back at Ginger.

Ginger opened the fridge and poured a glass of Kool-Aid. She placed it on the table in front of me. "Dinner should be ready in a few.

If you don't mind, Anna's joining us. She came over so I could tell her how to go about applying for this job at a nursing home not too far from here. It's the nursing home my girl Leslie works at and she got the hook up."

Anna sat quietly until Ginger fixed my plate, came over to the table and leaned in for a kiss. She softly spoke, "I'm so proud of you for working things out with your son. You have no idea what it means to me."

Ginger placed her lips on mine and stuck her tongue deeply into my mouth. When I saw Anna stand up, I backed away from Ginger.

"I...I really need to get going," she said, as the words barely made it out of her mouth.

Ginger rose up, "Anna, I thought you were gonna stay for dinner. Kiley and me get chummy with each other all the time. Don't pay us no mind."

Anna hurtfully walked towards the kitchen's doorway. Knowing that she'd probably never speak to me again, unless I cleared this up right here and right now, I reached out and grabbed her hand. Ginger backed up as Anna snatched her hand away and furiously glared at me.

"Please stay so I can explain this," I said, looking at her.

Ginger's forehead wrinkled, "Explain what?"

"That I've been seeing Anna, Ginger." I turned my head to look at Anna. "I lied to you about who I was because..."

"Motherfucker, you what!" Ginger yelled. I couldn't get my explanation to come out because Ginger yelled so loudly. "After all I've done for you, you've been sleeping with her!"

Anna rolled her eyes at me and walked away. I stood up to go after her as she headed towards the door. Ginger dug her nails into my chest and forced me backwards.

"Anna, wait," I said. "Just let me explain."

She walked out and Ginger took her hand and slapped me hard. "Get out of here! I'm not going to argue with you anymore and I'm damn sure not going to kiss your ass to be with me!"

Intending to leave anyway, I told Ginger not to touch me again. I headed towards the bedroom to pack my things. As I started to remove my clothes from the closet, Ginger came in and yelled again.

"I am in disbelief, Kiley! How long have you been fucking around with her, huh! How long!"

I got frustrated. "Look, don't worry about it! I'm leaving your place so it don't even matter."

"It matters to me, damn it! Just in case you forgot, I was there for you, nigga, when nobody else was! I put a roof over your head and fed you every day! Instead of giving that bitch an explanation, you fucking owe me one!"

"I don't owe you shit, Ginger! Maybe, a good ass kicking for fucking up my son's life and for stealing my damn money that didn't even belong to you! You've been repaid for your services, so shut the fuck up talking to me!"

Ginger challenged me and kept up with the bullshit. For the next half an hour or so, we went back and forth as I continued to gather my things to go. When she decided to put her damn hands on me again, that's when she brought out another side of me she didn't want to see. I punched her hard in her face and she fell backwards on the bed. Angry, she charged at me again, and I gave her an even harder blow than the one before. That was enough to quiet her, as she held her eye and cried. Having no sympathy for her, I hurried to gather my things and go.

Ginger got up and went to the bathroom. She slammed the door and sobbed out loudly. I pulled the suitcase from underneath the bed and when I noticed more of my money gone, that sent me over the edge. I knew how many stacks I had, and when two bundles of five thousand dollars in cash were missing, I slammed the suitcase down and hurried to the bathroom door. I knocked hard.

"What in the fuck did you do with my money? You've been buying drugs with my shit, huh?" I yelled. She didn't respond. "Ginger, I will kick this damn door down...

"I spent it, you bastard! Na! Get the hell out of here and go live with your other bitch!"

I put my foot on the door and kicked that motherfucker as hard as I could. It broke off the hinges and wood flew all over the place. Without saying one word, I grabbed Ginger by her neck and shoved her out of the bathroom. She dug her long nails deeply into my arms and scratched my skin off. When we got to the bedroom, I pushed her on the bed and reached for my gun on the dresser. I aimed it at her and thought seriously about pulling the trigger.

"Bitch, I don't care how you get it, but I want my damn money back! You got by next weekend to come up with it, or else I will blow your brains out—DO YOU UNDERSTAND!"

Just then, Desmon walked into the room. He aimed his gun at me with an irate and disturbing look on his face. "Motherfucker, don't you ever put your hands on my mama! I will kill you, nigga, and if she die, you die!"

"Shoot him!" Ginger yelled. "Kill his no good ass, Desmon!"

I turned the gun towards Desmon and spoke calmly. "Don't be no fool. If she really cared, she wouldn't have just asked you to kill me. And if you do, that makes you like me. Remember, you don't want to be like me." I slowly lowered my gun. Desmon's hand shook as he continued to aim his gun at me.

"Get out," he said calmly. He reached in his pocket and tossed my keys to me. "Please, get out of here."

I nodded and took my suitcases off the bed. Ginger sat on the bed crying and trembling as if she'd been beat-down for no damn reason at all. Desmon comforted her, and after I took my belongings to the car, I left.

ON MY OWN

For the next several days, I stayed at Al's place. He owned some property on the Southside of St. Louis, and once he cleared out one of his houses, he agreed to let me stay there for a little of nothing. I kicked him out a lil something extra, and since I agreed to have the placed fixed up, we called it even.

Always wanting to have the finer things in life, I had the place fixed up to my likings. It was a brick house that started at the living room, worked its way through the kitchen and had two separate bedrooms in the far back. The master bedroom had a bath and there was another bathroom in the hallway right next to the kitchen. The house wasn't nothing fancy, but for now, it was surely a place I could call home. Once I had my Italian leather living room furniture delivered, my 100" TV and booming entertainment center, I felt better. I knew I wouldn't feel completely at home until I had my bedroom in order, and after my king-sized gray and black marble bedroom set was delivered, I was pretty much satisfied. Now, the only thing I had to work on was getting Desmon to come live with me. I'd called the house a few times but Desmon wouldn't talk to me. As soon as he heard my voice, he told me never to call him again and hung up on me.

I couldn't believe after all of the progress I'd made with him, it turned out to be a waste of time. I knew he was more than angry with me for putting my hands on Ginger and I could only imagine what her face looked like after I'd punched it—twice. Thing is, I didn't have no regrets. The only thing I regretted was allowing my son to see me that angry. Ginger, though, she had it coming. For now, I'd hoped she was trying to figure out a way to get my money in order. If she didn't come up with it by Sunday, she'd fosho have to pay again.

When Saturday rolled around, I knew Desmon's school was in the playoffs. The game was at the *Edward Jones Dome* and I'd already gotten my ticket earlier on in the week to go. I didn't care if he knew if I was there or not. I was anxious to see him do his thing so I had every intention of being there. I was also sure Anna would be there, but since I knew she was upset with me for lying to her, I was in no mood to explain myself to her. As far as I was concerned, the pussy was cool while it lasted. I didn't have much more time to stress out over females and their bullshit. Being with them caused too much drama for me, and my number one priority was mending my relationship with Desmon.

It was a bit chilly outside so I put on my hooded sweatshirt and jeans. I looked at my gun on the dresser and hesitated to take it with me. I hoped nothing bad went down, but just in case, I slid it down inside the front of my pants.

On the drive to the game, I moved my head to the beat of a song that played on the radio. When my phone buzzed, I quickly turned down the radio to answer. It was Rufus. There was much static in my phone so I really couldn't hear.

"What you'd say, Killer? I can't hear you."

"Nigga, I said that I'm in the Lou. Where your punk ass at?"

I smiled, as I clearly heard him tell me he was in St. Louis. "I'm on my way to Desmon's game. Why don't you meet me there?"

"That's cool. So, you and the kid still getting along pretty good, huh?"

"Naw, not really. But, just meet me in front of the Dome. I can't wait to see ya. You know it's been...

"A long fucking time. So long, that I can't even remember."

"Shit, me either. I should be at the Dome in about fifteen minutes. I'll call you back after I find a place to park."

"See ya soon, partna," he said, and then hung up.

The parking lots were filled to capacity. I parked damn near a quarter of a mile away from the Dome and still had to pay twenty dollars for parking. Rushing, I hurried towards the front entrance and called Rufus to let him know I'd made it. After I gave him directions, he said he was on his way.

Teenagers were all over the place. I waited patiently for Rufus and when somebody came up from behind and poked me in the back, I knew it was him.

"This a hold up, nigga. Give me all of yo money."

I turned around and smiled. "My motherfucking, Killer," I said, giving him a hug. We embraced each other and Rufus gave me a few pats on my back. Shortly after, we let go.

"Kiley, man, I can't believe it's you. Look at you, nigga. How in the fuck did you get so big?"

"The Exercise Yard while in prison, man. Look at yo ass, though. You than tightened up too. And, what's up with that fro?"

Rufus patted his Afro that was at least eight to nine inches high. "Do you like? If you don't, my girlees do." He smiled and his front grill was solid gold. He was the oldest of the bunch, and almost thirty-nine, you'd never know it by the way he looked and dressed.

"So," he said looking around. "How do I get a ticket?"

"Shit, I don't know. I think you had to get them before the game, but let me see."

I walked over to the ticket booth and the lady behind it said that no tickets were for sale. Wanting Rufus to kick it with me, I stopped this young cat outside and asked to purchase his ticket. At first he said no, but when I offered to give him two hundred dollars for it, he took the money and jetted. Rufus and me laughed.

"You might have changed and so have I," he said. "But the power of money for damn sure hasn't."

"You got that shit right," I said as we headed up the escalators to find our seats.

Rufus' Afro was so huge that it was hard for us to go unnoticed. Every time we walked by, people eyes roamed and many stared. Rufus liked the attention, and when we took a seat, this white man behind us joked about not being able to see the game. He offered Rufus his hat to put on and Rufus found no humor in his joke.

"Motherfucker you don't know me," he yelled. "Fuck naw, I don't want your damn hat! If you can't see, take your ass somewhere else to sit."

"Hey, look," the man said. "I was only kidding. Can't you take a joke?"

"Find somebody else to play with, fool. I'm not the one."

The white man and two other fellas who he was with got up and walked away. Rufus stared them down like they'd straight up offended him or something.

"Ole, silly motherfucker," he continued, underneath his breath.

"Man, you gone be au-ight?" I said. "You seem like you got a chip on your shoulder or something."

"Nigga, you know I ain't too fond of white people. Ain't no need to be all fake with me and shit. That was his way of telling me he didn't like my damn hair. And since he didn't, then it was only best that his ass not be around me."

I laughed, and before the game got started, I hipped Rufus to what had been going down. More than anything, he was angry with me for letting Ginger get away with stealing my money.

"Trust me, the only reason she hasn't died is because she's Desmon's mother. If she wasn't, her ass would be history."

"But, man, she's been doing that shit for years. The bitch is money hungry, and when you're that hungry, that's when shit starts to happen."

I nodded, and soon after, the game got on the way.

By the end of the first quarter, Desmon had jammed. He had three quarterback sacks and the whole defensive line was hyped up. His team led fourteen to zero and the game seemed to be going every bit of Desmon's way. As the second quarter started, I scoped Anna sitting to the far left of the stadium with I'd guess some of her family. Shannon, who Desmon took to Homecoming, wore his jersey, and his ex-girlfriend, the cheerleader, obviously had an attitude about it. When Desmon made good plays, she tooted her lips and turned her head.

During the second quarter, Rufus had gotten a phone call and stepped away to take it. He was only in town for a few days, and during that time, I offered to let him chill with me. He'd even offered to drop me some of the cash Ginger had taken away from me. Since I'd spent so much on the luxuries I'd bought for the crib that was cool with me.

As Desmon continued to do his thing, I sat there proud as hell of him. I knew he'd someday make it to the pros and I certainly had that much faith in him. When Rufus came back, he said that he had to go make a quick run. Knowing what he was up to, I gave him directions to my crib and told him to meet me there later. We slammed our fist together and he jetted.

During halftime, I walked to the concession stand to get some nachos and a soda. As I stood in the long line, Anna and a lady who resembled her walked up and stood in line too. She didn't say anything to me, and I didn't say anything to her. I kept completely quiet until the chick that gave me her number a few months ago walked up to me.

"Kiley, right?" she said.

I couldn't remember her name. "Yeah, um…

"Marissa. My name is Marissa. Had you looked at my number on that piece of paper I gave you, you would have known my name," she smiled.

"Hey, I'm guilty," I said, holding my arms in the air. "Guilty of throwing your number in the trashcan because I was seeing someone else at the time."

"Thanks for being honest. Did you come here by yourself, or are you with...

"Naw, I'm by myself. I came to watch my son play."

"Who's your son?"

I really didn't want to say because I didn't want nobody to know my business. "Uh, Abrams. Desmon Abrams."

Her mouth hung open. "You're Desmon's father? But I thought...never mind."

I puzzlingly looked at her. "You thought what? That I was in jail?"

"No," she paused, and ordered her food because the lady behind the counter asked for our order. I ordered mine, and after I paid for both of ours, we walked away. I gave Anna another look before leaving and she turned her head.

"So, what do you know about me," I asked, as Marissa followed me back to my seat. She sat next to me and sipped on her soda. After she did, she cleared her throat.

"Let's just say that way back whenever, Ginger and I used to be pretty cool. I thought Desmon was my ex-boyfriend's, Myles, son. She told me Desmon was his son, after she slept with him behind my back. But, I can see the resemblances in you and Desmon too. Don't get me wrong, again, he looks like you, but he got some of Myles features too."

"Hmm," I said, sitting back in my seat. "So, where's Myles at now?"

"He was killed many years ago. I think Desmon was only one or two at the time. From what I can remember though, Kiley, Myles did use to go see him."

I was quiet for a long time and thought about how I really wasn't around Desmon that much when he was a baby. I'd been trying to work shit out with Jada and didn't want her to know I'd had a son. The only time I did see Desmon was on the weekends, but Ginger never mentioned anything about not knowing who the father was. If I had known what I know now about her ass, I would've had a blood test. Now, though, it really didn't matter. Something wasn't adding up because Desmon and me had too much in common. There was no denying him because he looked too much like Kareem, Papa Abrams, and me. If anything, Ginger lied to Marissa and that other cat, Myles. Especially since Desmon always carried my last name.

"Kiley," Marissa said. "I hope I didn't open up a can of worms. Your girlfriend, ex-girlfriend, or whoever the hell she is to you, she's a…"

"I know all about Ginger, Marissa. There's not much you can say about her that I don't already know. In the meantime, do you have a picture of this Myles character?"

"Not on me. But, if you'd come by my place later, I'm sure I can dig one up for you."

"Give me your number again. I have company in town so I won't call you tonight, but I promise to call you soon."

"Would I be intruding if I ask if it's male or female?"

"Yes, you would be."

She stood up. "Well, if you're not too busy Sunday night, I'm having a birthday party at Club Classic. Why don't you drop in and wish me a happy birthday?"

"Club Classic…that's where Ginger works, right?"

She winked. "You got it. The same place I saw you at the last time."

"We'll see. I'll try to make it," I said.

Shortly after Marissa walked away, the crowd was on their feet as the players came back onto the field. Again, they were hyped and the score was now twenty-one to seven. On the second play of the quarter, Desmon sacked the quarterback and he fumbled. Desmon recovered the ball and as he picked it up to run for the touchdown, another player on the other team grabbed Desmon's leg and made him fall. After Desmon fell to the ground, the other player twisted his leg back and came crashing down on it. I hopped up and so did everyone else in the crowd. The referee threw the flag down, but Desmon didn't get up. I could see he was in dying pain, so I rushed onto the field to see what was up. Of course, I didn't make it too far as security was all over me.

"That's my son," I said.

"Sir, you need to back up. You can't just come onto the field like this."

"You didn't just understand what I said, did you," I said, giving the security guard an angry look. "Now, get your fucking hands off my chest and let me go see about my son."

The guard backed away and I ran onto the field to where Desmon was. He had his helmet off and was moving back and forth on the ground while holding his leg. It was obvious he was in detrimental pain.

By the looks of it, I could tell his injury was serious. How serious was the question. The coaching staff called for the trainer, and shortly after, they took him off the field. Before going into the locker room with him, I politely walked over to the other side of the field where the other team stood waiting and watching. I walked up to the player who had purposely injured Desmon's leg and gave him a threat I truly intended to live up to.

"If he doesn't play football again, or if this injury prevents him from being all that he can be in this game, you're gonna lose both of your legs. You messed with the wrong one this time, partna, and you'd better hope like hell this ain't as serious as it looks."

The lil punk motherfucker had the nerve to roll his eyes at me, and since I didn't want to get arrested, I hurried off to the locker room to see about Desmon. When I got there, I could hear him screaming as I stood outside of the door. I knocked, and after one of his coaches let me in, Desmon turned his head to the side and looked at me.

"Why…why don't you just leave me alone, man?" he said. I could see the pain in his eyes, as a few tears had fallen from the sides of them.

I ignored Desmon and talked to the trainer. "So, what's going on with his leg?"

He shook his head. "It doesn't look too good. An ambulance is on the way and we're gonna take him to the hospital for x-rays."

Desmon held his eyes tightly together and continued to grab his leg. I walked over and took a look at it. It certainly wasn't a pretty sight. "Can't you all give him something for the pain?" I asked.

"We will. As soon as the ambulance gets here."

"I don't won't no…no damn medicine," he said, as he started to cry. "I wanna finish my game. Man, help me up so I can finish my game."

I was too hurt to say anything. The assistant coach walked over and talked to Desmon. "Not right now, man. We gotta get you taken care of, and then you can finish the game."

He opened his eyes. "Where my mama? Would you go call my mama for me?" Desmon asked his assistant coach.

"Sure. I'll go call her right now."

A huge part of me was really hurt. There I was standing right before him and he had the nerve to call for Ginger. She didn't even have the decency to have her ass at his game, yet alone, show up at the hospital when his coach asked her to come. I didn't say shit because I knew exactly what was about to go down.

I followed the ambulance to the hospital and stayed in the room with Desmon until the doctor came back in. We hadn't said two words to each other, but as long as he knew I was there, that's all that mattered to me. The doctor said Desmon had torn ligaments, but said he certainly could play football again as long as he allowed his leg to heal. Loving football as much as he did, Desmon was crushed. He acted as if it was the end of the world and when I reminded him that he could play next year, he told me to stay the fuck out of his business and asked me to leave. The doctor soon left the room and let us have at it.

"What did I tell you about disrespecting me, huh?" I said.

"And what did I tell you about being in my business. I don't even know why you're here. Don't you get it, man? I want you out of my life. You have caused my mother and me nothing but pain and suffering and I don't want anything else to do with you."

"You almost sound like Ginger. I guess she's manipulated you into believing I'm no good for you? You're a smart kid, Desmon. And, as soon as you wake up and see things for what they are, you'll be even smarter. Now, I'm deeply sorry about what happened to your leg. But maybe, this will allow you some time to get your grades in order. Those come first, and you need to remember that."

"Get the hell out of here with that! I don't need your advice— Dad! I'm gonna play football whether you or the doctors like it or not. So, see ya. Go back to wherever you came from. These past few weeks have been peaceful without you."

The assistant coach came into the room and said he'd left Ginger a few messages on her answering machine. He stayed for a while, and after they put a splint on Desmon's leg his coach left.

Desmon waited around for Ginger to come, and when I asked to take him home, he declined. I told him I'd see him later and left. Not intending to go anywhere until I knew he had a ride home, I waited on the parking lot for Ginger to come. I could see Desmon sitting in the waiting area and I watched as he made his way back and forth to the pay phone to call. I even called the house myself, but still got no answer. After another hour had gone by, I finally pulled my car in front of the hospital and blew the horn. He looked out at me and came outside. Being stubborn, he pulled the handle on the door and tried to get in without any help. When I got out of the car to help him, he insisted that I get back into the car. I let him handle his business, and soon after, he was inside of the car. His crutches were on the back seat and he reached for his jacket to get something out of his pocket.

"Would you mind stopping at the pharmacy to get my prescription filled," he asked.

I took the prescription from his hand. "Is this your pain medicine?"

He nodded.

I drove to the pharmacy and once I got his prescription filled, I walked back to my car. Desmon was on my phone and when I got inside of the car, he ended his call. He handed my phone to me.

"Where's your phone at?" I asked.

"I'on know. It might be lost." He paused. "Did you know that we lost the game?"

"Yep. Without their number one player, it was bound to happen." I looked over at him and smiled, as he turned his head to look out of the window.

I drove off and when we got halfway down the road, Desmon turned and looked at me. "Do you wanna know why I'm really mad at you?" he asked.

"No, I really don't care why you're mad at me."

"Yes, you do."

"Really, no I don't. Your being mad at me don't mean a damn thing to me, Desmon. I just hate you got all of this anger inside of you for nothing."

"Yeah, whatever. But the reason I'm so mad at you now is because, not only did you have my Moms face all fucked up, but why...why did you have to go fuck my best friend's aunt. She's like a mother to Antonio, and out of all of the women, why her?"

"Aw...so, you know about Anna? Did Ginger tell you about her?"

"Yep. And, I talked to Anna too."

"What did Anna say?"

"Other than that you're a no good, low down, back stabbing ass liar."

"Yes. Other than that, did she say anything else?"

"Yeah, she said a whole bunch more. But, it's gonna cost you if you want to know."

"Then, I don't want to know."

"Cool," he said. We didn't say another word to each other until we pulled in front of Ginger's townhouse.

Anxious to know what Anna said, I parked the car and turned off the headlights. "So, how much is it gonna cost me?"

He smiled. "I need some new threads, man. My shit getting out dated and a new pair of tennis shoes wouldn't be a bad idea either. My car down and so is Antonio's. We really could use some money to get them fixed."

I looked over at him. "Those cars will stay broke, but how much, Desmon? Stop beating around the bush."

"A thousand doll...

"Shit, you out of your motherfucking mind."

"So, are you telling me, you wouldn't pay a thousand dollars to hear what Anna told me about you. I think you'd really want to know."

"Well, ain't nobody paying you to think."

"Alright," he said, opening the door to get out. "Your lost and not mine."

I grabbed his arm. "Okay. Close the door. I'll give you five hundred dollars if you tell me."

"Nine-Hundred."

"Seven."

"Eight-Fifty."

"Eight...and that's my last offer."

He closed the door. "You would really pay me eight-hundred dollars to find out what she said about you?"

"Yes. Now, tell me what she said."

He hesitated and then looked at me and grinned. "She said that she was in love with you."

"Man, I already knew that. Tell me what else she said."

"That's it. She just told me she'd fallen in love with you. So, give me my eight-hundred dollars."

"Man, I ain't giving you no money for something I already know. I thought she said something else about me."

"So, that's how I get played. I told you what she said, and now, you holding back on the money."

I reached in my back pocket and counted out one thousand dollars and gave it to Desmon. The look of excitement was written all over his face.

"I can't believe you'd kick me out like this for telling you Anna loves you. That's crazy, man."

"Desmon, wise up, okay. I will give you the shirt off my back if you asked for it. The money I gave you has nothing to do with Anna. If you want to buy yourself some clothes and shoes, then go do it."

Desmon put the money in his pocket and opened the door to get out. I got out to help him and grabbed his crutches from the back seat of the car. As we walked towards the door, he turned and looked at me.

"Listen. That's my Moms flavor of the month car over there," he said, pointing to a brand new white Lincoln in one of the parking spots. "Please don't come in here and cause any trouble, okay."

I hesitantly nodded.

"Promise me," Desmon said.

"You have my word," I replied.

Desmon unlocked the door and limped inside. Music came from Ginger's bedroom and the door was closed. I could tell the lights were out because I couldn't see it from underneath the door.

"They must be sleeping," Desmon said, still standing, while putting little pressure on his injured leg.

"Aren't you going to wake her to tell her what happened?"

"I'll tell her later."

"Why wait," I said, getting ready to walk towards the door. "Let's tell her now."

Desmon grabbed my arm. "Let me tell her. Why don't you just go home and I'll call you later. Seriously, I don't want no trouble."

"Man, it ain't gone be no trouble. Trust me. In the meantime, you need to think about coming to live with me. I got a nice place, you can have your own room, and I promise to stay out of your business."

"Maybe, but go home. I'll let you know soon."

I turned towards the door, and soon after, changed my mind about leaving. "You know what, I think I got some unfinished business to take care of. Why let it wait until Sunday when I can take care of it today."

I walked past Desmon and went straight to Ginger's bedroom door. I lightly tapped on it and when she asked who it was, I told her it was me.

"What do you want? I'm busy," she yelled.

Desmon interrupted. "Hey, I got hurt at the game today. I've been calling…

She opened the door and closed it behind her. She stood in front of the door and tied her robe so I wouldn't see her naked body underneath. "Hurt. How'd you get hurt?"

"I injured my leg," Desmon said. She walked past me and went into the living room. When she turned on the light, she looked down at Desmon's leg.

"I told you about playing that damn football, Desmon. What happened?" She picked up a cigarette and lit it.

"It's a long story. I'ma take my medicine and go lay down for a bit. Will you fix me something to eat?"

"Yeah, baby," she said, blowing the smoke out of her mouth. "I'll fix it in a lil bit, okay."

Desmon turned and headed downstairs to his room. Before he did, surprisingly, he looked over and thanked me.

"Anytime," I replied and then turned to look at Ginger.

"Do you got my money yet?"

"I got some of it. If you want all of it, you'll have to wait."

"I'm not going to wait for long. So, you lay on your back as many times as you have to, to get it. And if you get tired of laying, then get on your knees. I got a feeling, though, as if that's not going to be a problem for you."

"Is that all you want?" she said. "You'll get your damn money back, Kiley. And I hope you and your little Hispanic bitch have a happy fucking life together."

I snickered, and since I promised Desmon I wouldn't cause any problems, I left.

TROUBLE IS ON THE WAY

Rufus and me were at my crib getting fucked up. He had some weed that was the motherfucking bomb and we stayed up for hours talking about old times while smoking blunts. Before his departure on Monday, I asked if he wanted to kick it with me tonight at Club Classic and he agreed to go. I wasn't tripping off Ginger working there, but I damn sure was tired of living this sheltered fucking life I lived.

Rufus couldn't stop pouncing on me moving back to L.A. And, from all of the good things he'd told me was going on it sounded all good. For now, though, it was about Desmon. I wanted to make sure everything was cool with him, and by at least offering him a decent place to stay, that was a start.

What Marissa told me had been heavy on my mind. Again, there was no denying Desmon, but sometimes, you just can't be too sure. I guess I need validation for myself that he is truly my son, so it was in my best interest to seek further for the truth. It really didn't matter to me because whether he is or ain't, I still love him no matter what.

Rufus and me parlayed around the house all damn day. I was slumped over on the living room couch and he was leaned over in a chair snoring his butt off. I kept flipping through the channels on the television, and tried to find something to watch. There wasn't much on, so I stood up and went to my nasty girl collection. I slid in a porn movie and sat back down to watch. My dick was lonely. It hadn't been sucked on, stroked, or played with in quite some time. The movie had me rock hard and there was no doubt somebody was going to get a piece of me tonight.

I gazed lustfully at the scenes on the TV, and trying to make Rufus snoring stop, I raised the volume to wake him. He slowly opened his eyes, and turned his head to look at the TV.

"Damn, man, it's too early for that shit, ain't it?" he said. He stretched his arms and continued to look at the TV.

"It's almost four-thirty in the afternoon. You have been knocked the fuck out."

"Four-thirty! You kidding, right?"

"Look at the clock, fool."

Rufus looked up at the silver and glass clock I had above the entertainment center. "Shit, you ain't bullshitting, is you? My ass ain't slept that good in ages. See what a lil herb will do for ya?" He reached for an already smoked blunt in the ashtray in front of him. He lit it and took a few more hits. After that, he passed it to me. I reached for it and placed it into my mouth.

"Kiley, this is my last and final offer. St. Louis is cool, but I hate to see you here all by yourself. Mo than anything, it's not you. You're bored all the fucking time, you ain't got no every day pussy around the house, and as for the drama, now, you gotta have some drama in your life."

I inhaled the smoke and swallowed. "Nigga, I got enough drama already. I wouldn't mind going back with you, but I gotta see about Desmon, Killer."

"Then, bring him with you. Desmon needs a new change, trust me."

"Yeah, change is what I'm afraid of. He would instantly turn into what I used to be and I ain't trying to let that happen. I know your kids are in the game and shit, and no offense, but I don't want Desmon to go out like that."

"Hey, whateva. My kids enjoy being in the game. We're living how we should be living and I'm leaving a legacy like Papa Abrams left for y'all."

I looked Rufus straight in the eyes and tried to be serious considering the buzz I already had from the weed. "That legacy died years ago, Killer. It was short lived and I thought it would last forever. When Kareem was killed, it was coming to an end then. After Quincy, it was all over with. There's no more money, no nothing. Now, you tell me what kind of legacy is that."

"But, you got to carry it on, Bro. Don't you know what you're capable of putting together around here? Man, you could blow St. Louis off the map. Desmon, you, or anybody else you'd trust to roll with you. And, if you came back to L.A., I can only envision what things would be like. The brothas there want you back bad. All they talk about is when Kiley was here and Papa Abrams was alive. Papa Abrams' legacy is back in L.A. It still lingers in all of us, man. It ain't no good if you ain't there to share it with us."

I sat there and didn't say another word. Maybe Rufus was right. Things weren't really looking up for me in St. Louis, and Desmon would surely love to move to L.A. Either way, I told Rufus I'd think hard about it. If anything, I knew what kind of man I'd become if I moved back, and being that kind of man again, I knew my life would be short lived.

After conversing with Rufus a lil while longer, still a bit sleepy, I leaned back on the couch and faded.

Rufus woke me up and told me he'd be back around ten so we could get ready to go out. When he left, I lay my head back and continued to get some rest.

I woke up around eight-thirty. Awfully hungry, I went into the kitchen and put together a quick sandwich. I put the sandwich in my mouth, and then, went into my bedroom to find something to wear for tonight. I opened my closet and looked at all the fancy and expensive clothes I had neatly hung up. At first, I pulled out my casual attire, which were a pair of jeans, a button down shirt, and another one of my tan linen outfits. Quickly changing my mind, I pulled out a black on black, silk shirt, tie, and *Gucci* suit that still had the price tag on it. After I chowed down on my sandwich, I put the suit on to see how it looked. The tie was cool, but it wasn't needed for the occasion. I took it off and unbuttoned the black silk shirt. Looking damn good, I turned in the mirror and looked at how the suit clung to the muscles in my arms and my shoulders. Not only that, but it made my butt look so good that I knew the women would barely be able to keep their hands off of it tonight. Fully satisfied with the look, I took it off and hurried to take my shower.

By the time Rufus got back, I was in the bathroom trimming my goatee and putting a shine to my baldhead. He stood in the doorway and watched me rub my handsome face.

"Man, are you wearing that suit you got laid out on your bed?"

"Yeah. Why?"

"Well, damn! I thought we were gonna just throw on some jeans or something. I ain't going nowhere with you looking like this."

"Then, wear something nice."

"I didn't bring no suits with me, nigga. If I had known, I would have."

"Then, pick something out in my closet."

"Fool, that's a bitch move. I ain't wearing another motherfucker's clothes. What time do the malls close around here?"

I looked at my watch. "I think you're out of luck."

"Shit, I think I might have a lil somethin-somethin in my trunk. I'ma go out there to check in a few minutes."

Rufus followed me back into the room and picked my suit up to look at it again.

"This is a cold ass suit, man. If I can't find me nothing decent to wear, your ass is going alone."

"Just wear what you got. Don't even trip off me."

"Yeah, whatever," he said, and then walked off. He left to look for something in his trunk.

Shortly after, Rufus came back in with a casual two-piece solid colored outfit. It was brown and had a button down elbow length shirt and flimsy loose-legged pants to match. It wasn't nearly as sharp as the suit I had, but you could tell Rufus paid a pretty penny for it.

"This cool," I said, holding it in my hands.

"You think?" he hesitated.

"Yean, man. Besides, I don't think a suit will do you any good with that big ass fro ya wearing."

"Nigga, don't talk about my fro. That's liable to get you hurt. Besides, I like my damn fro," he said, while patting it.

"Then, pat that shit down a little, shower, change clothes and let's go."

Rufus took his outfit into the bathroom with him and closed the door. Before I put on my clothes, I sat on the edge of the bed and reached for the phone. I called Desmon's cell phone to check on him because I hadn't talked to him since yesterday. When I called, his phone was disconnected. I called Ginger's house and was surprised when he answered the phone.

"I can't believe you're at home," I said.

"You can't do too much with a messed-up leg, can you?"

"I guess not. But, I just called to check on ya, that's it."

"I'm cool. I'm moving around a lil better, but other than that, I'm cool."

"What's up with your cell phone? Did you know it was turned off?"

"Of course I knew. I just swindled you out of some money so I can get it turned back on."

"Fool, please. You didn't swindle me out of nothing. You'd better take that money and put it to good use because you damn sure won't be getting any more any time soon."

"Aw, I'm gone put it to good use. That's one thing you don't have to worry about."

"Then, good. Have you, uh, thought about what I said?"

"You've said a lot, so I don't know what you're talking about."

"About moving in with me."

"Nope, I haven't thought about it. You and me won't be able to get along, Kiley. I like things my way and you like them yours."

"Then, we'll compromise."

"I don't do that too well either."

"Just think about it, okay? I'm getting ready to go out tonight so I can get me some puss—

After I paused, he laughed. I felt as if I was talking to one of my boys. "What were you getting ready to say?" he asked.

"Nothing. I said I was going out tonight."

"Yeah, well, finish it up. If you're going out to get some twang that's yo business. Mine is right here with me, but she's taking a nap. A leg injury certainly has its rewards, as Moms is waiting on me hand and foot, my girls are just throwing all kinds of goods at me, and you fill my pockets with money. Had I known I'd have this many people feeling sorry for me, I would have hurt myself along time ago."

"I don't feel sorry for you, Desmon. I just care about you, fool, so again, think about what I said and call me sometime this week. I want you to spend some time with me too, au-ight?"

He laughed and hung up. I really wasn't sure how this relationship between us was working out, and at times, his disrespect was quite unbearable.

By eleven, Rufus and me were dressed at our best. He'd trimmed his fro down a tad bit, and the outfit he had on, made him look much better. Me, on the other hand, I knew my shit was off the chain. Before leaving, I got one last glance at the mirror, and it certainly didn't lie. I straightened my goatee with the tips of my finger and headed for the door.

I drove my black Caddy since Rufus didn't know his way around town. And when we got to the club, there was roughly no place to park. Not wanting to have my car parked where some thugs could get a hold to it, I handed the keys over to the valets.

As soon as we made our way inside, heads turned and brothas checked us out like we were crazy or something. Completely forgetting to leave my gun in the car, the metal detectors went off as I went through.

Before the bouncer felt for it, I reached for it and pulled it out of my pants.

"Hey, look, I forgot. I'll got put it back in the ride."

"No need," a voice said from behind. "He with me."

I turned as Dominique and a few of his partners had walked in behind us.

The bouncer moved aside to let me in, and I waited to thank Dominique after he'd made his way in.

"I appreciate that," I said, shaking his hand.

"Anytime," he said, and then looked at Rufus.

"Dominique, this my man, Killer."

Rufus hesitated but held his hand out to shake Dominique's.

"Sup," Rufus said. "I didn't know my partna had friends in St. Louis."

"Good friends," Dominique responded. "Friends that, if needed, got his back like he had mine."

Rufus looked at me and shook his head. "Na, uh, uh. Don't nobody got his back but me. He know that...right Kiley?"

"I ain't met nobody else yet, so, uh, again, thanks Dominique. I'll holla at ya before I go."

We slammed fist together and Dominique and his partnas walked off. Rufus looked at me with a disgruntled look.

"Who the fuck was that ole poot-butt ass nigga?"

"I'll tell you about it later. Until then, lets get this show on the road."

He smiled and we walked over to the bar.

There wasn't no place to sit so we stood and waited for the bartender to take our order. I noticed Marissa and several of her friends sitting at a table in the VIP section, so I told Rufus I'd be right back.

From what I could see, Marissa looked pretty nice for a thick gal. She had on a pair of red fitted pants and a knee length jacket to match it. Her hair was slicked back into a neat shiny ponytail and showed the prettiness of her round shaped face. By the time I made it over to her, she'd already scoped me coming. Her pearly whites showed from a distance and she held her arms out to give me a hug.

"Thank you for coming," she said, hugging me tightly.

I kissed her cheek, "I told you I'd think about it. So, uh, Happy Birthday. So far, I hope you're having a good one."

"Oh, you just don't know," she said taking her arms from around me. "Trust me when I say that it just got so much better. You look fabulous."

"Thanks. You look nice too."

All of her friends at the table looked at me and stared. Marissa placed her hand on my back and rubbed it. "Everyone, this is Kiley. He's a good friend of mine."

"Hello, Ladies," I said. They spoke back and continued to stare.

"I am so excited you're here," Marissa said. "Come on, let's dance."

"In a minute, okay. I got my boy with me and he's from out of town. I wanna make sure he's cool."

"So, it was a male you were waiting on, huh?"

I smiled at Marissa and after giving her another hug and kiss on the cheek, I went back over to the bar.

Rufus had just gotten our drinks. Still not having any place to sit, we stood by the bar and checked out the scenery. Of course, I'd already scoped Ginger walking around doing her thing. I didn't know if she'd seen me already, and frankly, didn't give a damn. When I pointed her out to Rufus, he was stunned.

"So, that's Ginger, huh?"

"Yep, that's her ass."

"Man, I must tell you...that bitch is fine. Why you ain't tell me she had an ass like that?"

"Trust me, it ain't at all what it seems. That's all she got is a body. The rest of her is airless."

We both laughed and Rufus quickly asked me about Marissa. I told him I barely knew her, but hopefully soon, I'd know her much better.

As soon as the DJ kicked up another song, Marissa couldn't wait to make her way over to me. Rufus and me were in the midst of conversing with these other two females who stood by the bar with us, and Marissa interrupted.

"Come on, I thought you said we were gonna dance."

"We will—I promise you we will. Just give me a few more minutes, okay?"

"If he won't dance with you, baby, I will," Rufus said, slightly tipsy.

"Well, come on," she said, snapping her fingers. "I'm here to have some fun tonight."

She took Rufus' hand and they made their way to the dance floor. I continued my conversation with the ladies until Ginger came over and stood in front of us.

"Hi," she said, sharply, while holding the beverage tray close to her hip.

"What's up?"

She looked at the two chicks who stood by me. "This my baby daddy. Do y'all mind if I talk to him for a minute?"

One of them looked at me. "Goodbye, Kiley. We'll catch up with you later, alright?"

"That's cool," I said. They walked off and Ginger stood with her lips tooted. She looked me up and down.

"You look nice, but why you up in here?" she asked.

"Do I need permission or something to be up in here?"

"No. But, if you're here about your money, I said that I'd have it for you soon."

"Ginger, look. Now is not the time or place. I'm here to have a good time, so, how about you just get the hell away from me?"

She took a hard swallow then turned her head. After she spoke to this brotha who past by us, she turned back towards me. "What are you doing after you leave here?"

"Why?"

"Because I want to talk to you about something, that's why?"

"If it's not about my money, then there's nothing for us to talk about."

"It's not about your money. It's about how I want to work this out with you. I miss you, Kiley, and I miss having you around."

"Say you do, huh? Well, I haven't started missing you yet. If or whenever I do, I'll be sure to let you know, okay?"

"So, it's that easy for you to let what we had go. If that's the case, then you must have never loved me."

"I never said I did, did I?"

She gave me a cold stare. "So, what about Anna? Did you bring her with you tonight, or did she come alone?"

"I didn't know she was here. So, let me shut you up real quickly. I haven't heard from her or seen her since I moved out that day. Now, would you get back to work and let me enjoy my night?"

She raised her finger at me. "Remember, I am still the mother of your child. You will respect me in your presence and if you act a fool in here tonight with any of these bitches, I will clown on yo ass and I mean it." She rolled her eyes and walked away.

What a fucking joke, I thought. That bitch was crazy. If she thought for one moment I was going to give her some respect, she was sadly mistaken. My respect for her went out the door the day I got my ass out of jail.

As my eyes searched the crowd, Ginger didn't lie about Anna being there. I saw her on the dance floor near Rufus and Marissa dancing with a tall and slender brotha with dreadlocks. I pretended not to see her and looked in the other direction.

I stood drinking and taking periodic looks at the dance floor until one of Marissa's friends came up and asked me to dance. Ready to get my party on, I accepted. No sooner had we got on the dance floor, Marissa switched partners. She moved her friend away from me and started to dance.

"So, are we hyped now," she said.

"As hyped as I'm gonna get," I responded. She turned around and pressed her ass against me as she dance. My dick instantly responded, as I moved from side to side with her and watched her do her thing.

Marissa was an excellent dancer and we'd danced through at least three songs together. When the DJ switched to something slow, she placed her hand on her chest.

"Well, it's about time. I've been waiting all night for him to set the mood."

I really didn't feel like slow dancing, but I didn't want to keep playing her off, especially on her birthday. So, instead of leaving the dance floor, I put my arms around her waist and we started to dance. Surprisingly, Anna had done the same with her partner. She danced right next to me and wanted my attention so badly.

For a while, I was able to ignore her. My conversation with Marissa flowed, as well as our plans to hook up tonight. But, when Anna stared me down to get my attention, that's when I looked over Marissa's shoulder to see what Anna was saying.

"Meet me outside," she mouthed.

Playing hard to get, I shook my head and looked back at Marissa to continue my conversation. After the song was over, I thanked Marissa for the dance and we parted ways.

"Don't forget about me later on," she said.

"I promise you I won't," I responded, and then walked near the bar where Rufus was.

I interrupted his conversation with a female. "So, Killer, what you think? Is this place off the hook or what?"

"It's cool. You know ain't nothing like the clubs in L.A. but this a lil mo mellow."

I looked at the chick standing next to him. "I see you've managed to swoop up something good," I whispered.

"Like I said, it's all good. If you don't mind, though, I think I'm gonna catch a ride home with Saujay tonight."

"Hey, that's fine with me. I got plans anyway, nigga."

Rufus laughed and I walked off to the restroom.

I took a quick leak and as I washed my hands, Dominique came in with some brotha he was having it out with. They came busting through the bathroom door and most of the fellas in the bathroom cleared out instantly. Trying to see what was up, a few other spectators and myself stood closely by the door as Dominique already had a knife up to the brotha's throat.

"You are lucky that I don't feel like killing nobody today!" he yelled. "You need to fix my damn car the right way or buy me another one!"

As they were leaned against the sinks, the brotha struggled to get away from Dominique. "Look, man. Why don't you just get somebody else to fix it? I did the best I could," he said fearfully.

I kind of felt sorry for the fella. Dominique punched him hard in his stomach and he fell to the floor. With his long leather shoe, Dominique kicked him in the ribs and the brotha started spitting up blood. All I could think of was how he was about to lose his life over something as stupid as fixing a fucking car. With that in mind, of course, I had to interrupt.

"Dominique," I yelled. "That's enough, man."

He looked up at me as if hell had swarmed over him. "Kiley, do you know this motherfucker or something?"

"Yeah, something like that," I said, and then walked up to him. I held my hand out for the brotha to take it. "Man, get up."

He reached for my hand and made his way off the floor. He held his side, and after Dominique looked at him again, he took his fist and punched him hard in the stomach again. Unable to sustain the pain, the dude fell down on one knee. For whatever reason, I was pissed. I placed my hand on Dominique's chest, and could tell by the look in his eyes that he was about to kill him.

"Let this one go for me, au-ight?" I said.

"Man, this nigga messed up my fucking car. Do you hear me? Him and his friends stole my shit, fucked up my sound system and cut my leather seats up because they didn't have shit else to do. Instead of taking his life when I found out he did it, I gave the sucker an alternative. I said either fix my shit, or suffer the consequences. Instead of fixing it, his ass made matters even worse. My shit burned up because he messed up the wiring. I'm sorry, but this one I can't let go."

"Well, you gone have to. Because if you hit him again, it's gone bring about some drama between you and me. Now, you don't want that, do you?"

"So, it's like that, huh?"

"It don't have to be, so let the brotha go. If he'd fucked over your family or your boyz or something, then I'd say to hell with him. But a car ain't worth taking no life over. That can all ways be replaced."

"You're right. How-eva, he fucked me over and that's good enough reason for a nigga to die."

Dominique hesitated no longer and slashed the brothas throat right in front of me. That caused everyone in the bathroom to scatter, and before the cops showed, I gave Dominique one of the hardest looks he'd probably ever seen before and made my way to the exit.

"Kiley," he yelled as I was on my way out. I turned around. "Nice suit. I see you spent my money well. Just remember, though, I'm in charge around here. Don't you ever forget that, you hear me?"

"There's always a price to pay for being in charge, Dominique. And your money was chump change for what I did for you. It's a shame you wasn't willing to make an exception for me and that ain't good, my brotha. That for damn sure wasn't good."

I walked out and looked around for Rufus. I couldn't find him for nothing because people ran like crazy trying to get out of there. As soon as I got outside, I rang him on my cell phone. He answered.

"Man, where are you?" I asked.

"I'm chilling in a car with a ghetto girl. Why all these folks running wild like the place on fire or something?"

"Because somebody got killed. Thanks for making sure it wasn't me."

"Shit, I knew it wasn't you. Not with that piece you got tucked away in your pants it better not had been you."

I laughed. "Gone ahead and tend to your ghetto girl. If you need a key to my place, it's an extra one underneath the doormat."

"Au-ight, Dog. I'll catch up with you later."

I stood outside and looked for the valet so I could get my car keys and go. The police started to arrive and by the time I had my keys in my hand, they were walking around questioning people about what had happened.

As I put the key in the door to unlock it, one of the officers came up to me. Before he could ask for my name, Dominique walked out with a few of his boys by his side. He pretended as if he didn't see me, but he turned and listened in as I told the officer my name and that I hadn't seen anything.

"Mr. Abrams," the officer said. "So, are you sure you didn't see anything? A few other witnesses said you did."

I could see Dominique from the corner of my eye. "No, I didn't see anything. Your witnesses must have been talking about somebody else."

"Are you positive?" he pressed. "The only way we can begin to cut back on crime is when people start coming forward."

"Sorry, but, I can't help you."

117

The officer nodded and gave me a card. "If you have any information for me, give me a call." I took the card and he walked away.

Knowing that he was probably on Dominique's payroll, I got inside of my car and closed the door. Dominique's eyes and mine met up and he could see me looking at him through my lightly tinted windows. He grinned and nodded his head. Mad, about the whole fucking ordeal, I shaped my fingers like a gun and aimed it at him. I mouthed "pow" and had every intention of following through with my threat.

Soon after, I backed up and pulled off. No sooner had I made it down the street, I noticed a white car following closely behind me. When I turned, it turned. And when I ran a red light, it did the same. I sped up, and when it sped up after me, I slammed on the brakes and placed my hand on my gun. I quickly hopped out and fired two shots into the car's windshield. The car slammed into the rear of mine, before I noticed it was Anna in the car. I heard her loud screams as she dropped her head and bent down in the front seat. I rushed to the car and opened the door.

"Did the bullet hit you!" I panicked and yelled at the same time. "Damn, did it hit you!"

"No," she sobbed while still leaned over. I pulled her from the front seat and held her trembling body in my arms.

My heart raced fast. "I am so, so sorry! I didn't know it was you. Don't ever follow me like that!" I yelled.

She continued to cry, as I held her with a tight embrace. After I walked her to my car to get in, I got in the car she drove and parked it close to the curb.

When I got back into my car, Anna was still shaken up. Her hands covered her face and tears poured down her face. There wasn't much I could say to her because I felt bad. Instead of saying anything else, I drove her home and got out to open the car door for her. At first, she didn't move. Then, I moved her hands away from her face and slowly pulled her out of the car. I wrapped my arms around her again and continued to apologize.

"If I had known it was you, you know I wouldn't have done that. My windows are tinted and I couldn't see—

She moved away from me and walked towards the door. Wanting to talk to her, I followed behind her. She turned and looked at me.

"Come by tomorrow. I...I can't talk about this right now," she said nervously.

"Tomorrow is never promised. I need to talk to you now."

Anna opened the door and we walked into the living room. She turned on a lamp and sat down on the couch. I stood up by the door and waited for her to get herself together.

"What is it that you wanted to talk to me about?" I asked. She didn't respond. "I'm sure you wasn't following me for nothing."

She looked up with her puffy red eyes. "Why did you have to lie to me? I was honest with you—

"I lied because I didn't want you to know who I was. So there. It just wasn't in my best interest to tell you I was Desmon's father."

"You know damn well you could have told me the truth. You pretended to be someone that you weren't. You tricked me into telling you things about Desmon. And, you used me for sex whenever things got heated between you and Ginger. How could you do that to me? I thought you really cared—

"Look, you know damn well how I feel about you! I told you and I didn't lie about it! Like I said before, it just wasn't in my best interest to tell you the truth at the time!"

"Stop, fucking yelling at me bastard! I've been going through nothing but hell trying to fight these damn feelings for you! You never called or tried to give me an explanation!"

I pointed my finger at Anna. "I did try to explain this shit to you! When you were in Ginger's kitchen, I tried to explain everything to you! But, you walked out! Remember! So, now, I'm walking out! I'm sorry about the damn windshield and I'm sorry if you think I used you for sex! I promise not to hurt you no damn more, au-ight!" I opened the door and walked out. Anna came after me and hopped in on the passenger's side of my car.

"Get out," I said. "I'm going home."

"And...and I'm going with you. Since you want to live such a secret fucking life, who in the hell are you living with now."

I cut my eyes at Anna and drove off. During the drive to my place, I didn't say anything to her and she didn't say anything to me.

119

When I pulled in front of my house, I turned off the ignition and looked over at her.

"Do you want to come inside to meet my wife?"

"You're married?" she yelled.

"Yes. So, since you want to know everything about me, then why don't you start by meeting my wife."

Anna angrily looked at me and got out of the car. She slammed the door and started down the street.

I hurried out and followed behind her. "Where are you going?"

"I'm going home," she said, tearfully, shaking her head. "You are just full of surprises, aren't you?"

"And full of shit sometimes too, so come on," I said, grabbing her arm. She resisted, so I pulled her to the front door with me.

She stood with her arms folded as I unlocked the door.

"What do you want me to do, fight her for you? I'm not going to fight anybody over you," she said.

"Maybe she'll want to fight you for me, huh? Remember, you're the one who said that you wanted to know everything about me."

I pushed the door open and we walked in. Anna stood by the doorway with her arms still folded like she was prepared to meet my imaginary wife. Making sure the coast was clear, I walked through my place to make sure Rufus and his date wasn't there. While in my bedroom, I removed my jacket and silk shirt. I left my white t-shirt on and unbuttoned the top button on my pants.

When I walked back into the living room, Anna lustfully looked at my body, and then turned her head. I stood tall in front of her and took her hand.

"My wife is dying to meet you," I said.

She snatched her hand away from me and followed behind me. As I walked through the doorway to my bedroom, I moved aside so Anna could see there was no one in the room.

"Now, as you can see, I live alone. Is there anything else you'd like to know about me?"

She gave me a furious look, turned and started to walk out of the door. I quickly snatched her up and pushed he backwards onto the bed. I immediately hit the light switch and hurried to put my body on top of hers.

"Get off me," she yelled, while pounding my chest.

I grabbed her hands and held them down. When I tried to kiss her, she moved her head from side to side.

"I don't want you to kiss me," she yelled. "I want you to get up off me!"

"I will, once you calm down," I said calmly.

"I am going to calm down, once you get up!"

I continued to lay on Anna until she calmed down. After she stopped trying to kick me off her, I let her hands go and got ready to get up. She smacked my face hard.

"Don't ever force yourself on me like that again," she said calmly. "It felt as if you were about to rape me."

I stared at Anna in the partially dark room, and then kneeled down beside the bed. I took her shoes off and lightly rubbed up her legs.

"Do these hands feel anything like hands that's trying to rape you?"

She didn't say a word, until I reached up her skirt and touched her panties.

"Kiley, not now. We have so much we need to talk about first."

"We can talk during sex and afterwards...how about that? Let me just feel your insides for a while."

I reached for her panties again, and this time, she rose up to let me take them off. After I did, I stood up, removed my t-shirt and pants and then pulled her up towards me. I unzipped the zipper on her skirt and pulled her shirt over her head. She unhooked her bra, and after she took it off, she pressed her breasts against my chest. I tightly wrapped my arms around her back and rubbed it. She did the same to mine.

"Damn, you feel so good in my arms," I whispered. "What is it about you that makes me feel this way?"

"Please don't say those things to me. I'm so confused now, Kiley, that I...I—

"Shhh," I said, and then turned her around. I pulled her skirt to the floor and stood up behind her. I reached my hands around the front of her body and massaged her breasts together. When she leaned her head back and tilted it to the side, I took my tongue and lightly licked around her ear. She moaned and I pecked my lips down the side of her neck. Feeling my hard dick pressing against her ass, Anna was anxious for me to fuck her. She cut my foreplay short and placed her hands on the bed so I could fuck her from behind. I was just as anxious as she was, and as soon as I put myself inside of her, I was so ready to come. I slowly backed out and stood still for a moment. After I maintained my composure, I went back in and Anna moved slightly forward.

"Does it hurt," I asked.

"Yes. But, it's okay. Just don't expect me to move much in this position."

Taking some of the pressure off Anna, I raised her right leg and placed it on the bed. I put my leg up as well and balanced myself on one leg as I stood closely behind her. I slowly made my way inside of her again and her pussy got even wetter. It was so wet, that it allowed me to go deeper. In the midst of it all, her juices made an exciting noise that turned me the fuck on. And before I knew it, I released weeks of backed up cum against her walls.

I pulled out and quickly wiped myself off with a towel. Wanting to feel her for a tad bit longer, I lay on the bed and placed her hand on my thang so she could massage it. It took several minutes for me to work myself back up, and after I did, I straddled my muscular thighs across Anna's face. I then buried my face between her warm legs. As we tasted each other, I rolled her body on top of mine and continued to work on her insides. Of course, I got cheated when she rose up on her knees and let out soft moans. She placed her hands between her upper thighs to pull her coochie lips even further apart. I'd already had them as far as I wanted them to go, but since she insisted on helping me, I went in deeper with my tongue. Feeling how excited she was, I took her fingers, along with mine to tickle her insides. My intentions were to loosen her insides up a bit more, but she soon pulled her fingers out and released her juices into my mouth.

By now, we were even. She'd come once and so had I. I rolled Anna over once again, and placed her legs on my shoulders. I leaned forward, and after I inserted myself, I pressed her knees as close as I could to her chest. I started with slow strokes, and when she started to hang, I picked up the pace. She couldn't keep up with my new rhythm, but I stuck with it anyway.

"Why do you fuck me like this, Kiley? Baby, tell me, why?" she whispered.

"Because I enjoy fucking you, that's why," I responded. "Now, you'd better start fucking the shit out of me too, or else...

"Or else what?"

"Or else, I'm gonna find somebody else to fuck me. You don't want me to find somebody else to give it to me, do you?"

"No," she said. "Never."

With that being said, I switched positions and fell backwards. I put Anna on top of me and let her go to work. For the most part, she got down. That was until she got tired from riding me. I had my hands on her hips to hold them down and continued to dip my ass in the bed so I could rise up to the occasion with deep strokes up inside of her.

"Why are you stopping?" I asked, as I could tell she was tired.

"I'm not in physical shape like you are Kiley. I am sorry if I've disappointed you, and I hope that you wouldn't have sex with someone else because—

"Anna, don't take everything I say so seriously. I was only kidding, okay baby. I just wanted you to give me all you got. I got it, so I ain't complaining."

She smiled and started to move on top of me again. After several more minutes into it, we both came together. I squeezed her tightly in my arms and we lay there silently throughout the entire night.

A NEW START

Anna stayed the whole week at my place with me. Since I'd broken the window to her cousin's car, I took it to Al's earlier in the week to get it fixed. I also saw my boy Rufus off to L.A. and I'd promised him again I'd think hard about what we'd discussed. When I gave him the down low about Dominique, he agreed with me that trouble was certainly on the way. I told him I could handle myself, and if I couldn't, he made it clear that all I had to do was say the word.

As for Desmon, I'd been calling to check on him during the week. Sometimes he was cool, but most of the time, his conversation was shitty. Deep down I knew he was angry about not being able to play football, so I didn't press the issue. I did, however, remind him about spending some time with me and he insisted that he would. Both him and Antonio knew Anna had been with me all week and neither of them seem to trip. Anna was worried about Antonio not being receptive of our relationship, but it didn't seem to matter to him one way or the other. The other day while I was talking to Desmon, Antonio took the phone and told me to take care of Anna. He didn't have to worry about her because I intended to do just that.

My feelings for her surprised the fuck out of me. She really wasn't my type of woman but I couldn't figure out what it was about her that I liked so much. Normally, I desired to have a thick sista. One with a juicy round butt and hips to go right along with it. I wasn't too much of a breast man, but it didn't hurt to have a nice set of those to go with it. Anna, however, was none of that. Her ass was nowhere near the Jada's and Ginger's of the world, but she at least had enough breasts that I could enjoy. As for the sex, well, on a scale from one to ten, I'd give her a six or seven. She still had a lot to learn, but I wasn't really tripping. I understood her situation with the rape ordeal and I knew that a big part of her was afraid to let go and give me all that she could. She seemed comfortable with me, but I still sensed a bit of nervousness with her during sex.

On Saturday morning, Anna was still in bed resting from the smack-it-up and lay-it-to-the-side sex I put on her last night. I was doing everything in my powers to enhance our sex life, but every time I'd try something different with her, she'd insist the position was too painful. No doubt, I was packing but I ain't never had a woman who insisted she

124

just couldn't handle me as much as Anna complained. The width, she said, is what hurt her the most, but there was nothing much I could do about that. Besides, after all the fucking we'd been doing this week, I was sure things were starting to look up. But, what did I know? Her body was just different and if I wanted to be with her, then I just had to accept it.

After I got out of the shower, I slid into my black stretch jockey shorts and tied a white and black bandana on my baldhead since I didn't feel like shaving it. I quickly trimmed around my goatee, and rubbed myself with some moisturizing lotion. Since I'd been thinking heavy about Desmon coming to see me, I went into the living room and sat back on the couch. I reached for the phone and called Ginger's house. I hated she answered, and since she did, I asked to speak to Desmon.

"He's outside talking to somebody," she said in a snobby voice. "In the meantime, what happened to you the other night?"

"I got the hell out of there like everybody else did. After that, I went home."

"Yeah, I bet you did. I'm sure some bitch found her way to your bedroom that night."

I ignored Ginger's comment and told her to have Desmon call me.

"Call you for what?" she asked. "You need to stop pressuring him, Kiley. He will spend time with you when he feels like it."

"And, he gone feel like it today. I've waited long enough. Tell him I'll be over there to get him around two."

"I ain't telling him shit. However, I will tell you to ask your bitch to stop coming around here looking for you. I told her that you don't live here anymore, but she came by here again just last night."

"Who in the fuck are you talking about? Don't nobody know—

"The fat bitch...Jada. If she come over here again, I'm gonna let her have it. I've been trying to be nice, but I don't like her ass."

"Did she say what she wanted? I haven't talked to her in a while so I haven't a clue as to what she wants."

"Naw, she didn't say. But, by the looks of her face, I thought you kicked her ass or something."

"Umm...really? Seriously, though, I haven't seen her. I'll give her a holla, but since we're on the subject, have you figured out a way to repay me my money."

Ginger was silent for a moment, and then, she hung up the phone. I was going to deal with her later, since I wanted to find out what was up with Jada. When I dialed her number, her voice mail came on, so I left a message and my number for her to call me.

In deep thought, I leaned my head back on the couch and closed my eyes. I folded my arms in front of me and thought hard about this fucked up life I was living. Always needing something to relax me, I reached for the papers on the table and looked around for my bag of weed. It must have fallen on the floor, so I leaned over to pick it up. As I was in the midst of preparing a nice and healthy joint, I looked up and Anna stood in the doorway with her arms folded. Her hair was in a bouncing ponytail and her face was quite beautiful even without make-up. She was a cross between Jennifer Lopez, without the booty, and Eva Menendez. There was no doubt that I was lucky to have her, so I placed the joint on the table and patted my lap.

"Come join me," I said.

She headed my way with my long white t-shirt on. "Must you smoke weed as much as you do?"

"Must I tell you how much this stuff relaxes me?"

She sat sideways on my lap and wrapped her arms around my neck. Before I could say another word, she pecked my lips.

"As much as you smoke, one would assume you're under a lot of pressure. Tell me what it is that you're so worried about."

"I'm worried about my son, my life, my future…and of course, you."

"Why are you worried about me?"

"I don't know. I…I just am."

"Look, don't worry about me. I'll be cool, okay?"

I pecked Anna on the lips again, and then leaned forward to grab my joint. She looked at me and shook her head.

After I lit it, I took a few hits and she removed it from my hands. She smashed it out in the ashtray and told me to lay on my stomach. No questions asked, I did just that. Anna straddled my butt and massaged her hands deeply into my back. I closed my eyes from the feel of her hands and moaned.

"Um, um, um…that feels so good."

"I knew you'd like this. If I can't please you one way, there's always another."

126

I opened my eyes and turned my head to the side. "What do you mean by not pleasing me? I really wish you'd stop saying that."

"I can't help it," she said, continuing to massage my back and shoulders. "Ever since you said you'd get somebody else to screw you I—

"Can't you take a joke? I said that I was just playing."

"Okay…if you say so."

Anna worked her hands all over my back, neck and shoulders. I was all into it until my phone rang and broke my concentration. When I looked at the caller ID, the call was coming from Ginger's place so I answered.

"Hello," I moaned, as Anna continued to work my back.

"Yo," Desmon said. "Did you call?"

I smiled at the sound of his voice. "Negro, I…I'm always calling. I'm pleased to see that you haven't forgotten my number."

"Yeah, well, don't get too happy. I had to think about it for a minute. Anyway, the old lady said you supposed to come get me around two. I got something to do so I won't be able to make it."

"Something to do like what, Desmon?"

"Like…like something to do."

"I'm sure that whatever it is, it can wait until another day. Besides, I just wanted to hang out with you for a bit."

"Well, ain't that special. But, sorry, it can't be today. Maybe next week, au-ight?"

I was disappointed. "Next week ain't gone work for me. I live for today and not for tomorrow. Did I ever tell you about the day I went to jail?"

"Nope. What about it?"

"It's like this, I…I had a choice. Either I was going to go visit this chick I was seeing, or I was going to go visit my son. I chose some ass first, and then thought I'd have plenty of time to visit with my son later. Ya see, that hour of the day never happened. I was arrested and I didn't get a chance to see my son until almost ten years later. I've been put off long enough, Desmon. Cancel your plans or I'll cancel them for you."

"You know what…sometimes, you get on my damn nerves. I really don't have any plans, but I don't feel like going anywhere. My leg is sore from walking around too much, and I'd like to get some rest if you don't mind."

"You can rest here. I'll see you at two o'clock so be ready."

I hung up and moved my butt muscles to make Anna bounce on me. She laughed and fell forward to hold on. She then placed her head on my back.

"You are so strong, Kiley. I just love your body so much."

"And, what else do you love about me," I said. I turned around and Anna stayed on top of me. She rubbed her hands on my biceps and smiled.

"Along with your body, I lovvvvvve your…you know?"

"No, I don't know."

"Your, that."

"That? What the hell is that?"

"Your thing."

"What thing? I don't have a thing."

She stared down at me and smiled. She then leaned forward and whispered in my ear. "That thing that's poking me between my legs."

"Aw, this," I said, reaching down to grab my dick.

She rose up, "Yeah, that."

"Is that all you like?"

"Oh, there's so much more. But most of all, I love the way Desmon's voice makes you smile. I hope more than anything that someday you'll have that same smile whenever you hear my voice and think about me."

"And, I do. You might not know it but I do," I said, and then sat up.

"Where are you going?" Anna said. "I thought we were going to…you know, mess around."

I smiled and placed my hands on the sides of her face. I brought it to mine and kissed her lips. As our kissing got intense, I reached underneath the oversized t-shirt Anna had on and rubbed her naked body. I massaged her butt cheeks together and reached around to her front and touched the minimal hair she had covering her pussy. Before getting too excited, I lowered her shirt and kissed her forehead.

"I gotta go get my son. We'll finish this up next weekend, okay."

"Do you promise?" she said.

"Yeah, I promise."

"Then, you must know better than anybody that your promises ain't worth a damn, Kiley."

"And, I agree. So, don't hold me to it."

Anna snickered and rose up off me. I hurried to put on some clothes and patiently waited for her to get hers on as well. I could tell she didn't want to leave, but I wanted some time alone with Desmon.

When I pulled in front of Anna's apartment, I leaned over to give her a kiss. She hesitated, and afterwards, she clinched her hands together in front of her and looked at me.

"Don't make me wait too long to see you again. I don't know how much longer I can do this, Kiley."

I took a deep breath. "I pro...I mean, I'll make ever effort to get back here soon. The reason I wanted you to stay the week with me was so you could see that there's nobody else in my life. I barely have time for you, so how can I make time for somebody else. You gotta believe me when I say that my distance is not about being with someone else. I just need time to figure out a few things, au-ight?"

"I guess. I...I just be so lonely when you're not around. Again, don't make me wait too long, okay?"

"Hopefully, I'll see you next weekend. Until then, stay sweet."

I leaned in for a kiss, and afterwards, Anna got out and walked to the door. Before going inside, she kissed her hand and held it out towards me. I nodded and gave her a wink.

By the time I got to Ginger's place, Antonio and Desmon were standing outside talking. I saw Desmon's eyes roll, but I seriously didn't give a fuck. He had on a blue jean outfit and was held up with one crutch underneath his arm. I got out of the car and headed his way.

"What's going on, Pimpster?" he said. "Did Moms tell you that one of yo lil honeys stopped by the crib looking for you?"

"Fool, I ain't no pimp. You the pimp. I'll leave that profession up to you."

"What's up, Kiley?" Antonio said, reaching out to give me a slamming handshake.

"Nothing much, bro. How you living?"

"I'm hoping large like you. Dez told me you the man to see if I needed a lil cash."

I looked at Desmon, and then, back at Antonio. "You can't believe everything Desmon tell you, Antonio. And you fools ain't about to swindle me out of my money. Now, after I go inside and holla at Ginger for a sec, I'll be ready to go. If you don't mind Antonio, I'd like to spend some time alone with Desmon."

"Hey, that's cool," he said. "If you would just drop me off at my gal crib on the way I'll be cool."

I nodded and opened the door to go inside. As usual, the place was a mess. Ginger had clothes all over the fucking place and plates with leftover food on them were still on the table. I walked back to her bedroom, and since the door was halfway closed I knocked just in case I interrupted something.

"Come in," she said, while lying across the bed on her back. She had a towel wrapped around her naked body and gazed up at the ceiling as if she was in deep thought.

"Why did you hang up on me when I asked about my money?"

Not saying one word, she got up and walked over to her dresser drawer. She pulled out some money and tossed it on the bed.

"That's two grand right there. The rest I'll get to you as soon as I can. I hope once you get all of your money that you'll get off my damn back."

"And, I hope you realize that you can't steal money from me and expect to get away with it. You need to get yourself some help if you're at the point where you gotta steal from motherfuckers to support your habit. I've said it before and I'll say it again, the only thing that's preventing me from hurting you is the fact that you're Desmon's mother."

"And the only thing that's saved you is you're Desmon's father. If you wasn't, I would have had your ass back in jail a long time ago."

"Damn! Are you positive I'm Desmon's father? I came up on some information a few weeks ago about a man by the name of Myles. You wouldn't know who that is, would you?"

Ginger looked shocked and tooted her lips. "Yeah, I know who Myles is. And, he wasn't Desmon's father. I know that for a fact."

"Yeah, that's what they all say. In the meantime, you'd better hope and pray your facts are straight this time. If not, somebody…anybody have mercy on your soul."

"Look, nigga, I'm tired of your threats. Why don't you take your damn money and leave? I know who the father of my child is and if you can't see how much you and Desmon resemble each other then bastard have mercy on your soul."

"Looks can be deceiving, after all, I somehow managed to hook up with you, didn't I?"

Ginger didn't say a word and I reached for the money on her bed. I loudly counted it out and placed it in my back pocket.

"You got a long way to go. Whatever the hell you doing to get this money, please keep on doing it and hurry it the fuck up. I got some things I need to do and your procrastination is costing me time."

Ginger leaned against her dresser and gave me a cold and hard look. "I can't remember the last time I hated anybody this much. You gone get yours, Kiley. And whenever you do, I pray to God my son is nowhere around."

I wanted to stay there and cuss her ass out even more, but I could hear the radio from my car blasting out loudly. When I walked to the door and opened it, Desmon and Antonio were inside of my car checking out my sound system. I went up to the car and got in. I quickly turned the music down and looked at both of them.

"Don't touch my shit, au-ight?" I said. Ignoring what I said, Desmon reached for the volume to turn it back up. I quickly smacked his hand. "Did you just hear what I said?"

"See, that's what I'm talking about. This visiting bullshit with you ain't gone work out. What about compromising? You said that you'd compromise with me, remember?"

"Okay, then lets." I looked in my CD collection and found a soothing jazz song by Wallace Roney. I slid it in and blasted it out loudly.

"Who the hell is that?" Desmon yelled.

"It's my compromise. My music and your volume."

Desmon looked at Antonio in the back seat and they both shook their heads. By the time we reached the end of the street, they simply couldn't take it. They made up their own rap lyrics to drown out the sound in the car. It sounded pretty smooth, so I lowered the music to listen. I bobbed my head to the beat and gave them props when they finished.

"Ay, that was pretty smooth. I didn't know you two gangsters could rap."

"Slo Motion and me been rapping since we were kids. As you can see, we haven't been too successful, but who knows?" Desmon said.

"Slo Motion?" I said. "I know Antonio ain't Slo Motion."

"That would be me," he said, sucking in his bottom lip and slowly grinding on the back seat. "The ladies call me Slo Motion cause I like to do it Slo."

Him and Desmon cracked up and gave each other five. I couldn't help but smile, as the thought of Quincy, Kareem and me flashed before me.

"Hey, Mr. Abrams," Antonio said. "Would you mind stopping at the corner store so I can get some chips or something for my girl? When I called and ask what she wanted, she told me to bring her some chips."

I looked in the rearview mirror at Antonio and could tell he was lying. I wasn't quite sure what he wanted at *Jake's*, but I stopped for him anyway. When we got there, he scooted close to the front seat and tapped my shoulder.

"Say, Mr. Abrams—

"It's Kiley, man. You brothas sholl know how to respect somebody when y'all want something. So, what is it?"

"Okay, Kiley, then. But, I ain't got a dime. Can I borrow ten dollars? I'll give it back to you the next time I see you."

Desmon looked out of the window and whistled. I hesitated, and then reached in my pocket for five dollars. "Y'all need some jobs. Don't ask me for shit else, au-ight?"

Antonio took the five dollars. "But, I asked for ten—

"Well, five dollars better get whatever it is that you need. If not, then you'd better find another way to get it."

Antonio and Desmon got out of the car. They giggled and really thought they were getting over on me. I had my reasons for doing things the way I did, and hopefully, they'd soon realize it.

As I sat in the car waiting for them to come out of *Jake's*, my phone vibrated. I looked to see who the caller was and it was Jada. I answered to see why she was so anxious to see me all of a sudden.

"Yeah," I said, holding the phone close to my ear.

"Hi," she said, softly.

"Hey. What's up?"

"You."

"Naw, couldn't be me. I believe you're the one with something on your mind."

"Yeah, sort of."

"Wha...what's up," I said, getting irritated.

"I'm getting a divorce."

"And?"

"And, I wanted to know if we could meet somewhere and talk."

"Today?"

"Yes."

"I can't make it today."

"Please, Kiley. I...I'm going through something right now and I really need somebody to talk to."

"Jada, I'm with my son right now. I just picked him up and we're gonna spend some time together. How about I give you a call...tomorrow or Monday."

"I need you now, Kiley. My husband beat me up because he found out about my involvement with you."

"With me? You know damn well what happened between you and me only occurred one time since you've been married. I hope you haven't told him it was more to it than just that."

"I told him the truth. And, the truth is I don't love him, I love you. You can't deny—"

"Jada, look. What we had is over, baby. Now, I don't know what it is you want from me. You got married and you moved on. I'm sorry things didn't work out, but you can't come running back to me because your marriage failed."

"Just call me in a day or two. Please."

"We'll see," I said, and then hung up. Desmon and Antonio were heading back to the car just as I ended the call. They hopped in the ride and said they were ready to go. Antonio had a small plastic bag in his hand, and when I asked what was in it, he pulled out three candy bars and a card.

"I didn't have enough to get what I came for so I had to improvise," he said.

"I thought you wanted some chips," I said while driving off.

"Naw, I really needed some condoms but I didn't have enough to get them. So, the card is to apologize to my girl for not being able to give her some because of my lack of condoms. The chocolate is to make her feel better when I have to let her down."

"Fool, then you should have said so. I'll give you some money to get some condoms," I said, already turning the car back around.

"No problem, Kiley. I already got'em." He laughed, and then reached in his pocket and pulled out a box of condoms. Out with the condoms came some KY Jelly and a stick of gum.

"You gangstas in there stealing? What you got in your pockets?" I asked Desmon, as I could already see how fat they were.

"Let's see," he said, pulling some shit out of his pockets too. "I got some chap stick, some batteries for one of my games, and some condoms too." He reached in his other pocket. "In door number two, I got some shoe laces for my shoes and some Tylenol for the pain in my leg."

I stared at Desmon in disbelief. Maybe Antonio didn't have money to pay for his shit, but I knew Desmon had some money. He got a kick out of the shit and him and Antonio took pride in what they'd done. I pulled the car over to the curb and reached for the items he'd pulled out of his pocket.

"What you doing?" he laughed, and didn't know how furious I was. "Go get you own condoms."

"Give me this shit, man!" I yelled. "What the fuck is wrong with you! I gave your punk ass some money and you around here stealing shit like a thief in the night."

"Man, what you tripping off of? They ain't gone miss those few lil items I took. Besides, they shit overpriced just so they can make up for thievesses such as myself."

"Well, Mr. Thievesses, or whatever the hell you call yourself, you gone take your ass back in that store to apologize. Then, you gone break out the money I gave you and pay for the shit. If the manager decides to arrest your ass for being so stupid, then that's gonna be your problem and not mine."

"Shit, motherfucker you crazy. I ain't going back in there to get arrested."

"What the hell did you just call me?"

"I ain't call you nothing. I just said that I wasn't going back in there."

"Yeah you did. I know you didn't call me no motherfucker, did you? He didn't call me no motherfucker, did he Antonio?"

"I, ah, wha...I didn't hear what he said. I don't think he did, though, Kiley."

"Stand by your man, huh? You got yourself a good ass friend back there, but since I heard you call me a motherfucker, I'm gonna make it real hard for you now."

I drove back to *Jakes's* and before I could get out of the car, Desmon opened his door. He couldn't go too far, so I watched as he hopped out and tried to get away while limping. Antonio stayed in the car and watched. I grabbed Desmon by the back of his neck and opened the back door for Antonio to get out.

"Come on, Mr. Abrams. Don't make me go back in there. If I get arrested, Anna gone be mad at me."

"You should have thought about that before you and Mr. Thievesses here went on a crime spree."

I marched back into *Jake's* and demanded to speak to a manager. When he came out Desmon had his mouth poked out and I could feel Antonio's body trembling as I held him tightly by his arm.

"May I help you?" the tall slender brotha asked.

"Do you all have security in this place?" I asked.

"Yes, sir, we do."

"Then, he or she needs to be fired. My son and his friend came in here and took these items from your store." I placed the items on the counter. "Now, I don't know what kind of system you got going on in here, but it's evident your metal detectors don't work. You're losing a whole lot of money if they don't, and I'm sure the kids around here are having a field day. What I'm really trying to say is," I stepped away from Desmon and Antonio who were no doubt upset with me. "What I'm trying to say is, I don't want these two boys arrested for stealing. I want this to be a lesson learned so go get your security guard and pretend that the police is on the way."

"But, sir, if they've stolen some merchandise from our store, I intend to call the police."

"See, that's not gonna work. Since your store has non-working metal detectors, and I'm sure they haven't been working for quite some time, I might just have to report that. You wouldn't want to make yourself look bad being upper management, would you? Besides, I intend…we intend to pay for everything that was taken."

He shook his head. "Good. Stay right there and I'll go get Smokey."

"You do that," I said, and then walked back over to Antonio and Desmon.

"Antonio, I'm gone call Anna to she if she'll come bail you out tonight. Desmon you know damn well Ginger ain't coming no where and I'm not gone waste my money on something as petty as getting you out of jail. It's time that you two learned a valuable lesson."

Desmon turned towards the exit doors and so did Antonio.

"If you two are stupid enough to leave, that's robbery. Your misdemeanor case turns into a felony, and from what I heard, judges are giving out five years right off the back for robberies."

Just then, the manager and the security guard Smokey came up front. The store was crowded and many people stared at us to find out what was going on. If anything, I could tell Antonio and Desmon were beyond embarrassed.

"You two brothas wanna come with me," Smokey said in a deep voice. If his voice wasn't enough to intimidate them, then his thick neck and incredible hulk build was.

Desmon looked at me.

"Man, I'm outtie," I said. "I'll see what's up with you in a few days. You gone learn just like I had to."

"Damn! I'll pay for the stuff. Why y'all tripping?" Desmon said. He reached in his back pocket and pulled out his wallet. I could see how full it was with money and shook my head. "Here." He handed some money over to the manager.

"That's not good enough," the manager said. "He has a serious attitude and he hasn't even apologized. Actually, neither of them has."

People continued to look at what was going on, and even though Desmon and Antonio didn't want to, they both apologized to the manager.

"I didn't hear you," the manager said. "What did you say?"

"Sorry," they both said in synch.

"Good. And please don't come back in here again. If you do, you'll both be arrested."

Antonio and Desmon both looked relieved. The manager handed the paid for items over to me and we all left the store together. Neither of them said one word to me until I reached Antonio's girlfriend's house. He thanked me for dropping him off, and before he got out of the car, I tossed the box of condoms to him.

"Here. You might need those," I said.

"Thanks. And, can I have my KY Jelly too?"

"What in the hell do you know about some KY Jelly?"

"Before having sex I like to be rubbed with it. I also like to wet my condom—

"Hey, whatever," I said, giving it to him. "Y'all know y'all just fuck me up. Things have changed and I—never mind. Just make sure you call Anna to let her know you're okay."

"Always," he said. He gave Desmon and slamming handshake and jetted.

Desmon remained quiet all the way to my place. I wasn't going to kiss his ass to talk to me, and even though I didn't say it, he knew it. When we got inside, I pulled my shirt off and tossed it on the couch. I walked over to my booming ass system and turned it up loudly. I then sat on the couch and tried to make use of the joint Anna had smashed out earlier. Seeing that Desmon was still standing by the doorway, I looked over at him.

"Make yourself at home. I got plenty of food in the fridge and if you'd like to lay down, go check out the room I fixed up for you."

He didn't say anything, but I could already tell how impressed he was by the way I had shit fixed up. My place was nothing like Ginger's shack and was decorated with contemporary furniture.

I took a few hits from my joint and watched as Desmon slowly made his way throughout the house to check it out. I watched as he went from one room to the next, but when I didn't see him come out of his room, I got up to see what he was doing.

I stood in the doorway and looked at him as he sat on his king-sized bed and gazed at the ten-foot wide fish tank I had built into the wall. His furniture was black lacquer and was trimmed with silver. The bed was made like a wall unit with glass that nearly covered one entire wall. To make the room even more luxurious, it had a plasma TV on the wall, a silver and glass radio system, a flat screen computer and football trophy's I had made for every year of his life that I'd missed were on a shelf I had designed for his accomplishments.

He continued to stare at the fish tank, and seemed unable to get any words to come out of his mouth.

"So, do you like it," I asked.

He turned and looked at me. "It's cool, but I wish you'd stop doing stuff like this for me. It's like you trying to buy me, man, and I can't be bought."

I walked into the room and sat on the bed next to him. "I don't know what else to do, Desmon. I know you can't be bought, but I'm willing to do whatever I got to do to have my son in my life. Don't tell me it's too late because I don't believe that for one minute. I'm not trying to change who you are, but I want you closer to me. Is there something wrong with that?"

"Nope. But all this stuff makes me feel unworthy. You...you know I don't deserve all these things. After I looked in that closet I had to take a chill pill. Man, why you buy me all that stuff?"

"I'on know. I just felt like doing it. I think about you all the time so why not?"

"Because, Kiley!" he said angrily. "I don't understand all this love you say you got for me. Why can't I feel that kind of love for you...for Moms? Honestly, I care but it's not like what I feel for my best friend Antonio. I know you're trying, but I just can't reach out like that, man."

My eyes watered, as his words hurt so badly. He was the only person who had that type of effect on me, but I turned away so he wouldn't see my hurt. I took a hard swallow and responded to him as best as I could. "Time, Desmon. Just allow us time together. I have to grow on you like you've grown on me. And even though we've been apart for many years, I never forgot about you. You were too young to remember everything about me, but I held on to everything that I remembered about you. Ginger even sent pictures of you as you grew up, but you didn't see my face again until several months ago. Again, if you just allow us time together, you'll see what kind of father and son relationship we can have."

"So, what you want me to do? Move in with you?"

"Only if you want to. But before you decide to, I want you to know that I have rules. Rules that you're gonna have to follow."

"Name 'em."

"For starters, you must go to school."

"No problem."

"No more disrespecting me...calling me names like motherfucker this or that. And, all of the cussing needs to stop too."

"Bet."

"No carrying a gun anymore. I want you to give it to me so I can put it in a safe place."

"No problem cause I already got rid of it. One of my boys needed it and I sold it to him."

"Stupid move, but you'd better not be lying."

"I'm not. Do you wanna call him?"

"No, but I'll find out. And, finally, no smoking weed or fucking in my crib."

"Now, we got a problem. Why is it that you can smoke weed and I can't? And, why can you have sex in the crib and I can't?"

"Because I'm grown and this is my house, that's why."

"But, you're the one who said we'd compromise."

"I lied. Parents don't compromise with kids. They tell you how it's gone be and that's how it's gone be."

"They don't lie to kids either. So, instead of compromising can we work out a deal?"

I laughed. "What's the deal?"

"I'll cut back on the weed if you allow me to bring females to the crib."

"I never said that you couldn't bring females to the crib. All I said is you can't screw them here."

"Well, where else am I supposed to do it? Before you answer that would you do me a favor?"

"What?"

"Just close your eyes."

"What!" I yelled.

"Just close your eyes," he insisted. I closed my eyes. "Okay, now think back to when you were my age. Think about smoking blunts with your pops and later creeping off into the bedroom to bust that cherry. You can feel the explosion as you're in deep thought."

I opened my eyes. "Sorry, that didn't happen."

"Quit lying. You told me—

"Okay, maybe I did. But, I want things to be different with you Desmon. I don't want you to be like me."

"And, I don't want to be like you either, but help a brotha out. Setting this issue in stone now will cut back on much confusion in the future. Besides, I'm gonna do it anyway. Whether it's here or somewhere else, I'm gonna have my smoke and my girlees." He placed his hand on his chest like Kareem used to do. "You want honesty, so I'm just being honest."

I stood up. "One or the other Desmon. Decide now and be done with it."

"Cool. I choose sex. I cut back on the weed anyway since my coach said it'll mess me up if I wanted to continue to play football. And since I cut back, you need to cut back too."

"Never," I said, reaching my hand out for his. I pulled him off the bed and gave him a tight hug. "Let's make this work this time around, au-ight?"

He moved back. "Yeah, but I got a feeling that Moms ain't gone like this one bit. I don't know if I should call or send her a post card."

We both laughed and I told Desmon we'd break the news to her together. Realistically, I felt as if she really wouldn't give a fuck either way.

TURNING BACK THE HANDS OF TIME

Ginger didn't start looking for Desmon until late Wednesday evening. I'd been taking him back and forth to school and since I hooked him up with many nice outfits, he didn't have to go home to change. When she called, I told her he was with me. She was furious, but there wasn't a damn thing she could do about it. I gave Desmon the phone and he told her that he was staying with me until school let out. He promised her he'd stop by and visit, but for her, she claimed it wasn't good enough. She'd even started to cry like she really was going to miss him and when she made him feel guilty, that's when I took the phone. I even promised her myself I'd make him stop by, but she knew better than anybody that a promise from Kiley Jacoby Abrams wasn't worth a damn. Either way, she agreed that maybe we needed to spend time together and she claimed Desmon being with me would surely give her a break.

Through my eyes, though, she had too many breaks. Desmon was seriously messed up. Being with me for these several days allowed me to see so much more about him. He was lazy, didn't want to clean up, didn't want to go to school, and had mega issues with sharing. When he'd cook something, he'd only cook for himself. He never offered to cook for me or to go the extra mile for me like I'd gone for him. I wasn't going to trip because I knew it was hard to change a kid who'd been so accustomed to doing shit his way.

On Thursday, I dropped Desmon off at school and headed to *IHOP* to meet Jada for breakfast. She'd been bugging the hell out of me since I hadn't made arrangements to meet up with her. So, we made plans. The thought of getting in touch with Marissa was heavy on my mind, but I hadn't decided if I wanted to know the truth about Desmon yet. Something inside told me to leave well enough alone, but then, there was something that wanted to know if he was really my son or not. I'd been staring deeply at him every time I got a chance. He'd even noticed my stares and questioned me about them. Basically, I told him I was happy he was with me and I left it at that. To me, there really wasn't no denying him. He looked like me, acted like me, and it was hard not to recognize an Abrams man when you saw one. If I had to place a million dollar bet, Desmon, no doubtfully, was made by me. Maybe, though, Marissa knew something I didn't know, but I wasn't going to rush into possibly making my life more chaotic than it already was.

When I pulled into a parking spot, I could see Jada standing inside of the door at *IHOP* waiting for me. She smiled as I headed towards the door and hurried to open it.

"You're late," she said, holding her arms out for a hug.

"Have you ever known me to be on time?"

"I guess not."

I held her with a tight embrace and kissed her forehead as I let go. Soon after, the waiter walked us to a booth so we could take a seat. As soon as we did, Jada looked over at me and smiled.

"If you don't mind me saying…you look good. I mean damn good," she said.

"Thanks. And, you look good too. With the exception of the black eye you're sporting."

"I can't help the eye. I'm just glad to be getting a divorce from that crazy ass nigga."

"You didn't know he was crazy before you married him?"

"A little. This ain't the first time he's put his hands on me. He did that shit two weeks after I met him. He told me he'd never do it again, and for the most part, he hadn't."

"So, he did it this time because he found out about you and me, huh?"

"Actually, he didn't find out, I told him. I got angry with him and told him what went down between you and me."

"Jada, that was so damn stupid. You can't tell no man no shit like that. You should've remembered from our previous relationship that a man will kill over his pussy. Now, you got me all tied up in the bullshit."

The waiter came over and interrupted us. After Jada gave her order, I ordered a stack of pancakes and some cheese eggs. The waiter placed our drinks on the table and walked away. I took a sip from the glass of water and placed it on the table.

I cleared my throat. "Again, I'm not sure what you want from me. I feel for you baby, but you know it's not in my best interest to intervene."

Jada reached her hand across the table and placed it on mine. "How can you just let go of what we shared? We were together for years

Kiley, and you always had my back, as I had yours. Even while you were in jail, I still came to see about you. You just can't give up on me—on us that easily, can you?"

"This ain't about giving up. I'm always gone be your friend, but I really don't see much else going on between us, baby."

Jada's phone rang and when she looked at it, she excused herself from the table. She walked off towards the bathroom and spoke softly to someone on the other end. No doubt, baby-girl still looked good to me. Ass and thighs were thick, breasts were meaty, and her round full face was still pretty enough to bring back good memories of our relationship. Sadly, though, it wasn't enough to make me want to take her in my arms and embrace her again, especially after all the wrong she'd done.

Jada ended her call and walked back over to the table. She told me the phone call was from her cousin who informed Jada that her husband was looking for her.

"Why is he looking for you? I thought the two of you were separated?"

"We are. I stopped by his place last night and got the rest of my things. He told my cousin I took his damn watch."

"Did you?"

"I took what was due to me. That nigga didn't give me one damn dime when I left. He lucky that his watch is all I took."

At first, I didn't say a word. What she'd said took me back to the time when I kicked her ass out and she took shit from my place as well. It amazed me that after all these years, some things just never change. History had a way of repeating itself, I guess for her and me as well.

Soon after conversing for a while, the waiter finally brought our food. Since I was hungry, I dived right into it and listened to Jada tell me how badly she wanted our relationship back. I continued to tell her how I thought it wasn't a good idea for us to see each other again, but she always insisted on having her way.

"I'm not giving up on us, Kiley. There's got to be something inside of you left for me."

I smiled, as the thought of fucking her had crossed my mind. I knew it would lead to something I couldn't handle, so it was certainly just a thought.

By the time we finished, it was almost eleven o'clock. I paid for breakfast and walked Jada out to her car.

"Take care of yourself," I said. "And the best thing you can do for me, and for yourself, is to stay the hell away from that fool. I'll be angry with you if you go back to him and something happens to you."

She touched my goatee with the tip of her finger and softly spoke. "I'm never going back to him, especially since I know how you feel about me now."

I removed her hand from my face. "Look, I told you—

"Yeah, you told me a lot. But what you said don't jive with how you've been staring at me. I know that look, Kiley. I know you want to taste me like you used to and I can see the desire still burning in your eyes."

I snickered. "What you see is a man who hasn't seen his ex in a while. Of course I'm gone look, and of course, I thought about hitting that but—

"Then hit it. Make arrangements with me to hit it—soon."

"Naw, that's—

Before I put down my rejection, a car skidded on the parking lot right next to us. A tall and medium built brotha hopped out of a Lexus SUV with a brown short leather jacket on. He quickly slammed the door, and by Jada's reaction, I could tell he was her husband.

"Dwayne, I don't want no shit—

He walked up to Jada and pointed in her face. "Bitch, shut the fuck up! Don't open your big mouth unless I tell you to!"

"Nigga, you better get your hand out of my face," Jada yelled back in her defense. "You know damn well you ain't gone talk to me like that!"

Knowing that the shit was gonna get deep, I slightly backed up. Before I could take two steps backwards, Dwayne turned to me.

"You want my bitch, nigga?"

"Naw, man, I don't want your bitch. I thought her name was Jada, though. In the meantime, I'm Kiley. You don't have to refer to me as a nigga, so for future references my name is Kiley."

He smiled and looked back at Jada. "You couldn't wait to call this motherfucker, could you?"

"Don't worry about who the fuck—

As Jada spoke, he took his hand and slammed it hard across her face. Stunned by the blow, she held her cheek and dropped her head. Before I could do anything, he quickly turned around and lit my ass up

144

with a blow to the face with his fist. I must admit, the son of a bitch had some power that caused my face to turn as well. He reached up to hit me again and that's when I grabbed his fist with my hand. I tried to break it, and after twisting it far back, I heard it crack.

Jada moved away from the car because she knew what was about to go down. Dwayne screamed out loudly from the pain of his wrist, and feeling as if my job wasn't complete, I twisted his arm behind his back and slammed his face against the trunk of the car.

I leaned my body against his and spoke calmly to him. "See, I was gonna let you and your woman handle y'alls business until you put your fucking hands on me. Now, not only am I going to break your damn arm for punching me, but also, I'm gone take your wife somewhere and fuck the shit out of her for you. While you're in the hospital getting all taken care of, you be sure to remember my name, motherfucker, and remember the pain."

I pulled his arm back and I'll be damn if it didn't crack. Dwayne screamed out loudly again, and as I backed up, he fell to the ground on one knee.

"You...you dead," he stuttered, as he couldn't get the words to come out of his mouth.

I leaned down to him. "I...I...I'm what? I'm dead? Naw, I ain't dead, nigga." I pulled my gun out from the back of my pants and aimed it at him. "You are."

"No, Kiley!" Jada screamed. She ran up and grabbed my hand. "Baby, no!"

I heard the police sirens coming and saw all of the people from the inside of *IHOP* looking out of the window. "Go get in my car," I yelled at Jada. She ran to my car and I placed the gun down inside my pants. I leaned down and spoke to Dwayne again.

"Today was your lucky day. If you ever put your fucking hands on her again, it'll be the last time you breathe."

He didn't respond so I took my fist and slammed it against his face. His head hit the back of the trunk and the blow sent him plunging to the ground. I gave him one swift kick in the ribs and hurried to my car, as the sirens got closer. After getting inside, I sped off the parking lot and hit the nearest highway.

Jada sat on the passenger's side in a panic. I was beyond livid and didn't say shit to her. I knew some good Samaritan had gotten my license plates number and it was just a matter of time that they'd be looking for me. The car was registered in Al's name, so before I did anything, I called to give him a heads up. After I ended my call with him, Jada turned to look at me.

"I'm sorry for getting you involved," she sobbed. She wiped the tears from her eyes. "I didn't think he —

"Well, you thought wrong!" I yelled. "I got enough shit to worry about and now this!"

"What are you so worried about? Dwayne's not gonna tell—

"Fuck a Dwayne! Fuck you and fuck your damn man, Jada! I wish you'd just leave my black ass alone!"

"And I wish you'd stop driving this car like a bat out of hell. If you want to get arrested, just keep on driving like you're driving. I apologize for what happened, but I didn't tell you to go break his damn arm."

I looked at Jada and wanted to punch her in her damn face for being so stupid. Instead I kept quiet until I pulled over at a gas station to get some gas. As I pumped, I watched Jada as she looked in the mirror at her face. It had bruised up even more and she dabbed some makeup over the bruise to cover it up. When I got back into the car, I slammed the door and looked over at her.

"Where do you live?" I asked.

"Why?"

"So I can take your ass home."

"I don't want to go home. I want to stay with you."

"Well, you can't stay with me damn it!" I drove off.

"Then, take me somewhere and fuck me like you told my—

I shook my head. "I can't believe you, Jada. After what just went down back there, that's all you can think about is getting a dick inside of you?"

"*Hampton Inn* is right down the street. I promise I'll make it up to you if you stop."

I drove down the street and when I saw *Hampton Inn* I passed it up. Jada placed her hand on the steering wheel and I slammed on the brakes.

"Would you stop playing?" she said. "Let's just go inside and chill, alright?"

"I'm not playing, Jada! My damn pressure is up because of your bullshit!"

"I said I'm sorry. Now, back up and lets go inside."

I hesitated and then backed up the car. When I pulled into a parking spot, Jada had a look of satisfaction written all over her face.

"I'll pay—

"Don't say shit to me," I yelled. "I don't want to hear your mouth!"

We opened the car doors and got out. After the clerk gave us a key to a room, we walked to it without saying one word. As soon as we made it inside, Jada put her purse on the dresser and I walked up behind her. I turned her around and grabbed for the button on her tight jeans.

"Damn!" she said. "Can't we—

"Didn't I tell you not to say anything to me!" I yelled, as I continued to remove her pants. She stepped out of them and pulled her shirt over her head, as I eased her black silk panties down to the floor. She stood naked, and before I took off my clothes, I back her up against the wall and held her breasts in my hand. I placed her healthy left breast in my mouth and squeezed it as if I was a baby looking for some milk.

Feeling my touch, as I'd lowered my hand to fondle her insides, Jada reached for my belt and removed it from around my waist. She unbuttoned my pants and reached her hands down inside to massage my ass. When my pants dropped to my ankles, I stepped out of them and pressed my body against hers up against the wall. I dug deeper with my fingers and lifted one of her legs to hold it in my arm.

"Suck me, Kiley," she moaned, while closing her eyes and rubbing my baldhead. "I want you to fuck me and suck me good, baby."

I didn't say a word. She opened her eyes and stared at me. "You are so fucking fine when you're angry like this. Hurry up and put your dick inside of me."

I lowered Jada's leg and stepped backwards to remove my jockey shorts. As my long and fat hardened dick plopped out, Jada looked at it and smiled. She placed her hands on it and pulled it to her. She placed it between her legs, and teasing her just a bit, I rubbed it against her soaking wet walls. I felt her moistness, and the feel of her pussy lips curved to my dick and stiffened me even more.

Able to handle her weight, I picked her up and held her legs in my arms while her back was against the wall. She reached down and directed my thang inside of her. As it found its way, I kept my rhythm at a mediocre pace until we got more in to it. Soon, I sped up and listened as our bodies smacked hard against each other. Jada held tightly around my neck and squeezed her eyes together, as the feeling was as good to her as it was to me.

"That's right, baby," she screamed, as I pounded her harder. "Fuck your pussy how your want to. This pussy is yours and will forever be yours."

I hated that her words excited the hell out of me. They excited me so much that damn near every muscle in my body worked hard and caused sweat to drip from both of our bodies. Getting tired, I lowered her legs and got down on my knees. Jada pulled up a chair beside her, and placed her foot in it to keep her balance. After she did, I dived right into it. I sucked her juices when she came and I backed against the dresser behind me so she could return the favor. She got on her knees and worked me with her hands first. And as she took me deeply into her mouth, I closed my eyes and took long deep breaths. Working me like a porn star, Jada had my dick slippery wet and she moaned about how good it tasted. I'd damn near lost my balance, as I made my way to the back of her throat. Before I came, I wanted to pull out. Jada wouldn't let me, though. Since she didn't, I exploded and watched as my juices came dripping from her mouth.

"Damn," I yelled, and unable to hold back my emotions. "You are so good at that shit!"

Nowhere near finished with her, I helped Jada up from the floor and placed her hands on the dresser. Her ass is what I admired the most, so I stood behind her and smacked my dick against her butt to give myself a rise. As my thang grew, I couldn't wait to put it inside of her. I separated her butt cheeks and maneuvered my way in. The feel of her insides were so moist and warm that I couldn't even move.

"Ju...just stay in this position for a minute and don't move," I said, taking slow strokes inside of her. Of course, she didn't listen and started bouncing her ass against me. I squeezed her hips tightly and concentrated on my insertions.

No doubt, Jada and me were throwing down. She continued to talk her dirty shit, and soon, I joined in with her. I couldn't help myself, but it had been a long time since I'd gotten my fuck on with anybody like this. I loved being with Anna more than anything, but I wanted to sweat, I wanted to fuck how I wanted to fuck, and more than anything, I needed some pussy that could work me like I wanted it to. Jada's was doing just that, and for the moment, I desired to be nowhere else but right here with her.

Time flew by. I had to pick Desmon up from school around three so I hurried to wrap shit up with Jada. I'd already come three times within the hours and she was on come number five. Her legs were high on my shoulders and as I gave it everything I had, her body started to tremble.

"You have been too damn good to me," she said, while gritting her teeth. "Don't you want to fuck like this for the rest of your life!"

I didn't answer but it sure as hell didn't sound like a bad idea. Jada came, and afterwards, I dropped her legs on the bed. I took deep breaths and so did she. We were drained, but the evidence of two satisfied individuals was written on both of our faces.

I wiped the sweat from my forehead and removed myself from between her legs. I helped her off the bed and wrapped my arms around her.

"Do you think we have time for a shower?" she asked.

I looked at my watch. It was two o'clock. "I don't think so. I gotta go get Desmon from school."

"Then, when are you going to take me home?"

"Now. Put your clothes on so we can go."

"I at least need to go wash up. Give me a few minutes, okay."

Jada and me quickly washed up, and before I knew it, it was already two-thirty. I rushed her because she seemed to be taking her time. I was about to pull off and leave her, but she quickly jumped into the car.

"Damn! I can't move no faster," she griped.

I gave her a funny look and disagreed after what she'd just put on me.

"Okay, so maybe I can. I know what you're thinking, Kiley."

"You're not my mind reader, au-ight? I know what I'm thinking too, and you don't have a clue."

"Yes I do. You're feeling guilty. You hate that you gave in to me, but you need to understand you and I have a lifetime bond. One that will never be broken no matter what."

"No, sorry, that's not what I'm thinking."

149

"Then, what are you thinking?"

"Do you really want to know?"

"Yes, I really want to know."

I hesitated. "Na, you really don't want to know. It might hurt your feelings."

"It won't be the first time you've hurt my feelings and I'm sure it won't be the last. However, if you want to sit there and deny that you didn't just enjoy what went down between us, then I don't want to hear it. You're a damn liar if—

"Aw, I thoroughly enjoyed myself. No doubt, baby-girl, that coochie you working with is off the chain. I know better than your husband how it can make a nigga clown. Remember, I've been there before."

"Then what's your gripe about?"

"Who said I had a gripe? You just asked what I was thinking about and I said that I didn't want to tell you."

She folded her arms. "What's on your mind, Kiley? I can all ready tell whatever it is, it ain't good."

"Aw, it's good. Maybe too good."

Jada pushed my shoulder as I drove. "Let it out. Tell me what's on your mind."

I sped up to make it to Desmon's school since I was already five minutes late. "If you must know, I'm thinking about this young lady I've been seeing."

"Please. After I just gave you what I did, you have the audacity to be thinking about another bitch?"

"She ain't no bitch, na. But if you really want to know, I was thinking about her the whole time I was fucking you."

"Kiley, don't play with me."

"I'm not playing. I...I was thinking about how I wish she had the capabilities of fucking and sucking me like you do, but I guess I can't have it all, huh?"

"So, you messing with an inexperienced ho that can't even satisfy your manly needs."

"No, she's far from being a ho. Actually, she's a beautiful woman that don't deserve to have a man like me in her life. As we did our thang, that became more and more clearer to me. It was kind of like a wake up call, you know?"

"No, I don't know. However, I do know that if she can't keep up then she's bound to be replaced. Her replacement is sitting right next to you and I ain't going nowhere anytime soon."

I ignored Jada's comment, and soon, made it to Desmon's school. He stood by the steps and talked to this chick who sat on the steps next to him. When he saw my car, both of them headed my way.

Jada stared at him. "He is so cute, Kiley. Damn! I can't believe how much he looks like Kareem. That shit is scary."

"Do you think he look that much like Kareem?"

"Hell, yeah! He look like you too, but the color of his eyes make him look more like Kareem."

No doubt, I was glad to hear that. Desmon opened the back door and leaned his head down.

"Do you mind if she come to the crib and help me with my homework?"

"Who is she?" I asked, as I knew homework wasn't on his agenda.

"Lamyah. Lamyah Melrose. I need some help with my math and—

"Just get in the car," I said.

Desmon got in and she scooted in next to him. As we drove off, Jada turned around and spoke to him.

"Hey, what's up?" he said.

"I'm Jada. A long time friend of your daddy's."

"I didn't think my daddy had any friends. But, you learn something new everyday. Ain't that right, Kiley?"

"No doubt," I said, looking in my rearview mirror at him.

He looked out the window at the car waiting at the stoplight next to us. It was Gabrielle, the cheerleader he'd been seeing off and on, in the car with another brotha. I could already see the brotha, but being in the backseat, Desmon couldn't get a good look at his face.

"Hey, man, edge up a lil bit," he said.

"For what?" I said, as if I didn't know why.

"I need to see something."

Before I could edge up, the light turned green. Trying to spare his feelings, I waited until the car made a left and took off before I moved.

"Did you hear what I said?" he asked.

"I heard you, but I was thinking about something and got side tracked."

He sat back on the seat in deep thought. He mumbled something to himself and I asked him to speak up.

"I was just saying that I know whose car that was."

"What car?"

He caught my eyes in the rearview mirror and just stared at me.

Jada gave me directions to her cousin's place where she was staying. When we got there, she leaned in for a kiss before she got out. I didn't want to kiss her because I knew it would bring about many questions between Desmon and me. Jada noticed my hesitance and took my face in her hands. She gave me a smack on the lips and asked when we would see each other again.

"I'on know," I said.

"What you mean, you don't know?"

"I mean, I don't know."

"How about the weekend?"

"I got plans."

"With who?"

"None of your business. Now, go handle your business and I'll call you later."

"You'd better. And if you don't, I know where to find you," she said. She opened the door and got out.

Desmon got out of the back seat and got in the front with me. I waited until Jada got inside of her cousin's house, and after she did, I drove off.

I knew Desmon couldn't wait to question me. "What's up with big booty?" he asked. "She kind of got an attitude problem, don't she?"

"She ain't the only one with an attitude—is she?"

"Na, but...but things didn't work out with you and Anna?"

"Yeah, they working out. And before you get started, Jada and me are just friends."

"Friends, huh? Friends that...you know, get down every chance they get?"

"Na, we don't get down like that. She had some issues and needed somebody to talk to."

"So, basically, y'all ain't fucking?"

"Man, why you all up in my business?" I said, getting irritated. "I don't need to discuss who I'm laying the pipe to with my son, do I?"

"Hey, look, Mr. Attitude, I thought we were cool like that. I guess I was wrong."

"We are cool, but some things I don't care to discuss with you."

"Then, tell me now. Things like what? That way, you don't get all bent out of shape when I bring certain things to your attention."

I took a deep breath. "Desmon, not now, okay. We'll discuss all of this a lil later on, au-ight?"

He didn't say another word, but I knew he was trying to put the guilt trip on me about Anna. He didn't have to because I was already starting to feel bad about my decision not to see her again. Moreso, I knew she was looking forward to spending time with me this weekend, and unfortunately, that wasn't going to happen.

THE BEAT DOWN

I was tired as fuck. After I took Desmon's *tutor* home the other night, I thought I was going to come back home and get some rest. That didn't happen because he stayed up all night arguing on the phone with Gabrielle about who the hell she'd been seeing. Evidentially, she hooked up with another one of the football players on the team and Desmon was irate. He'd called Antonio up and told him about it, and I had to listen to him go on and on about how she played him. That totally fucked me up because he was definitely the one playing her. He'd had his share of females and had even taken another chick to Homecoming with him. If many others sporting his jersey and calling here wasn't enough, then the *tutor* he brought here with him the other day certainly was.

Now, she did help him with his homework, but it wasn't until I heard the music blasting that I realized what was actually going down. When I walked up to the door to ask him to turn in down, I could hear the moans and groans coming through the door. I didn't want to be nosy, so I stepped away from the door and went back into my room to watch TV. That night, when I dropped her off at home, my suspicions were confirmed. Her hair was a mess and all of the make-up she had on was cleared from her face. Desmon gave his goodbyes with a kiss and I was so sure I'd probably never see her face again.

When Saturday rolled around, Desmon asked me to drop him off at Ginger's place so he could drop in to say hello and later go to the mall with Antonio. When I asked if he'd make his way back home, he said he didn't know and promised he'd call me later. Since his hoop-tee wasn't working, he asked me if I'd take a look at it to see what was wrong. I didn't want to work on his car in front of Ginger's place, so I called Al's to see if he'd have it towed back to my place for me. He came within the hour and towed it to my house. He also told me the police were looking for me and had paid him a visit several times. When I asked if there was a warrant out for my arrest, he assured me that there was.

I wanted to tell the police what really happened, but I was going to wait until they caught up with me. I'm sure Dwayne's story was full of shit, but I was also sure they didn't have no sympathy for an abusive drug dealer either.

Either way, I didn't trip. It was too beautiful outside, so I put my torn faded jeans on and my red wife-beater. I tied my bandana around my head and searched for my tools. After I found them, I went outside and got busy on Desmon's car.

As usual, time had gotten away from me. By now, my hands were black as dirt and so was my face since I'd rubbed it a few times to wipe the sweat from my forehead. Realizing that Desmon needed a whole new engine, I called it a day and headed back into the house. As I was about to step in the shower, the phone rang. I looked at the caller ID and it was Jada. I didn't answer because she'd been bugging the hell out of me since we'd last got together. Thing is, she didn't want shit. Her messages were clear that all she wanted to do was fuck again, and for the moment, I wasn't interested.

I hopped in the shower to wash all the grime and dirt off my face, body and hands. When I finished, I dried off and wrapped a towel around my waist. Since this was the perfect opportunity for me to get some rest, after I made a sandwich, I fell backwards on my bed. I looked up at the ceiling and took large bites into my sandwich. It was gone in four bites and I was still hungry. Trying to decide on sleep or more food, I continued to lay back on the bed and stare at the ceiling. I started to think more about Desmon, so I reached for Marissa's number on my nightstand to call her. She answered, but I could barely hear her from the noisy background.

"Who is this?" she asked.

"Kiley," I responded.

"Hey, Kiley. Give me your number so I can call you right back."

I gave her my number and waited for her to call back. Within ten minutes she did.

"Hello, there," she said.

"Hey, what's up?"

"You know I gotta ask you this, but, what happened to you last Sunday night? I looked all over for you but you were gone."

"I left after that incident. Somebody got killed, didn't they?"

"Yeah. My friends and me got the heck out of there too. I did look around for you, but I figured you'd left as well."

"I looked around for you too, but there was so many people that I couldn't find you no matter how hard I tried."

"You could have called. It's evident you still have my phone number."

"No doubt. I've been kind of busy with Desmon. His leg still trying to heal, so I've been taking care of him on that end."

"I see. Since I know you've been busy, no need to apologize."

I didn't respond because my intentions weren't to apologize. Marissa cleared her throat. "So, what you got up for the evening?"

"Nothing. I just called to see if we could finish the conversation we started at the game about Desmon."

"Oh, that. Well, along with that, I was hoping you'd let me take you to dinner or something."

My stomach growled from the sandwich I'd eaten, but I really wasn't up for dinner. "Thanks, but I'm not in the mood—

"So, basically, the only thing you want from me is information about Desmon."

"Yeah. That's only if you got vital information."

"Kiley, like I told you at the game…Ginger was the one who said Myles was Desmon's father. I dated him for years so I know how much he and Desmon looks alike. After you see the picture, you be the judge."

"Would you say that Myles looks more like Desmon than I do?"

"I really can't say. You have to be the judge of that. All I can do is give you his picture, then you decide."

"Where do you live?"

"By the Halls Ferry Circle. But, since you won't have dinner with me, I'm gonna step out for the night. Why don't you let me bring the picture to you."

I was skeptical, but I gave Marissa the address to my place. She said that after she picked one of her lady friends up, she'd drop the picture off for me to see it.

A bit nervous about seeing the picture, I poured myself a glass of Vodka and rolled up a Bahama-of-a-mama joint. I was fucked up by the time Marissa made it to my place, and when I opened the door, the looks of an unstable man was written all over my face.

"Kiley, are you okay," she said, walking in.

"I'm cool," I said standing in the foyer. "Where the picture at?"

Marissa looked out at her friend in the car and dug into her purse. "She's been rushing me so I hope you appreciate me bringing this picture to you."

"I do. I very much do," I said, leaning against the door.

Marissa handed the picture over to me and I looked at it. The picture looked a lot like me, but Myles' eyes and eyebrows were quite different.

"See," Marissa said, pointing to the picture. "Desmon's got his features all up in here."

"I don't see all that, but thanks for bringing this over. Do you mind if I keep it?"

"Sure. Just let me know if there's anything else I can do for you. If you're that worried about it, Kiley, then why not have a blood test? That will determine everything."

"Maybe I will. In the meantime, if there's anything else you can do, I have your number."

"And I have yours too," she said, on her way out.

I thanked Marissa again and she jetted.

By midnight I was tow-up from the flo-up. I'd gazed at Myles' picture at least a million times. It seemed as if the more I looked, the more Desmon looked like him. I'd even put their pictures side by side, and still there were some resemblances. When I got my picture and placed it next to Desmon's, he was all me. I was fucking confused, but I knew there was only one way to get to the bottom of this.

The phone awakened me, as I lay naked on the couch in a deep sleep. I glanced at the clock on the wall and it showed a little after midnight. When I answered, it was Desmon.

"Wake up," he said. "You ain't sleep already, are you?"

"Yeah, I was," I mumbled, as my head was banging hard. I sat up and rubbed my hand down my face.

"Kiley," Desmon said.

"What!"

"Why you yelling? You the one who told me to call if I was gone stay out."

I took a deep breath. "Yeah, I know. So you not coming home tonight?"

"Naw, I'm gone stay at Antonio's girlfriend's crib. I just got into a fight at the mall a few hours ago."

"A fight? With who," I said, discouraged.

"With Gabrielle."

"Man, why you fighting girls? You know better than to be fighting girls."

"Okay, Pops, when I show you how badly she scratched my face, you gone want to fight her your damn self. You should see these scratches she put on my face."

"First of all, what are you doing out at the mall with an injured leg? You need to stay off that leg and let it heal."

"I be bored, man. I just wanted to get out for a while."

"Are you coming back tomorrow? I need to talk to you about something important."

"I might. If so, it'll be late."

"Don't make it too late. Until then, stay out of trouble and...I love you."

He hesitated. "Um...uh, Antonio wants to speak to you. Hold on." He passed the phone to Antonio.

"Hey, Mr. Abrams, I don't mean to be up in yo bitness or nothing, but what's up with you and Anna?"

By Antonio's tone, I could tell he was high. "Nothing, why? We cool."

"She don't seem to think so. I ain't liking to see hu upset all the time. I'on know what's up, but you told me you'd take care of hu."

"Antonio, please don't get in the middle of this. I'm digging Anna, but I got so much shit on my mind right now. It has nothing to do with her."

"Then, why don't you just tell hu?"

"I have. I told her to be patient with me, but I don't know what else to say."

"Well, whatever you've been saying to hu ain't working. She be tearing up all the time and you got to know how much it hurt me to see hu like that."

"Antonio, I'm sure you know Anna is very emotional. I will deal with her when I can. Again, don't you take this personal and please don't come between us."

"I'm not. Just do the right thing, okay?"

"If I knew what that was I would."

He gave the phone back to Desmon. "Are you in the dog house," he laughed. "I got a feeling Jada, the baby-girl with lots and lots of back, got you in trouble."

"Did you tell Antonio about Jada? Man, tell me you didn't."

"See, it slipped. I—

I hung up on Desmon. That's why I didn't want his punk ass in my business. I knew he'd run his mouth and I hoped Antonio wasn't stupid enough to hurt Anna's feelings even more by telling her.

Curious to find out, and even though I said I wouldn't, I picked up the phone and dialed Anna's number. I could tell she was asleep by the way she answered.

"If I woke you, I can always call you back later," I said.

"No, I'm fine."

"Are you sure?"

"Why wouldn't I be?"

"I don't know. Antonio said you were upset about something."

"I don't know what Antonio is talking about."

"So, you're not upset with me about not calling—

"Look, Kiley, I don't know what kind of game you're playing. I've said it before and I'll say it again, but this shit is not working out for me."

"So, you are upset."

"Are you intentionally trying to screw me around so I will get upset?"

"No, I'm not. I've just been busy."

"Too busy for somebody you say you care about? That doesn't make sense to me. I don't even think it makes sense to you."

"By the sound of your voice, I can tell how much you've missed me."

She paused and continued to speak in a higher pitched voice. "Miss you? Yeah, I've done that a lot. Missing you does me no good, though, especially since I don't even have a phone number to reach you. You call here privately like you're trying to hide something."

"What time would you like for me to pick you up tomorrow?"

"Don't bother."

"Why? I thought you wasn't upset with me."

"I'm damn upset with you. You gotta stop doing this shit to me, man. I can't be on your time like this, I just can't."

When I heard her voice crack, I could tell Anna was starting to cry. I didn't want to hear it, so I made a quick attempt to end the call.

"How about lunch, shopping, dinner, a movie, the racetrack, and sex tomorrow? I'll pick you up around eleven so we can get an early start."

"If you do not show up tomorrow, Kiley, I swear to God that it will be the last time you ever see me. I will not—

"I hate threats," I said, calmly and clicked Anna off the phone. I dropped the phone on the floor and lay back on the couch to continue with my rest. I was glad she didn't have my number because I knew she'd call right back. In addition to that, I knew once I picked her up tomorrow, she'd have an earful of bullshit for me to listen to.

By morning, I got up early because I had a busy day ahead of me. I put on my comfortable white sweat suit and white new tennis shoes to match. After I grabbed my keys off the dresser, I jetted. I stopped by the supermarket to get Anna some roses so I could purposely be late. She just didn't know how much I loved a challenge and how dare her threaten me to be on time. Still a bit early, I went to Al's place and messed around with him for about an hour or so. He said the police hadn't been back looking for me, but claimed that Dwayne and some of his partners were. Apparently, Al knew Dwayne from working on his car, so he gave me a heads up and told me to be careful. I wasn't the least bit afraid because any man who beats on a woman for no reason is a punk. Now, I admit, Jada can work a motherfucker's nerves, but I only resorted to putting my hands on her when she'd put her hands on me.

I didn't reach Anna's house until almost noon. When she opened the door, she still had on her nightgown and turned away from the door. I walked in and sat on the arm of her couch. I held the roses out to her, and she stood across the room with a mad look on her face.

I held the roses out in front of me. "I stopped at the store and bought these for you. Here."

She walked over and snatched them from me. One by one, she tore them apart and dropped them on the floor. She walked away and headed towards the kitchen. "Get out!" she yelled. "And don't forget to close the door behind you."

I rushed up to her and grabbed her waist. "Would you stop all this nonsense and go put on some clothes?"

She snatched away from me and her robe came loose. "Nonsense! What's nonsense is you hanging up on me last night and

160

coming here late with some freaking flowers thinking I'm going somewhere with you. You are crazy, man, I swear you're crazy."

I looked at her naked body and she quickly gathered her robe and tied it. "I apologize for hanging up on you, but I don't take threats too lightly. I'm late because I stopped to get your flowers and I saw a friend of mine at the supermarket. Please know that I'm not gonna kiss your ass, Anna, but I'm asking you to get dressed so we can go. If not, then I'm out of here."

She rolled her eyes and turned to go upstairs. I followed behind her, and when we got to her room, I sat on the edge of her bed while she got dressed. There wasn't no need to get all hyped about what had gone down between us because it was obvious Anna was going with me the moment I stepped in the door. Her perfume I could smell a mile a way. Her makeup had been freshly done, and when we made it to her room, her outfit was already laid out on the bed. The drama that women bring about just fucks me up sometimes. It didn't make sense to go through all that bullshit when she knew damn well she was going with me. One minute, they be chewing a brotha's head off, and the next, they be loving his dirty underwear. This was some confusing shit, but I guess we all had to go through it.

Anna took her time getting ready. She stood in the bathroom and played around with her hair while looking in the mirror. When she couldn't decide how she wanted it, she stepped outside of the bathroom and called my name as I paged through a magazine.

"What?" I said looking up. She was naked and held her hair up with her hands.

"Up or down?" she said, and then let her hair fall.

I looked at the tiny gap between her legs. I then looked at her breasts and back down between her legs. "Down," I said.

"I was talking about my hair. Do you like it up or down?"

My eyes continued to search her body. "Up," I said.

"Forget it," she said, walking back into the bathroom. I watched as she stood on the tips of her toes and leaned in to look in the mirror. She teased her hair with her fingers and slid on some more lip-gloss. The nice small curve in her ass looked awfully good from the side and before she put her clothes on, I got up and walked to where she stood. I leaned against the doorway and continued to watch her get ready. She looked at me through the mirror.

"Can I help you?" she smiled. She knew that she had my undivided attention.

I nudged my head toward the bed. "Do you feel like taking care of something before we leave."

She turned to look at me. "Uh, no. I am smelling and feeling too fresh and I'm not about to mess myself up. Besides, you can wait until later, can't you?"

"I guess. But, hurry up and put on some clothes. You haven't a clue what you're doing to me now."

Anna smiled and walked out of the bathroom. She slid into her turquoise silk panties and bra. Before she put her jeans on, I walked over and took them from her hands. I laid her back on the bed and wrapped her legs around me.

"Please," I begged. "I can't wait until later."

She rubbed my face. "You look so pathetic when you beg. But, this is payback for not being on time. I said later, so we're going to wait until later. Now, please get up so we can go."

Normally, this shit wouldn't go down like this. I'd play with the pussy until it was ready to give in to me. However, I knew Anna was different. She'd be offended if I tried to go any further so I had to be careful that I didn't hurt her feelings. With that in mind, I got up and went downstairs until she got dressed. Nearly a half an hour later, she was ready to go.

For Anna to be such a beautiful woman, she dressed kind of plain. Today, she had on a pair of faded jeans and a pink t-shirt with white letters on it. She looked cute, but I knew underneath it all that she could also look like a lady. Honestly, I can't think of one time I'd seen her in an outfit I was overwhelmingly pleased with. So, instead of having lunch first, I took her to Saks Fifth Avenue. I didn't know much about women's clothing, but when I saw this white silk knee length fitted skirt and white and black strapless halter to match on a mannequin, I envisioned it on Anna. I pulled her into the store and the sales associates came flocking. It didn't dawn on me as to why, until Anna went to the fitting room to try the outfit on.

"So, what football team do you play for?" the sales associate asked.

"I don't play football."

"Baseball?" she laughed. "Your face looks so familiar."

162

"You might have seen it on *America's Most Wanted*. I don't know, I'm not quite sure where you've seen it."

She laughed. "Oh, you're so funny. I'm gonna go check on your wife and see how she's doing."

She walked off, and as I looked around and saw some more things I wanted Anna to have, I picked them up and placed them across my arm. Shortly after, she came out of the fitting room with the black and white outfit on. The skirt curved to her hips perfectly and the top made her breasts look down right suckable. I placed the items in my hand on the chair in front of me and walked up to give her props.

"You look amazing," I said.

"Doesn't she looked gorgeous," the sales associate chimed in.

Anna smiled and looked down at herself. "I feel so...I don't know how I feel. I like it, though."

"Turn around," I asked.

"Kiley," she said as if I'd embarrassed her.

"Honey, let him see your tush," the lady interrupted again. "That's how men really can tell if they like the outfit or not."

Anna turned around and I felt like I was in heaven. "We'll take it," I rushed to say. "And, we'll take this other stuff too."

"Kiley, do you know how much this...this outfit cost? I will not...you will not buy this for me."

"I buy what I want to buy. Leave the outfit on, and put the jeans and the t-shirt in a bag that the sales associate is gonna give you."

I hadn't even purchased anything yet and the sales associate had already run behind the counter to get a bag.

"Here you go, hun. And I have the perfect shoes to match that outfit. Would you like to see them, sir?"

I nodded and she walked me over to the small shoe department.

"What size shoe does she wear?"

Anna walked up from behind with her arms folded. "A size six, but I'm not wearing this outfit today."

"Baby, come on, you look good. Stop being so difficult and just relax."

"Kiley, there's no need for me to look like a million bucks and I don't have it. I could use this money for Antonio—

"Here you go!" the lady shouted. "A size six it is. You are going to look fabulous with these shoes on."

I had to admit, the shoes were as sharp as the outfit. They had a thin three to four inch heel and strapped up with thick black and white ribbons.

Anna took the shoe from the lady and held it in her hand. "How much is this shoe?" she asked.

The lady cleared her throat. "I...I think it's like two or three hundred dollars. I'm really not sure." She turned to look at the box. "Two seventy-five. But you can match it up with so many things."

"I don't want the shoes," Anna quickly said.

"Why not?" I asked.

"Because they're too expensive. Besides, I can't walk in a heel that high."

I turned to the associate. "Do you have anything else with a smaller heel?"

"You don't want to go too much smaller with a skirt like that. Maybe an inch smaller but that's as low as she'd want to go."

The associate found another shoe for Anna that had a black frame and silk white straps that crossed over the top. It matched the outfit even better.

"We'll take them," I said.

Anna rolled her eyes. "I'm almost afraid to ask but how much are they?"

The sales associate was about to speak up, but I stopped her. "It doesn't matter. I said we'll take them."

"Good good good," she said, rubbing her hands together and heading for the counter.

Anna sat on the leather chair behind me and slid into the shoes. When she stood up, she walked up to me and slid her arm into mine.

"I'm killing you when we get back to your place. You didn't have to do this."

I smiled at how beautiful she looked and waited for the associate to come with a total. As she scanned in the other items, Anna pinched my arm.

"I don't like that shirt," she said, as she tried to convince me not to buy it.

"I do," I said to the associate, "so go ahead."

"Those pants are ugly," she said as the next item was scanned.

The associate ignored her as well as me. When all was said and done, the total came to three thousand ninety-five dollars and some odd cents. Anna released her arm from mine.

"I'll be waiting for you outside. This is so ridiculous," she said, walking off.

I reached in my pocket and pulled the money out from my wallet. After I paid the associate, she was all smiles. She walked the bags around to me and placed them in my hand.

"Thank you, sir. I can't remember the last time I've seen a woman look so magnificent."

"Me either," I said, and then left the store. Anna was sitting outside in the mall on one of the benches. She moved her curly hair away from her face and placed it behind her ears.

"Did I look that bad where you felt the need to clean me up?"

I sat next to her. "Na, baby. It ain't nothing like that. I just wanted to do something nice for you, that's all."

"Thanks," she said, and then kissed me on the cheek. "Where to now?"

"You wanna grab a bite to eat while we're here?"

"That sounds good," she said, and then stood up. "Besides, I'm starving."

Anna and me walked to a restaurant that was at the other end of the mall. I can't remember a time when I'd gotten so many stares. Everybody was looking and I assumed they were thinking what in the hell was she doing with a black ass brotha such as myself. Either way, she was uncomfortable with all of the attention, but I loved every bit of it. It took me back to my earlier days in L.A. when we'd get dressed at our best for a kick ass night on the town. At the time, Jada was my sidekick, and she had no problem flaunting the two or three thousand dollar fit she'd bought with my money. She was a big spender and so was I. It wasn't until I moved to St. Louis when all of that shit came to a halt.

Dinner was nice and quiet with Anna and me. We didn't have time to make it to the movies because I wanted to make it to the racetrack before it got too late. Every once in a while, I had to get my gamble on. I enjoyed going to the tracks, and since Anna had never been, I thought the atmosphere would be perfect.

By the time we got there, the place was jammed pack. I let Anna pick the horses and I told her I'd split the cash with her if the horses she picked won. Before we took our seats, I stood in line to get some popcorn and Anna went to the restroom. As she walked away, I stared deeply at her from behind and thought about our eventful intercourse later on tonight. As happy as she was, I knew she'd get loose with me tonight. I had a good feeling and couldn't wait to bring about some changes I wanted to take place in our sex life.

Just as I was in deep thought, looking at her as she opened the bathroom door, I heard a voice next to me.

"Now, that is a sight for sore eyes," he said. I turned my head and it was Dominique. He was pimped out in his black on black pants suit with two of his boys standing next to him. "Kiley, why you ain't tell me you was doing it like that? If I had known Anna could clean up like that, shit...

I just looked at him because the motherfucker seriously disgusted me. When the lady behind the concession stand asked what I wanted, I told her some popcorn and a soda. I could tell Dominique was pissed because I hadn't given him the attention he thought he rightfully deserved. And when Anna came out of the restroom, her hips swayed from side to side as she made her way towards me. She walked right past him, as he and his boys checked her out from head to toe. She came up to me and wrapped her arm around mine like she'd done all day long. As we waited for my popcorn and soda, she leaned her head against my shoulder.

"I love you," she said softly.

I kissed her forehead and didn't feel as if the time was appropriate. After I got my popcorn and soda, Anna and me headed for our seats. When we walked by Dominique and his boys, he spoke to Anna.

"Hi, Dominique," she said as we tried to keep walking but the crowd had everybody at a stand still. I couldn't help but hear one of his partnas call her a stuck up bitch. And then, he went on and on about how he'd rip her skirt off and tear her ass up.

Anna heard every bit of what he'd said and she looked over at me.

"Don't trip," she said. "Just ignore him."

The son of a bitch treated me like a punk and got louder with the shit. "Man, I'd wear that bitch out, you hear me!" he yelled. I tried to hold my peace, but after that, I couldn't. I removed Anna's arm from around me and maneuvered my way over to Dominique and his boys. Anna pulled my arm and begged me not to go. Instead, I snatched away from her.

"That's kind of disrespectful, ain't it?" I said, standing face to face with the brotha who couldn't keep his mouth shut.

"I don't know what you talking 'bout," he replied.

Anna pulled my arm again. "Kiley, let's just go. I don't want any trouble."

"And neither do we," Dominique said. "Lorenzo get to trippin sometimes and he didn't mean no harm."

Anna continued to tug at my arm and after I stared Lorenzo down even harder, I turned to walk away. I placed my hand around Anna's waist and I'll be damned if that motherfucker Dominique didn't reach down with his hand and swipe it across her ass. No hesitation on my part, I took my fist and slammed it into his mouth. The son of a bitch fell backwards and hit the ground. He rushed up towards me and so did his boys. I knew I'd soon be in a battle to save my life, but I'd been here and certainly done this shit before. Papa Abrams always taught me that if I were ever in a fight with more than one person, to focus on one of them and beat the shit out of them. That one person just happened to be Dominique. We scraped like two wild dogs in an alley fighting for some food. I'd busted the side of his face with my fist and karate kicked one of his partnas back into the concession stand. No doubt, I was winning this fight, until I felt something hard come crashing down on the back of my head. The hit was too powerful and quickly sent me staggering to the ground. I tried to get up, but I couldn't. I felt another punch in my back, on my side, in my ribs and then I watched as somebody's black long Stacy Adams was making its way to my face. I cradled my face in my lap and the shoe somehow missed. All I could hear were Anna's screams and I could see her trying to help me off the ground. I heard a smack, and I'd known somebody had hit my woman. When I'd realized I didn't want to die in front of her, I rolled over on the ground and hurried to get myself up.

My body was in so much pain, but that didn't stop me from holding up my fist.

"Look at here, look at here! This motherfucker got guts," Dominique said. He'd had enough of me so Lorenzo charged at me again. Since I knew it was time to give it everything I had, I took my fist and sent it flying with mega power behind it. So much power that it knocked Lorenzo the fuck out. Dominique and his other boy came at me with everything they had too and punches were being thrown everywhere. I couldn't even see who I hit, but I knew many of my punches landed cleanly. So cleanly that it was obvious the son of bitches had enough. Somebody yelled that the police were coming and we all did what we knew best—scattered.

I took Anna by the hand and shirtless and all, I made my way through the crowd. Everybody looked at us with disgust, and before the cops could find me, I hurried to my car to leave. I reached in my pocket for the keys and tossed them to Anna.

"Drive, please," I said, in detrimental pain. She hopped in the car and I got in on the passenger's side. I leaned down and reached for my gun underneath her seat.

"No, no, Kiley, please don't," she cried.

"Drive my motherfucking car," I yelled and reached further underneath my seat for the bullets. I angrily loaded the gun and held it in my hand as Anna made her way off the parking lot in tears.

"You are scaring me. Would you please put that thing away?"

"Would you drive this fucking car like I told you to," I yelled. I banged my gun against the dashboard. "Do you see what these punk ass fools did to me! Huh?" Look at me damn it! Do you see what the fuck they did?"

She continued to look forward and made her way to the exit. I searched the parking lot, and it was right up my alley when I saw Dominique and his boys heading for his car. Anna saw them too and sped up to exit the lot.

"Slow down!" I yelled.

"You are not about to do this with me in the fucking car! You're gonna have to shoot me because I'm not stopping!"

"No problem," I said, and aimed the gun at her. She slammed on the brakes and dropped her face into her hands. I opened the passenger's side door and walked towards Dominique and his boys as quickly as I could. They spotted me from a distance and that's when I aimed the gun and fired. I fired so quickly that the gun jerked my hand back as the bullets exited from it. The empty shells hit the ground and fire sparked from the tip of the gun. I watched Lorenzo's body drop first, but Dominique and his other boy ran pretty quickly. A bullet caught Dominique in the leg, and before I could send him off with his final goodbyes, I had to quickly reload my gun. I did it as fast as I could, but his other partna turned around and fired shots back at me. I dodged the bullets as they bounced around me and glass from people's car windows shattered everywhere. As I fired shots back at him, I backed up to my car. I stood completely still before getting in and concentrated hard as I aimed my gun directly at his chest. I pulled the trigger and it hit him in the upper part of his chest. His gun dropped from his hand and he fell backwards.

Anna was in a serious panic, and as soon as I hopped in the car, she sped off down the road. As the car was out of sight, she pulled over to the side of the road and put the car in park.

Her entire face was pale and the tears poured profusely down her face. Her hands shook and she let go of the steering wheel. She could barely get words to come out of her mouth. "I...I can't drive. Will you drive...please?"

I looked behind us and got out of the car. I ran over to the driver's side and she moved over. When I got back into the car, I sped off and made my way to the highway. I'd been a fool to take Anna home, so I took her back to my place with me. When I pulled up, I put the car in park, looked over at her and spoke calmly.

"This is why I didn't want to be with you. I knew some—

"All I want to do is go home. Just take me home and be done with it, Kiley."

"I'm not taking you back to your place. Going there will put your life at risk and I'm—

"Take me home, damn it!" she yelled.

I gave Anna a hard stare and seriously didn't have time to argue with her. I opened the door and placed one foot on the ground.

"If you want to stay in the car, then do so. I'm not taking you home, but if you want to go, you can always find another ride. If something happens to you, I'm not gonna hold myself accountable."

I got out and slammed the door. I slowly made my way to the front door and was relieved to see my couch. I closed the door and plopped down on the couch. I elevated my feet with my pillows and placed my arm across the top of my forehead. I knew I needed a doctor, but I refused to go. My ribs were aching and the back of my head throbbed with pain. I could barely see my entire face in the rearview mirror when I drove, but my vision was blurred from my nearly closed shut and swollen right eye. My jaw line was numb and I'd spit up enough blood to donate it.

Making sure that Antonio wasn't at Anna's crib, I reached for the phone and called her house. No one answered, and then I checked my messages to see if Desmon had called. Surprisingly, he had. He said he was crashing out at Antonio's girlfriend's house for one more night and said he'd holla at me tomorrow when he got out of school. I was relieved and closed my eyes to think about something else other than my pain.

A MAN AIN'T SUPPOSE TO CRY

By morning, I could barely move. I was able to turn my head slightly to the side to see Anna sitting in a chair directly across from me. She had my oversized white t-shirt on and her legs were up in the chair while pressed against her chest. After I looked at her, I turned my head and closed my eyes.

"Do you want me to call a doctor," she said.

I shook my head. "No."

"Aren't you hurting?"

"I've endured way more pain than this in my life. I'll get over it."

"Kiley, you just can't lay there in pain. Let me take you to see a doctor."

"I said no. I just need some sleep, that's all."

"Then, let me help you to your room. I put some clean sheets on your bed and fluffed out some pillows for you."

"I need a joint," I mumbled. "If you want to do something for me, you can roll me up a joint."

"No,"

"Then, I'll do it myself."

I slowly eased up and pressed my sore back against the couch. I then leaned forward, and reached for my bag of weed and papers on the table. My hands were cut and bruised, but it didn't stop me from putting together the joint I so desperately wanted. I placed it in my mouth, and after I lit it, I took a long and deep drag from it. So deep that it made me cough. And when I coughed, my body ached.

Anna stood up and removed the joint from my hand. She laid it in the ashtray and took my hand.

"Come take a bath with me. I think you'll feel so much better after you soak in the tub for at least an hour."

I stood up and slowly followed Anna to the bathroom. She started the water and helped me out of my pants and shoes. I felt helpless, but I was hurting too bad to even remove my own clothes. Anna got naked, dimmed the lights, and after she put her hair in a ponytail, she stepped into the tub. She reached for my hand and I stepped in and sat down right between her legs.

The tub steamed from the hot water and it felt good as she wrapped her legs around my waist and dabbed my chest with soap and water. I closed my eyes and leaned my head back against her chest.

"I don't even know where to begin to tell you how sorry I am," I said softly.

"It wasn't your fault. I guess you did what you had to do."

"I guess I did."

There was silence as Anna continued to wash my body. She lightly massaged my aching spots with her hands and had given me an icepack to place over my eye. Again, I felt helpless but it was damn good to have her with me to help a brotha out.

We stayed in the tub for at least two hours. She'd kept refreshing the hot water until it had basically turned cold. I stood up and she took a towel and wrapped it around my waist. She covered herself with one and we made our way to the bedroom. After she dried me off, she pulled the covers back so I could lay down. She dried herself off as well and climbed into bed with me. She moved in as close as she could and pressed her butt against me. I wrapped my arms around her and held her tightly around her waist. I kissed the back of her head, as she held my hands together with hers in front of her.

"Are you relaxed now?" she asked.

"Very."

"Then, let's get some sleep."

"No doubt."

My body felt so good against Anna's that I couldn't help but find myself in a deep sleep. She must have been tired too because she'd kicked off minutes before I did.

My eyes popped open at the first sound I heard coming from the kitchen. As I listened in, it was the fridge making ice and dropping it into the tray. I turned my head and looked at the clock behind me. It was almost two o'clock in the afternoon, so I knew Desmon would be making his way home soon. Yesterday when he called, he said he'd get a ride home. And, by the way I felt, I was glad that I didn't have to move.

After taking a bath earlier, and downing several Extra-Strength Tylenols, my body felt a tad bit better. No doubt, it still needed some work, but I was pleased to already be making progress.

I looked over at Anna as she was still in a deep sleep. She must have been exhausted and I'd figured she must have stayed up all night sitting in that chair. I hated she'd seen what I did, and more than anything, I never wanted her to see the beast I could become when I got angry.

Thinking about what had happened, I kissed the back of Anna's head two times. I then lifted the covers and looked at her naked ass that was still pressed up against me. In need of a quickee, I reached for her leg and placed it on my thigh. As her leg separated from the other one, I held my thang in my hand and gently rubbed my thick head between her legs. I could feel her wetness so I placed two of my fingers inside of my mouth and soaked them. After I did, I reached around the front of her and placed my fingers on her clitoris. I stroked it gently with my fingers and that's when she woke up. She turned her head slightly to the side.

"What are you doing?" she said, squirming from my touch.

"What does it look like I'm doing?"

"Are you sure you're up for this?"

"I'll soon find out, won't I?"

Anna held her leg in place, as it rested on my thigh, and she leaned slightly forward. I continued to manipulate her clitoris and made my way inside of her from behind as we lay on our side. Now, talk about a pussy curving to a dick, hers did just that as I went inside of her. There was no way that I could move fast, so I took slow deep strokes against her walls. When she grabbed my hand and moved it away from her clitoris, I knew she was already about to come. And every time I backed up and went in, her "Uh's" got louder and longer. Once she came, my side started to hurt so I rolled over on my back. She sat up on me backwards and turned her head to the side.

"Can you wait a minute," she said. "I'm still trying to recover from that."

I was anxious and really didn't want to wait. "Just let me put it back inside. You don't even have to move, I'll move."

Anna lifted her body up a bit and allowed me to go back inside. She slowly rode me, and to assist, I held her waistline and pushed her up and down to the rhythm I wanted. From the pain still in my mid area, I didn't mind that the pace was slow. Either way, I was kind of pissed by her performance so I instructed her.

"Go all the way up to the tip, and slowly come down on it. Take your time and don't move faster until you want to. Only work below your upper hips because moving the upper part of your body does nothing for me."

Anna did just as I'd asked, and each time she came down on it she let out a deep breath and a soft-spoken, "Ah." On occasion, an "Ah, shit" when I reached far up inside of her. As she sped up, I asked her to lean forward. When I separated her cheeks, I had a clear vision of her insides.

"Damn!" I yelled

She stopped, rose up and turned her head to the side. "What...what's wrong?"

"Nothing, baby. Just keep doing what you doing."

Anna turned back around and leaned forward again. I reached over to the drawer on my nightstand and opened it.

"What are you doing?" she said, stopping again.

"Nothing. I'm getting ready to come so stop cutting me off like that."

She got back into position and continued to work her thang on me. I separated her butt cheeks again, and before I came I asked her to come with me.

"Wait a minute," she said. "I'm not quite there yet."

Getting her there, I took deep strokes inside of her that damn near lifted her off me. I wanted to tickle her clitoris, but my hands were focused on holding her ass. Instead of me touching her insides, I asked her to do the work for me. She reached down and stroked her clitoris while keeping the rhythm going.

"Okay," she moaned. "I'm about tooooo—

Her body jerked and I released myself inside of her. I then placed the camera I had in my hand over my eye and took a picture. Anna quickly turned around and eased off of me.

"I know you didn't just take a picture of that, did you?"

"I couldn't help it. I wanted you to see what I saw."

"That is so nasty," she said, getting off the bed. "I didn't know you could get that nasty."

I ignored Anna and looked at the camera, as I waited for the picture to appear. When it did, I smiled and held it out for her to see it.

"Come look at this," I said. "You have got to see this!"

"No thank you," she said, pulling the shirt over her head.

I dropped the camera to my side. "You ain't no fun. If you don't mind, I just wanted you to see what it looks like when we share our love."

"That's bullshit and you know it," she said. She plopped down on the bed next to me so she could take a look. "This better be good."

"Trust me, you gone like it a whole lot." I picked the camera up and showed Anna the picture. She squinted her eyes and moved in closer to look at it.

"That is gross," she said. "I can't believe you would take a picture of something so gross."

"Gross? Are you crazy! Baby, look at the—

"I'm looking at it, damn it!"

"Then, tell me that my dick don't look good inside of your pussy."

"Kiley, it don't look good. It feels awfully good, but I can't agree with you about it looking good."

"Aw, my heart is broken. I can't believe you don't see what I see when I look at this picture."

"Okay, then, what is it that you see...other than—Shit, I can't even say it."

"I see...I see, cum and—

Anna covered my mouth. "Stop being so nasty. And if you show anybody that picture, I'm gonna hurt you. Do you understand?"

"Baby, this is for my eyes only." I placed the camera on my lips and kissed the picture.

"What a great sense of humor?" she said, getting out of the bed. "I didn't even know you had one."

I ignored Anna as she walked off into the other room. I put the camera back in my drawer and placed my hand behind my head. Anna came back in with a wet towel. She wiped me thoroughly with it, and then, leaned forward and pecked my lips.

"You don't have much food in the refrigerator. Do you mind if I use your car to go to the store and to go check on my apartment?"

"I don't want you to go alone."

"Kiley, I can't hide out forever. I told Antonio not to go there, but I need to go there to get a few things."

"Then, wait until I put on some clothes so I can go with you."

175

"I want you to get some rest. I'll be okay, trust me."

"I don't trust nobody. That's why if you leave, I want you to take one of my guns with you."

"It would be a waste of time because I don't even know how to shoot a gun, yet alone, hold one. Again, I'll be okay. I'll call you when I get there and I'll call you on my way out."

"Please, be careful," I said.

I didn't want Anna to live a sheltered fucking life because of me, but I damn sure wanted her to be careful.

After she put on her clothes, she held a piece of paper and pen in her hands. "What's the phone number here and give me your cell phone number?"

I looked at her and smiled.

"I know," she said. "It's a darn shame you haven't given neither of them to me."

"I'm not thinking about that. I'm smiling because you're wearing those pants that you said you hated so much."

"I didn't have anything else to put on. So, what's the number?" I called both my home and cell phone numbers out to Anna. Before she left, she gave me a long, wet and juicy kiss.

I hadn't seen Desmon since I dropped him off at Ginger's place on Friday. I was anxious to see him, but I wasn't anxious for him to see how messed up I was.

By the time he made it to the house, it was going on five o'clock. Anna called and said she was on her way back, so that gave Desmon and me a lil time alone. I was still in bed naked and had the covers pulled up to my waist. Desmon went to his room first, and then came into my room.

"What's been up?" he said, maneuvering over to the leather love sack in my room to take a seat. He was getting around pretty good without any crutches.

"Ain't nothing up," I responded while keeping my head straight so he couldn't see my right eye. "I'm just tired."

"You said that you wanted to talk to me about something."

"That was the other day. Since then, I forgot what it was that I wanted to talk to you about." I knew damn well it was about Myles, but I felt no need to dig into that issue right now.

"Why you tired, by the looks of it, you've been in bed all day long?"

"Because I had a fight yesterday."

He smiled. "You too? What chick did you have to put down? I hope to God you wasn't fighting with Anna."

I turned my face so he could see my eye. "If any chick is capable of doing this, you'd better stay the hell away from her."

"Damn!" he said rising up from the love sack. He sat on the edge of my bed to get a closer look. "Who in the fuck did that?"

"Some wanna-be pimp and his boys who think they got the Lou on lock down."

Desmon shook his head. "Whewww, man, they messed you up. Does it hurt? It looks like it really hurts."

I rubbed around my eye. "It really don't hurt, it just feel kind of numb. The bloodshot eye makes it look much worse than it really is."

"Why y'all get into a fight?"

"We was at the racetrack and—

"That was you!" Desmon yelled. "That shit was on the news last night. They said two brothas were killed and the other was in the hospital in serious condition. Here I am thinking you at home chilling and you out blowing moth—

"Desmon, do you know how foul your mouth is? You need to cool out on using so many curse words when you talk to me, man."

"Hey, look, I apologize, but don't try to change the subject. Did you shoot them fools or what?"

"No, it wasn't me. There were several people fighting so it could've been anybody. Besides, did the news say anything about suspects?"

"No, however, I suspect that you just lied to me. You know damn...darn well ain't nobody bust you up like that and they lived to talk about it."

"How was school," I said, quickly changing the subject.

"School is good. After a few more months, you can consider me an upperclassman."

I reached for the remote and turned on my TV. Desmon looked at my hands.

"Aw, yeah. Whoever was caught on the end of them blows, I'm sure it ain't nothing pretty."

"Desmon, get out of my room. Don't you have some homework or something else to do?"

"As a matter of fact, I do. Gabrielle coming over in about an hour or so. You don't mind if I have a lil company, do you?"

"Gabrielle? I thought you and her just had a fight."

"We did, but we made up. We all ways make up."

"Man, you gone learn from those fuck-me then fight-me relationships. Trust me, they ain't no damn good for you."

"Why don't you cool out on the cursing when you talking to your soon. He just might learn something from you," he said, and then got off the bed. He smiled and then exited to his room.

"But, I don't want you to be like me," I yelled out loudly so he could hear me.

He stood in my doorway. "And, I ain't trying to be like you either, but sometimes, shit just happens that way."

I pulled the pillow from behind my back and threw it hard at Desmon. He caught it and held it in his hand.

"You wanna pillow fight, man," he said coming up to me. My body was in no condition, so I declined.

"Man, don't play," I said. "My body is sore, so don't hit me with no pillow."

Of course, he did it anyway and we went at it with the pillows. I quickly got tired from holding the sheet around my waist while still in bed pounding him with a pillow. I sat back and held my arm up to block his pillow punches.

"Man, stop," I said, while holding my side.

Desmon held the pillow in his hand. "You messed up ain't you? Or maybe, that body of yours getting too old."

I smiled and cut my eyes at him. He then took the pillow and hit me in the face.

"I told you to quit playing, didn't I?" I said. He dropped the pillow on the floor and I grabbed him by his injured leg.

"Ahhh...don't play now. My leg ain't fully recovered yet."

"Good," I said and pulled his leg on the bed. I put my body weight down on it and didn't move.

"Oooo, Kiley, man, don't do that. Please don't do that."

"You gone stop playing?"

"Yes, I...I quit. Now, let my leg go."

178

"Please."

"Please, let my leg go."

"Daddy, please let my leg go."

"Okay, Kiley, please let my leg go."

"I said...Daddy, let my leg go."

"Oh, Daddy, I love you so much so would you please let my leg go."

I couldn't resist his bullshit choice of words and released his leg. He put his leg on the floor and limped towards the door. Before he left, he picked up the pillow from the floor and threw it at me.

Anna had made it back. She was in the kitchen cooking us something to eat while I lay on the floor and tried to do some sit-ups with a seventy-five pound weight laying flat on my bare stomach. The only way to stop pain was to bring more pain and I was doing just that as I strained to make it to five hundred. After I finished my sit-ups, I sat on the bed and pressed weights above my head. My arms and hands were still sore, but after a while, I didn't feel a thing.

Dripping with sweat, I placed the weights on the floor and got down on my hands and the tips of my toes. Before I started my push-ups, Anna came in and sat on the bed.

"Don't you think you're overdoing it?" she asked.

"Nope," I said, while kneeled down. "Would you like to help me?"

"Help you how? You seem to have everything under control."

I pulled Anna from the bed and laid her on the floor. I pulled up on my hands and tips of my toes, while she was underneath me.

"One," I said, lowering myself to do my push up. I kissed her on my way down. I rose up and went back down. "Two." I kissed her again. I rose up and lowered myself again. "Um," I mumbled, as my lips smacked with hers for a long time. "Um, um, um," I continued each time I made my way up and down on her. When I'd gotten to at least the twentieth "Um" Anna wrapped her legs around my waist to stop me. She placed her arms on my shoulders and pulled my head to her. We kissed for an even longer time and I rubbed my hands up and down her legs. I eased my hand to her inner thigh and moved her panties over to the side. Anna grabbed my hand.

"Kiley, no," she whispered. "Desmon is in the next room and I don't want him to hear us. Besides, the door is wide open."

179

Since we were close by the door, I reached out with my hand and closed it. It slammed shut.

"Now what's your excuse," I said, lowering my shorts to my thighs. I reached for her panties and moved them to the side again.

"I don't have an excuse, but we just did this earlier today."

"That was a quickie. It only lasted for about fifteen minutes."

Anna looked as if she really didn't want to do it, so I backed up and helped her off the floor. She sat on the bed and scooted back.

"Come on," she said hesitantly. "Let's finish."

"Na, that's au-ight. Don't go doing me no favors."

"Are you mad at me?"

"Naw, I'm not mad at you, but I don't think it's fair for you to come in here and tease me either. Then, change your mind and say you don't feel like it."

"I didn't say that I didn't feel like it."

"Well, reminding me that we already did it earlier means you don't want to do it now."

"Stop the tedious bickering with me and let's just do it."

"Don't ever feel as if you have to compromise yourself," I said, walking to the door. "If you ain't feeling me enough to let loose sometimes or get creative then maybe you should be with somebody else." I opened the door and walked out.

After I looked and saw that Desmon's door was closed, I went to the bathroom to soak in the tub. Earlier, it was the best thing Anna could have suggested, so before shutting down for the night, I wanted to have the feeling of relaxation as I did before.

I'd been soaking in bubbles and water for about an hour. I was leaned back with my head against the back of the tub. My eyes were closed and my mind was in deep thought. Sooner, more than later, I knew I had to shake, rattle and roll. I planned on calling Rufus tomorrow, so he could assist me in settling my differences with Dominique. Since he wasn't already six-feet under, I had to make sure he was put there. If I didn't, I'd already learned from my procrastination, when I suffered from the lost of Kareem. Therefore, I knew it was in my interest to make the next move and make it as soon as I could.

Still in deep thought, I turned my head when Anna came into the bathroom with the phone in her hand. She had a disturbing look on her face and was quite pissed off.

"Instead of telling her I don't please you, why couldn't you tell me? Honestly," she said, moving her head from side to side. "I don't even know why I'm still here."

She tossed the phone to me and it almost dropped in the water. I caught it as it almost slipped through my hands. I quickly placed the phone on my ear because I knew it was Jada.

"What did you say to her?" I asked.

"I told the non-fucking bitch like it is. If she can't handle the dick, then that's too bad. I can."

I hung up on Jada and hurried to get out of the tub. She continued to call back and that's when I picked up the phone and lost it.

"You're a stupid ass bitch, Jada! Don't call my fucking house no more!" I yelled.

"I wasn't no bitch when you were fucking me! Just—

I hung up and left the phone disconnected. I wrapped the towel around me and walked into the kitchen to where Anna was. She pretended to be occupied with dinner, but by the way she slammed shit around, I could tell she was mad.

"What did she say to you?" I asked, and took a seat at the table.

She wouldn't turn around but I saw her wipe a tear from her eye. "She told me that she'd been with you. She said that you went to the *Hampton Inn* with her and had sex. Did she lie?"

"You damn right she lied! Baby, Jada is always interfering with my relationships. We stayed together for a long time and she has a hard time letting shit go!"

Anna turned around. "Then, when did you...why did you tell her about you and me?"

"I didn't. The only thing I told her is I'd met somebody who I wanted to be with."

"Was that before or after you fucked her?"

"I said I didn't fuck her!"

Anna spoke in a soft tone. "You are such a liar. She told me what an eventful day she had with you and how well you and her sweated together. She also told me you said I didn't know how to fuck you and that you wish I could fuck you like she does. And you know what, Kiley, I believe her."

"Fine, Anna! Believe her over me! I'm telling you how crazy that bitch is and you won't even listen to me!"

"Oh, I'll believe you. After I get tested for STD's tomorrow, and I come back clean, I'll certainly believe what you say. Jada told me her husband gave her an STD and she gave it to you. If you haven't slept with her, then I should be okay, right?"

My heart dropped but I still kept with my lie. "Yeah…you gone be cool cause I ain't got nothing."

"The reason why I didn't want to have sex with you a little while ago is because I had a heavy discharge earlier. I wasn't sure what was wrong with me but I guess by now, we both know what it is. I'd hate more than anything to go to the doctor tomorrow and get even more embarrassed. Why don't you just tell me the truth so I can be prepared?"

I was silent, and in disgust, I dropped my head. I clinched my hands together and looked up at Anna. "I've tried so hard to make this right between us. I'm feeling for you like I've never felt for no woman in my entire life. Every time I attempt to show you how much I care about you, I fail. I…I enjoy making love to you, but I'm a brotha who likes to get down when I'm having sex. I like to kick up a sweat with my woman and get creative—

"So, that's why you fucked her?"

"I…yes, I did. Only once. However, it was an acid—

Anna moved forward and smacked the shit out of me. "You will never find a woman who will love you like I did." She slightly raised her voice. "I gave you all I could and it still wasn't good enough. I feel so sorry for you, Kiley, and it's a shame that you were too damn stubborn and stupid to know a good thing when you had it."

"I don't like that you're talking in the past. I know you ain't gone walk out on me over some bullshit like this. I never made a commitment to you or to anybody. I never said I was sleeping with you and only you."

"You just can't stop the lies, can you? And neither can I. Jada didn't tell me that she had an STD. I made that up to get the truth out of you. She did tell me about the hotel, but look what I had to resort to in order to get to the truth. Either way, I'm done with this, Kiley. You can screw whoever you want to screw, but it for damn sure won't be me anymore. Especially, since I'm not creative enough for you anyway."

She walked out of the kitchen and into my room. I followed behind her and sat on the bed as she pulled my oversized t-shirt over her head. She stood in her bra and panties and reached for her jeans.

I held my face in my hand, as I could feel a headache coming down. "Don't go," I begged. "I know you're upset with me, but there's so many things you just don't understand. For the record, making love to you takes me to a world that I've never been to. Of course I want us to be more creative, but I still enjoy being with you. I said something to that affect to Jada, and explained to her why I didn't deserve you after having sex with her. If you give me one more chance, I prom...I know I won't let you down."

Anna continued to put on her clothes and ignore me. I got up and stood in front of her. "Baby, do you hear what I'm saying to you? Don't go. Please don't leave me. I need you. I've needed you every day since I met you. I just had a hard time dealing with my feelings, that's all."

She reached for the phone on my dresser and called for a taxi. After she gave the dispatcher my address, she plopped down on the bed. She covered her face with her hands and wiped the tears that had fallen from her eyes.

I sat next to her and held her. "Don't cry like that. You make me feel like shit when you cry like that because of me. I've been trying hard to be right by you but I'm not perfect. Nobody's perfect."

Anna didn't say one word as I continued to hold her. And when I heard the horn from the taxi, I asked her again to stay. She stood up and reached for her purse on my dresser. She placed it on her shoulder, grab the few pieces of clothing she'd gotten from her place earlier and headed for the door. By this time, I didn't care if I'd made a fool of myself. I knew she was the only woman who'd ever truly loved me and I wasn't about to let her leave. I hurried off the bed and grabbed her arm.

"If you walk out that door, I'm not coming after you," I said. She snatched away and continued to make her way to it. When she opened the front door, she turned to face me.

"Goodbye, Kiley. I wish you well."

I was irate. I ran up to the door and pounded it as she stood in front of it. "I said don't go! Please! Do...Don't you know how much I love you! Can't you see it! Can't you feel it! Damn, baby, I tried!"

Just then, Desmon walked out of his room.

"What is up?" he asked. "What's all the noise?"

I ignored him and looked at Anna as my eyes watered. "Please," I said, for the last time as a tear had found it's way down my cheek.

Desmon stood and waited for an answer with me.

She pointed her finger at me and spoke sternly. "No more bullshit from you, Kiley. I don't like how you've put me on the spot like this and if you ever lie to me again, I'm leaving your behind for good."

"You got a deal," I said, feeling relieved. I pulled her to me and placed her head against my chest. Desmon yelled out at the taxi, "I don't think she needs you!" As we moved away from the door, he closed it and stood in the foyer.

"I must say, Dad, that was one hell of a plea." He laughed. I was in no mood to joke around with him, as I still had Anna in my arms.

"Desmon, go back to your room. Now ain't the time or the place."

He walked off to his room and closed the door behind him.

Still feeing a bit uneasy about her decision to stay, Anna loosened my arms from around her and walked back into my room. She got in bed with her clothes on and lay on her side. Allowing her some time to chill, I turned down the lights and went to the kitchen to get something to eat. After I ate, I lay across the couch and chilled in the living room for the rest of the night.

MAMA'S BABY,
DADDY'S MAYBE

It's time to shake, rattle and roll. That's what Rufus said after I told him about what had went down between Dominique and me. I even told him about Jada's husband Dwayne and Rufus insisted, as I did, that it was time for everybody to get taken care of.

Desmon hadn't gone to school because he claimed his leg was hurt from me leaning on it. I knew that was bullshit, but I wasn't up for arguing with him this morning. As for Anna, she was still asleep. I lie back on the couch and quietly spoke to Rufus because I didn't want Anna or Desmon to hear what my plans were with him.

"So, after we do this, you coming back home, right?"

"I told you I was. Ain't gone be no need for me to keep hanging around here."

"You know that cock sucker Dominique got some fellas down here running a petty game for him. I knew that bastard was a playa hater the day I saw him. I also had a feeling some shit was gone go down between y'all."

"I kind of had that feeling too. I'll get all his information for you and call you later on in the week with it."

"See, you need to think, Kiley. You should've had that shit a long time ago. If that motherfucker had taken you out at the racetrack, we would've been in the dark. And you know how much I hate being in the dark when it comes to shit like that."

"You wouldn't have been in the dark because Anna would have told you."

"Man, I'on trust no bitch to tell me nothing! How you know her ass ain't five-o? After what happened to you before, you should be a bit more skeptical about your selection of bitches. If she got a purse or something laying around there, go get it and give me her social security number so I can have her checked out."

"It ain't even that serious. You starting to sound more paranoid than me. Now, I'll call you back with Dominique—

"Too late. I already got it. See, why you been down there in the Lou playing house, I had your back. Dominique got a big mouth. So big that I heard it all the way here in L.A. Rumor had it that even though you saved his ass from Candi, he was worried about you ratting him out.

That's why I came to the Lou. I know where the nigga lives. I know where his mama lives, and where every last one of his kids live. If you wanna know the nigga net worth, I know that too."

"Killer, you sound like you got problems with me or something."

"I got problems because you let them poot-butt rooty-too ass imitation gangstas roll on you like that. And, in front of your bitch too? Those niggas are weak, man. Including Jada ole lousy ten thousand dollars per month making starving druggist ass fool."

I couldn't help but laugh at how upset Rufus was. "I thought it was a starving artist, playa."

"That nigga a starving druggist. He'll be broke by the end of the year. If not, dead."

We both laughed.

"Ain't shit funny," he said, laughing his damn self. "How much more time we got?"

"Give me a month. By then, every thing should have calmed down and nobody will suspect nothing."

"One month from today, I'm on my way to the Lou. I'm not even gone let you know I'm there, but my presence will be known. No later than two days after, I'll see you back in L.A."

"You gone throw me a party?"

"The biggest one you've ever seen."

"See you in a month, Killer."

He hung up and shortly after called back. "Did you forget something?" I asked.

"Naw, you did."

"What?"

"Nigga, get that pussy off your mind and go get that bitch purse."

"Man, you gone have to hold it down on the bitches. I told you how much I'm feeling Anna."

He snickered. "Are you telling me pussy comes before partna? Our motto has always been to never put pussy before partna."

I hesitated knowing how much I felt for Anna. "Rufus, you know you—

"I want you to think about something. The night you met Anna was Dominique there?"

I thought back to the first time I met her. "Yeah…yeah he was. He was there with Candi."

186

"Okay, now rewind the tape again. When we saw Dominique at the club, wasn't Anna there that night as well?"

"Yes. Yes she was."

"Good. Now, my last and final question...when you were getting the living shit beat out of you, who was there? Not only that, but at anytime, did that bitch pick up something and try to bust a motherfucker's head clean open for you? I don't know much about love, but if you lovvve somebody, in a situation like that, the ho should've helped!"

"Man, you grasping at straws. She ain't even like that."

"Jada would've helped. Any time we scraped, she scraped right along with us. There wasn't nobody who made it to you unless they went through her. I'on like that bitch either, but at least she had your back."

"That's because she's fucking ghetto. Anna ain't like that. And for your information, she did help me."

"And let me guess...she walked away from the whole damn thing with maybe a minor scratch on her face."

"Somebody did hit her," I said, in Anna's defense.

"What's the SS number?"

I'd already had Anna's purse in my hand and searched through it. I called her SS number off quickly to Rufus and he laughed.

"You my nigga," he said, and then hung up.

The house was still quiet so I crept slowly to my room to check on Anna. She was still in her jeans and shirt from yesterday and was knocked the hell out. Desmon's door was closed so I didn't want to bother him. Instead, I went into the kitchen and poured a bowl of milk and cereal. I took it back into the living room and turned on the TV. Seeing some rump shakers in a rap video, I sat back and watched.

When Anna came into the room, I was all into it. She actually cleared her throat to get my attention. I dropped my spoon in my bowl and placed it on the table. I then picked up the remote and turned off the television.

"Good morning," I said.

"I already said good morning, but you didn't hear me. It's a bit early to be watching porn, don't you think?" She sat in the chair and folded her legs up to her chest.

"That wasn't no porn. That was a rap video."

"Call it whatever you'd like, but it looked like porn to me."

I left the situation alone.

Anna looked down at the floor and I could tell she had something on her mind. I waited until she was ready to say what it was. Soon, she did.

"Is Jada prettier than me?"

"No," I answered without hesitation.

"Than Ginger?"

"No."

"So, she just has better sex with you than I do?"

I hesitated and then answered. "No."

"I thought I asked you not to lie to me anyone."

"Okay, then yes. Jada and me have good sex together."

"Better than you and me?"

"You just asked that question. I answered, and baby, it is what it is. I'm not wanting you to be Jada, though. I want you to be yourself. I love you for who you are."

She placed her feet on the floor and stood up. She came over to where I was and lay on the couch while resting her head on my lap. She looked up at me.

"When is the last time you told someone you love them?"

"Five seconds ago."

"I mean, before that."

"Last night."

She let out a sigh. "Before then."

"Almost a week ago."

"Who?"

"Desmon."

"What about a female?"

"It's been so long that I can't remember."

"So, you never told Ginger you loved her?"

"Never. And that's because I didn't. When I say those words, I mean them."

Anna turned on her side and stared in front of her. "I've never said I love you to anyone before other than you and Antonio. I truly mean it from the bottom of my heart and I hope you do as well."

188

Again, I kept quiet. I knew for damn sure that I didn't say "I love you" to anybody unless I meant it. Thing is, though, I wasn't going to spend my entire morning trying to convince Anna that I did.

"Have you noticed I haven't been to work since I've been here with you?"

"I didn't even know—

"I got that job Ginger told me about at the nursing home. I'm sure by now they've fired me."

"Who cares," I said. "I got plenty of money."

"How do you get it?"

I didn't answer, as our conversation was starting to sound all too familiar. I had flashbacks from Candi's and my conversations.

"What's up with all the questions this morning?"

"I've just been thinking—a lot. Thinking about how can you love me and you know so little about me."

"I guess the same way you can love me and know so little about me."

"I'm just trying to get to know you better."

When Desmon walked out of his room, he saved our conversation from going any further. He limped into the living room like his leg was in dying pain. He stood up and rubbed up and down his leg.

"Don't come in here trying to make me feel sorry for you," I said. "You might wanna call and cuss Gabrielle out for not leaving here until damn near two in the morning."

"Her moms had to work late. She couldn't come get her until she got off work."

"Then, I suspect that all the overtime must be why your leg hurt."

"You might have a point," he said while nodding his head.

"Both of you are crazy," Anna said. "Have you talked to Antonio, Desmon? I didn't get a chance to talk to him yesterday."

"Yeah, he's been over Michelle's house since you told him not to go home. I told that fool he might as well move in because he don't never go home."

"Never," Anna said. "I told him the same thing."

"What's a young man to do when he's in love? Antonio's been digging her since they were in third grade."

"He sure has. And she's a nice girl too."

Desmon cleared his throat, as if the statement Anna made wasn't true. When Anna pressed for more info, he pretended his leg was hurting from standing up and left the room.

"You two have a lot in common," she said.

Before I could respond, the phone rang. Before I could look to see who it was. Anna grabbed it. She didn't recognize the name so she handed the phone to me. It was Rufus.

"Hello," I said.

"What did I tell you?" he yelled.

My heart raced as Anna continued to lie on my lap. "About what?"

"About your bitch, nigga!"

"What about him," I said, trying to play it off. I was so ready to break Anna's fucking neck as she lay on my lap.

"I told you to watch yo back, didn't I?"

I raised my voice. "Just get to the point!"

Rufus laughed. "She all good. But, baby-girl used to be a BOOSTA! Way back when, she did two days in jail for shoplifting but for the most part she cool. She also got a warrant out, though, for some unpaid tickets. And lastly, my brotha, she did not finish high school."

"Straight," I said. "That nigga got a good head on his shoulders, though."

"I do, don't I. Sometimes, dropouts like myself might have it like that."

"You the man," I said. "You are no doubtfully the man. Thanks."

"Much love, Daddy O. I'll see ya in a bit."

Rufus hung up, and no doubt, I felt relieved about Anna.

I had much to prepare for and little time to do it. Since I had every intention of moving back to L.A., I still had some unresolved issues with Ginger. In addition, I wasn't sure how I'd break the news to Desmon or Anna. I wanted both of them to come with me, but I had a feeling it wasn't going to be that easy.

Anna was in the kitchen cleaning up, and Desmon had asked me to take him over to Michelle's house where Antonio was. I'd broke the bad news to him about his raggedy ass car and he had the nerve to ask me to buy him another one. Even though I wanted to, there was so many other things I had to do with my money.

Before we'd left the house, Desmon called Ginger to chat with her for a few minutes. He stayed on the phone with her for about ten minutes, and then, passed the phone to me.

"What's going on?" I said, after placing the phone on my ear.

"I hope you're happy that you've taken my son away from me."

"You've had him for over fifteen years. I'm sure these several weeks ain't been the end of the world for you."

"This place has been too damn quiet. Now, I ain't gone lie because I have enjoyed it, but I miss my baby too."

"Hmm..." I said, keeping it short.

"Listen, I got some more of your money. It ain't much, but it's something. If you want to stop by later on to get it you can."

"I just might do that. I need to talk to you about something else anyway."

"About what?" she said. Since Desmon was still close by, I walked into my room and closed the door.

"You can keep the money if you tell me the truth about something."

"I know what you're getting ready to ask me and I have told you the truth. Myles is not Desmon's father. Why can't you get that through your thick fucking head!"

"Ginger, I saw a picture of him. There are some resemblances."

"So what, nigga! I know who my baby daddy is."

"Do you really expect me to take your word for it? I just wanted you to know I'm gonna open up a can of worms real soon. Ginger, you better not had lied to me."

"Come get your damn money," she said, and then hung up.

Desmon was still messing around in his room, so I headed towards the kitchen with Anna. She still seemed a bit uneasy, so I didn't walk up and kiss her like I normally did. Instead, I stood in the doorway and told her Desmon and me would be back.

"Would you bring some detergent back with you so I can wash your clothes?" She stood at the sink washing the dishes and wouldn't turn around.

"Yes, I'll get some detergent. I'll wash them, though. You don't have to. Do you need anything else while I'm out?"

She moved her head from side to side. I felt bad because it was obvious she was still hurting. Not only that, but I knew she was feeling insecure about Jada and about not being able to please me like she wanted to. I walked up from behind and put my arms around her. Not saying a word to her, I kissed her cheek and down her neck when she tilted her head to the side.

"Don't look so sad," I said. "We got a lot to look forward to, okay?"

She nodded and I backed away from her. Desmon yelled that he was ready, and feeling as if Anna didn't want to be bothered, I left.

On the ride to Michelle's house, Desmon kept complaining about the splint on his leg and said that he wanted it off. I reminded him that his leg hadn't healed yet, but he insisted it was time. I told him about the time Jada cracked my wrist and how I cut the cast off with a knife. He laughed and said sooner or later, the splint would be history. Knowing that removing it would probably do more damage to his leg than good, especially since he still wanted to play football, I told him that was not a good idea. But, did he ever listen to me? Hell, no. I was sure the splint would be off by the end of the night.

I pulled in front of Michelle's house and Desmon couldn't wait to get out.

"Can I get a thanks or something," I said.

"Aw," he said, holding onto the door. "Thanks. And, ask Moms to give you my navy blue and white tennis shoes."

"I will. But, remember that you got school tomorrow. Don't stay over here all night."

"I might. I might catch a ride to school with them in the morning. If I do, I'll call you."

I didn't argue with him because Anna and me needed some time alone. Instead, I reminded him to call again and he said that he would.

Ginger's place wasn't too far away, so I turned up my system and made my way there. It was such a beautiful day outside and it was obvious that many other people thought so as well. Kids were hanging out, as if there wasn't any school, and grown-ups were chilling on porches because their houses were probably too stuffy.

When I pulled into a parking spot in front of Ginger's townhouse, these two young punks were making a transaction right in front of me. I started to scare them by telling them I was five-o, but instead, I left well enough alone.

I walked up to Ginger's door and knocked. I stood there for about two minutes, and when she didn't answer, I knocked harder. Since I'd talked to her less than a few hours ago, I knew she was there. I figured she was probably inside getting her fuck on.

I banged for a few more minutes, and after getting pissed, I turned the knob on the door. It was unlocked, but before I went inside, I pulled my gun out from inside of my pants. I didn't know what was up, but I had a feeling something wasn't right. A set-up? Maybe. I wasn't fosho, and I wasn't taking any chances.

Either way, I slowly pushed the door open and walked in. I immediately called for Ginger, but she didn't answer. I called again, still nothing. My eyes quickly searched the living room, and soon after, I made my way to her bedroom. There was no sign of her, so I walked past the dining room and made my way to the kitchen. Still, she wasn't there. After searching around for a few more minutes, it was evident that she wasn't. I guess she'd left and forgot to lock the door. Feeling as if my paranoia was starting to get the best of me again, I sat down in the kitchen to calm my nerves. I took a few deep breaths and placed my gun back down inside my pants.

As I'd sat in deep thought, I was kind of upset that Ginger told me to come get my money, but then, had the nerve to leave and not call. It also surprised me that her place was cleaner than I'd ever seen it and nothing seemed to be out of place.

Soon, after sitting a bit longer, I walked back into her bedroom to see if she'd left my money on her dresser or something. My money wasn't there, but cocaine residue was visible on her dresser and on the table next to her bed. I shook my head and headed downstairs to get Desmon's tennis shoes. I flicked the light switch at the top of the stairs, but the light didn't come on. I could see a sliver of light coming from the small window in the basement, so that allowed me to find my way down the steps. As I made it to the bottom, I saw Ginger lying across Desmon's bed.

"Didn't you hear me call your name," I said. She didn't answer, as she appeared to be sound asleep. "Ginger," I yelled, and then pulled on the light string from above my head. When the light came on, Ginger hadn't moved. I kneeled on the bed and turned her body over. It was limp and her eyes were rolled to the back of her head.

"Ginger," I yelled, while shaking her. Panicking, I felt her body for blood and looked to see if someone had strangled her. It wasn't until I saw an empty prescription bottle on the floor when I'd realized what she'd done.

Realizing it, I pulled her body to the floor and pumped hard on her chest.

"Damn you, Ginger!" I yelled. "Breathe!" I pumped harder and opened her mouth. I felt inside for anything that I could feel, but nothing was there. I quickly pulled her neck back and took long deep breaths into her mouth. "Breathe!" I yelled, each time I forced my air inside of her. Nothing came of it, so I started to pump her chest once again.

"You are not going to do this to my son!" I angrily yelled and pounded her chest harder.

After trying to revive Ginger for about fifteen minutes, I knew it was a lost cause. Sweat dripped from my forehead as I sat up on the floor with her head resting across my lap. I closed my eyes and heavily breathed in and out.

"Why did you fucking do this?" I said, talking to myself. "Damn!"

I sat silently for a moment longer, and then, slowly placed Ginger's body back on the floor.

This shit was starting to be too much for me to handle and I couldn't believe there seemed to be no light at the end of my tunnel. I'll be damned if history didn't just repeat itself. I knew how I felt when my mother committed suicide, and now I had to put Desmon through the same excruciating pain I experienced when Papa Abrams had to break the news to me.

I thought about why Ginger would do something so stupid and reached for the sheets on Desmon's bed to cover her up. When an envelope dropped to the floor, I reached down to pick it up. The front of it had Desmon's name on it, so I opened it up.

"My beloved son," it read. *"I'm sorry I had to do this, but I felt as if the time was right. You have Kiley now and after many years of failing you, I failed myself too. I know that a big part of you felt as if I didn't love you, but I truly did. I loved you how I wanted to, and at times my love wasn't good enough. Yes, I could have done things differently, but I was so wrapped up in my own life that I didn't have time for you. When I started using drugs two years ago, I began to hate myself even*

more. I allowed them to take over me and over the priorities in my life. I hurt you by letting my men misuse you and I know you'll always hate me for it. It's something I can't explain, but my stupidity prevailed. Lastly, my baby, I owe you the truth about something that has always been heavy on my mind. I know Kiley told you about him possibly not being your father. And like I said, I'm the one who owes you the truth. Kiley is the daddy that you will know and will always know. A man that I dated by the name of Myles Stein was your real father. He was killed when you were only two years old, and since I wanted you to have a father, I continued on with my lie. I never wanted you to know the truth as you grew up because Kiley was the father that I wanted you to have. He had money that I knew could take care of you, so therefore, I had to do what was best for you. I wanted the best life for my baby and I knew with him being your father you'd someday have it. Now, you're where you need to be and where you should always be, with him. I'm where I want to be and please don't hate me for it. Grow up and be a good man and never look back at this horrible lifet I somehow managed to create for you. Love, Mama.

I was zoned out while reading Ginger's letter and had backed into the wall. I was too numb to move, so I stood there as the tears poured heavily down my face. Wanting desperately to scream, I couldn't. Wanting to kill anybody...somebody, I couldn't do that either. The pain I had in my chest after reading her letter was unlike no other. After all this fucking time, Desmon wasn't even my own flesh and blood. I couldn't believe what Ginger had done to me, or to the only kid I'd known and loved as my son. I stood for a moment longer and that's when I lost it. My head started spinning around the room and I gave quick swift punches to the air in front of me. As the punches got harder and faster, I started making a complete mess of Desmon's room. I started with the trophies on his shelves and broke them in pieces. I tore the posters down from his walls and smashed his TV on the ground. I hurried to his closet, reached for his clothes and I pulled them apart with my hands. No doubt, I was beyond angry and couldn't stop myself from destroying his room no matter how hard I tried.

When I did calm down, I dropped to my knees and crawled my way over to Ginger's body. I dropped my head on her chest and loudly cried out.

"Why in the fuck did you do this to me?" I gagged, as the saliva dripped from my mouth. Softly I spoke, as I wished like hell she could hear me. "Damn you, Ginger. Motherfucking damn you!"

Soon, I rose up and wiped the flowing tears from my face. I tore the letter into tiny pieces, straightened my clothes and stood up. I staggered up the steps and walked to the front door. I left it wide open and got into my car. If anybody needed to kill themselves, it damn sure should've been me. After knowing the truth about Desmon, I had no purpose. He was my reasoning for wanting to live. And now, I had to stand face to face with him and tell him not only that his mother was dead, but that he didn't have a father either. I loved him too much to bring hurt to him like that. And I knew if I didn't tell him the truth it would cause him more hurt if he'd ever found out.

Either way, I wasn't prepared to do anything. I drove to the nearest payphone and called emergency so they could send somebody to get Ginger. When the dispatcher questioned me about who I was, I told the lady I was her brother and I'd been the one who found her. I even explained Desmon's room I'd messed up by saying how difficult it was for me when I found her. She said they'd send somebody right over and I got back in my car and headed for home.

Before going inside, I sat in the car for at least an hour. I was a mess and didn't want Anna to see me in this condition for the second day straight. It was obvious that life just wasn't going to get better for me. If it wasn't going to get better for me, then it damn sure wasn't going to get better for her. She didn't deserve all of this and I hated myself for not allowing her to walk out on me last night.

After maintaining some of my composure, I wiped my face with my hands again and got out of my car. I walked to the door and opened it. The house was dark and when I made it back to my bedroom, Anna was lying in bed naked while watching TV. I stood in the doorway and leaned against it.

"Baby, what's wrong," she said, reaching for the lamp to turn it on. She saw the weary look on my face. "Kiley, tell me. Are Desmon and Antonio okay?"

"They're fine," I said softly and then walked over to her.

"Then what—

"I'll tell you about it tomorrow. Just hold me tonight. Tell me you love me and convince me that tomorrow will be a better day."

Before I could take off my clothes and get in the bed with Anna, she stood up and wrapped her arms around me. She told me she loved me, and afterwards, she lay down with me and held me. She made me no promises about tomorrow because I guess she knew, as I did, the chances of shit getting better was slim.

RECOGNIZING MY PURPOSE

The sun was up and it beamed through the window. When I reached for Anna, she was already out of bed. She must have been cooking because the aroma of bacon was in the air. I hadn't gotten a chance to tell her what had happened, but I prepared myself to tell her everything after I got out of bed. I still wasn't sure how to break the news to Desmon, and after his phone call last night, telling him the truth seemed so much harder to do. I told him to make sure he found his way to the crib after school and he insisted he'd have one of his friends bring him home.

I stretched my arms far apart and stood up to look in the mirror. The swellen in my eye had gone down, and for the most part, I could finally see. I still had body aches, but nothing like they'd felt a few days before.

Taking my time, I slowly made my way to the bathroom. I freshened up a bit and put my toothbrush in my mouth. I stood naked and when I finished with my teeth, I gazed into the mirror again. The look of a tired, weary, and angry Black man stared back at me. Confused might have described me as well, but I had to follow through with everything I'd planned. Somehow, I had to make a way out of no way.

As I continued to look in the mirror, Anna walked in and placed her hand on my back. She rubbed up and down it, and then squeezed my hand with hers.

"Tell me what's wrong," she said.

"I will."

"When?"

"Give me a minute."

"Are you hungry?"

"Not really."

"But, you gotta eat something."

"I know. I'll be in the kitchen in a minute."

Anna rubbed my back a little while longer and then walked out. Shortly after, I followed and went into the kitchen to where she was. She'd cooked some pancakes, grits, bacon and eggs. It smelled delicious but my stomach wasn't up for it. I sat at the table and placed my elbows on my knees. I looked down at the floor and gripped my hands together.

198

I spoke in a low voice. "Ginger committed suicide yesterday."

Anna stopped in the midst of putting some food on a plate and turned to me. "Kiley, no. How...Why did she do that? Don't tell me because of you and me. For God's sake—

"No. It wasn't because of our relationship. She just didn't want to live no more."

Anna walked over and pulled a chair in front of me. She sat down, took both of my hands and held them with hers. "I'm sorry. I know how hard this is going to be for you and Desmon. Especially him. He's a strong kid though, Kiley. He's been through a lot. And you and I both will help him get through this. He's going to need you. You're his father and...

I lifted my head and looked Anna directly in her eyes. "I'm not his father, baby. Ginger lied. For all these fucking years, she lied, baby. Now, I got to tell him—

Anna got mad. "You will tell him no such thing! He's been through enough, Kiley. All he's ever known is you as his father and that's all he's going to ever know. I can't believe Ginger would lie about something like that. It just doesn't make sense."

"Well, she did lie. We look so much alike that I really hadn't given it much thought until somebody brought the issue to my attention."

"You both do look alike. She probably just made that story up to hurt you even more. I wouldn't believe that shit for one minute if I were you."

"You might if you see who she says is Desmon's father."

"What's his name?"

I stood up and walked to my room to get Myles picture. It was hidden away in the pocket of my leather jacket so no one would see it. When I went back into the kitchen, I gave the picture to Anna. She gazed at it, and then, looked at me. "So what, baby. You really can't tell much by looking at this picture."

"Anna, spare me. You know damn well that there are some resemblances."

"Yes there are, but like I said before, Desmon looks like you as well. Why mess up a good thing? Nobody ever has to know."

I sat back down in front of Anna.

"So you don't think I should tell him."

"No. Never."

"What if he finds out?"

"How?"

"I don't know. Anything is possible."

"Don't tell him. If he ever finds out, hopefully, he'll be old enough to understand."

I nodded.

There was silence. Anna took my hands again and lifted my face as I continued to look down at the floor. "I hate to ask you this," she said. "And I know how angry you can get at times, but you didn't hurt Ginger after she told you about not being Desmon—

"Do you really think I would do something like that? How could you ask me—?

"Baby, I know how angry you can get. Maybe you don't know, but I've seen with my own eyes how—

I gave Anna a hard stare. "I don't care what you've seen. I would have never taken the mother of my child's life. Especially, knowing how much pain it's gonna cause him."

Anna didn't respond. She looked away, but continued to hold my hands. "Are you afraid of me," I asked. "If you think I just go around killing people because I get a kick out of it then you must be afraid of me."

She looked at me. "I'm very afraid of you. I'm afraid for us and I'm afraid for Desmon. More than anything, I'm afraid that something might happen to you. You live a dangerous life, Kiley. Sometimes I really don't think you realize how dangerous it is."

"First of all, you never have to be afraid of me. I would never hurt you. Sometimes, I'm afraid too. Not for myself because I'm not afraid to die. I am, however, afraid for those who are around me. I feel as if I have to protect y'all and when things happen, as it did in the past, I just go crazy because I feel as if I've failed."

Anna leaned forward and gave me a hug. I rubbed the silkiness of her robe as I embraced her back. She asked me again if I wanted something to eat, and still realizing the difficult task of telling Desmon about Ginger, I declined.

Around five o'clock, I sat quietly in the living room when Desmon had finally made it home. Anna had left about an hour ago so that we could have some time alone. He came rushing through the door with his duffle bag on his shoulder. He dropped it in the foyer and looked into the living room at me. He held his hands far apart from each other.

"Look, man!" he yelled. "Do you notice anything different about me?"

I looked him up and down and noticed his splint had been removed. I slightly smiled. "You just couldn't wait, could you?"

"Nope," he said, strutting into the living room. He took a seat in the chair across from me. I gave him a long hard stare, as I wanted to see myself in him so badly. I'd been comparing him to Kareem all along, but maybe it was my way of dealing with the pain of missing him so much.

"What you staring at?" he said, looking behind him. "Do you see a ghost?"

"Na, I was just thinking."

"You always thinking. I told you before and I'll tell you again, you got issues. Big issues."

I was silent. Desmon thought I didn't want to be bothered so he stood up and said that he was going to his room.

"Sit down for a minute. I need to tell you something."

He sat back down. "I hope everything cool, man. We been getting along pretty good and it's a miracle that I haven't had to put you in your place," he joked.

"I've enjoyed my time with you too. You have no idea how much these several weeks have meant to me. I hope we can continue to have a father and son relationship that gets stronger and stronger by the day."

"We'll see," he said, smiling and nodding his head. "Living with you ain't as bad as I thought it would be. I just might decide to stay the summer with you, who knows."

"How about just staying the rest of your life with me?"

"Man, Ginger wouldn't like that. I got to share the love, don't I? Besides, who wants to live with you for the rest of their life? I hope to have my own crib someday."

"You know what I mean. I want you to stay with me until you're capable of making it on your own."

"I hear you. But I ain't gone be in the middle of you and Ginger arguments about—

"Desmon, I'm sorry. But, Ginger...Ginger ain't here no more. She committed suicide yesterday. I found her body when I went to her place after I dropped you off."

He took a hard swallow. "She what? Committed suicide? She...she wouldn't do nothing like that. Stop lying, man. You just want me to stay with you."

"I wouldn't lie about nothing like that, Desmon. I'm sorry—

"This is bullshit, man!" He hopped up. "I'm going home. Take me home, nigga!"

"I can't," I said, as I watched him about to lose it. He picked up the phone on the table and dialed Ginger's number.

"I'm gone have my Moms come get me," he said, waiting for her to answer. "I'm through fucking with you Kiley. After this, I'm through fucking with you!"

I stood up and slowly walked up to him. I place my hand on the phone to take it off his ear and he snatched it away. "Move," he yelled. He hung up and dialed the number again. I stood in front of him and said nothing, as there still was no answer. "Damn," he said, getting ready to dial the number again. I snatched the phone from him, and as I was about to put it on the table, he pushed the side of my face. My head turned.

"I hate you, man," he started to cry. "I swear to God I hate you!" He quickly made his way to his room and opened his door. I followed and watched as he gathered his things as if he was getting ready to leave.

"I can't believe you would do me like this," he said, slamming his shoes into a duffle bag.

"That's because I wouldn't. I don't know why Ginger did what she did, but I ain't going nowhere. I'm here if you need me—

"Well, I don't," he said looking at me with tears pouring down his face. He stopped stuffing his bag for a moment, picked up his football and threw it into the glass mirror on his bed. The entire glass shattered and crashed to the floor. "I wish I was dead!" He yelled. "I wish I was never fucking born!" I felt his hurt and tried to stay as strong as possible for his sake. "I don't need nobody.! No damn body! I'm tired of being fucked over! What did I ever do to deserve parents like this?"

"Nothing. We just fucked up, Desmon, and it had nothing to do with you. I promise to make it right. You have my word that I'm not giving up on you...on us. Just—

"Promise?" he yelled in a high pitch. He darted his finger at me over and over again as he spoke, "You promised when I was a kid that you'd never leave me, you've been promising for months that this shit was gone some day work out, Mama promised that she would never fucking leave me, but so much for that, huh? Not once have either of you lived up to your promises! I don't understand why y'all fucking brought me in this world to begin with! If you wasn't gone take care of me then you should have left my ass where I was!"

I walked further into the room and all I wanted to do was wrap my arms around him. I'll be damned if he didn't say the same things I said to Papa Abrams when he'd told me about my mother. Even though she'd hurt us by being the mother she'd chose to be, it was still a devastating blow because Kareem and I both knew she could never be replaced.

"I feel your pain," I said, walking towards Desmon.

"Oh, you don't have a clue!"

"Yes, I do. Your grandmother, my mother, left here the same way Ginger did. I was even younger than you, but Papa Abrams told us to be strong, and said that no matter what, we'd all make it. He was much like me, and the days, months, and years following my mother's departure, I made it because of him. Now, I made some mistakes, but every time I did, I always had him to turn to. What I'm saying man is, I can't turn back the hands of time, but I'm here for you now. For as long as I'm allowed to breathe on this earth, I am your father and that's who I will forever be."

Desmon sat on the bed and dropped his head. Tears continued to pour profusely from his eyes and snot drizzled from his nose. He turned his head to the side and looked at me. "Wha…what I'm gone do when you die? Then I ain't gone have nobody."

"I'm not gone die," I said, walking over and sitting next to him. "What makes you think I'm gone die?"

He wiped his nose. "Cause I dream about it. I dream about you getting killed all the time."

"Well, that ain't gone happen. I'm a survivor, Desmon. I've endured probably more than anybody you've known or anybody you'll ever meet. There's a purpose for my being around and I'm not quite ready to go yet."

"You might be a survivor, but you ain't invincible."

"No, I'm not. But, hey, nobody is."

I sat quietly next to Desmon, as he continued to let out his emotions. After he'd calmed down a bit, I told him to call his grandmother because I was sure she'd been looking for him.

The next few days ranked in the top five of the saddest days in my life. Desmon, along with Anna and Antonio prepared to attend Ginger's funeral. I couldn't stand seeing my son in any more pain than he'd already been in. I'd listened to his cries throughout the night and faced his weary and confused look every morning that he woke up. I was angry. Angry with myself for not being a better father than what I could have been, and angry with Ginger for bailing out and leaving me to deal with the effects.

At this point, I didn't even care that she lied to me about being Desmon's father, because as far as I was concerned, he never belonged to Myles, he always belonged to me.

Anna was a bit disappointed with me for not attending Ginger's funeral, but I explained to her my reasoning. The last thing Desmon needed was to see me fall apart in front of him. There was no doubt that I'd lose it, and I refused to let him know how unstable I really was. Besides, being around the police wasn't in my best interest either. I knew there were warrants out for my arrest and the last thing I needed was to be placed back in jail. Desmon fosho would be lost, so I had to keep a low profile until I made my way back to L.A.

When the funeral was over, Desmon, Anna and Antonio made their way back to the house. Desmon was suited up in all black and his black sunglasses covered the swollenness in his eyes. I greeted them at the door and was surprised when I saw him smile as he talked to Antonio. I hadn't seen him smile since I broke the news to him, so it was certainly a good feeling inside.

"Did you cook like I asked you too," Anna said, walking through the door.

"I sure did. I don't know how good it's going to taste, though." She gave me a peck on the lips, and after Antonio spoke, him and Desmon walked past me.

I wasn't sure if I should ask about the funeral so I waited until somebody said something to me. Desmon and Antonio went into his room and closed the door. Soon after, the music thumped loudly so I figured they were okay.

"How did it go?" I whispered to Anna and followed her to the bedroom.

"You should have come. It was tough…real tough, but I told you that Desmon's a strong kid."

"Just like his Daddy, huh?"

"Yeah," she said, reaching up on the tips of her toes to give me a kiss. "Just like his Daddy."

We walked into the kitchen and Anna looked around for the food. "I smell it, but I don't see it," she said.

"Have a seat," I said, pulling the chair back for her. She sat down and smiled. I grabbed a potholder and opened the oven. I pulled out one of the four chicken TV dinners I had inside and placed it on the table.

"It's hot, so be careful," I said.

"You've got to be kidding me. Is this what you call dinner?"

"I'm not a chef, baby. This is the best I can do."

She laughed and pulled the plastic film from over the top. "If I wasn't so hungry, I swear I wouldn't eat this."

Just then, Antonio and Desmon came into the kitchen. "What's up for dinner?" Antonio asked. I walked over to the oven and pulled out the other two dinners. They both looked at each other.

"Do you mind if I use your car to go get something else to eat?" Desmon asked. "That just don't look too good to me."

"Me either," Antonio said.

I hesitated, but then, told Desmon the keys were in my room on the dresser.

As Antonio waited for Desmon to get the keys, I went into my room and closed the door behind me. He stood by my dresser searching for my keys. When he saw them, he put them in his hand.

"Are you gone be okay?" I said, walking up to him.

"Yeah, I'm cool."

"If you need to talk, you know I'm here."

"How many times you got to say it." He smiled.

I pointed my finger at his head. "Until you get it though your thick head."

"I got it," he said, and then walked towards the door. He put his hand on the doorknob.

"I love you, Desmon."

He stopped in his tracks and hesitated to open the door. He stood for a moment and looked straight ahead. "I...I didn't realize until today how much I love you too." He opened the door and walked out.

My emotions almost got the best of me, so I tightened my eyes to keep the water from flowing. I was so happy to hear his words, and excited, I went back into the kitchen to mess with Anna.

She was cutting up some lettuce to make a salad.

"Are you still hungry," I said, wrapping my arms around her.

She cut her eyes at me. "Starving."

"Girl, I got something that will fill you up!"

"I was wondering when you were going to feed me. I've been starving for a very long time."

"I almost hate to ask, but do we have to wait until the boys get back and get settled for the night?"

"Of course. You know I wouldn't want them to hear you screaming like a baby, would I?"

I laughed and pinched Anna on her butt. I couldn't wait until tonight, and it was evident that Anna couldn't either.

It was almost midnight and Antonio and Desmon were still up messing around. Michelle and Gabrielle had come over and you could hear them in Desmon's room laughing and making much noise. Anna and me lay on the couch in the living room, while drinking shots of Vodka and messing around with each other under the cover so no one could see.

Anna was by no means a drinker. We'd played a trivia game and every time she or I didn't get the question right, we had to down a shot of Vodka. She was blasted and giggled while she rubbed on me from underneath the cover.

"You need to cool out," I said, smiling, but at the same time enjoying it.

"I am cool. I just feel sooo dizzy."

"You ain't gone throw up, are you?"

"How am I supposed to know?" She rose up off me and stumbled a bit. She held the shot glass in her hand and downed the last shot of Vodka. She then slammed the glass on the table and smacked her hands together.

"I betcha didn't think I could handle that, did cha?" she slurred.

I saw Anna about to fall, so I jumped up from the couch and flipped her over my shoulder. She laughed as I carried her to the bedroom. After entering the room, I use my foot to kick the door shut. I tossed Anna on the bed and she sat up on her elbows.

She moved her long hair away from her face. "You did this to me on purpose, didn't you? Jussst so you could take advantage of me?"

"Uh-huh?" I said, removing my sweat pants. Afterwards, I pulled my shirt over my head.

"You are going to tear it up to...tonight, aren't cha?"

"Uh-huh? And, so are you." I crawled my way on top of her. I sucked in Anna's lips with my mouth and both of our breaths reeked of alcohol. I was only tipsy, but I could tell she was messed up by how loose she was. The moment I found my way between her legs, she had her hands on my ass and gripped it tight. She removed her clothes within seconds and before I could dish out any foreplay, she had put my long awaited dick inside of her.

"Ahh, easy," she moaned, loudly, as we moved at a semi-fast pace. While still on her elbows, she dropped her head back as I manipulated her nipples with the tip of my tongue. "Ummm, I love this...this dick inside of me. But," she brought her head forward and looked at me. My strokes came to a halt.

"But, what?" I said.

"I'm not in the mood to make love tonight. I...I thought we were gonna fuck each other."

"So, you wanna fuck," I said, already turning her over. She hung halfway off the bed on her stomach and I slid down behind her.

"Uh-huh? That's what I wanna do," she loudly moaned as I took a hard pound inside of her. My body slapped against her ass and made loud noises. She backed her butt against me and loudly talked dirty.

"Shhh," I said, covering her mouth. I was no doubt turned on by her words, but I didn't want anyone to hear us. She moved her face away from my hand and sucked in her bottom lip. "Ummm," she said, trying to fight back her words. I laid my back on the floor and Anna scooted back with me. Her back faced me, as she placed her hands on the bed and worked her lower body to ride me. She jolted down hard on my thang, so hard that it kind of hurt. The loud sound of our body's smacking together aroused me even more. And, the wetter her insides got, the sound of her juices was enough to make me go crazy.

I didn't want to be the first one to throw in the towel, but I was so damn ready to come. I quickly sat up and held Anna tightly so she wouldn't move.

I then placed my head against her back. "Hold on for a minute." She ignored me and continued to slide herself up and down on me. And then, in a circular motion. Feeling myself about to explode, I leaned her over to the side. I placed one of her legs high on my shoulder, and no doubt, took advantage of the situation. I fucked her as well as I could while we were both now stretched out on the floor.

"I'm coming with you, baby," she screamed, as she felt my goods throbbing inside of her.

"Then, come on, baby. And make it good."

Soon, we released our energy together and were still laid on the floor while taking deep breaths.

Anna reached for a towel and wiped it between her legs. She then crawled over to me, lifted her thigh over my face and straddled it. She pressed her coochie against my lips and leaned forward on her hands. No hesitation on my part, my tongue left my mouth and attached itself against her walls. I used my index finger to go up inside of her and my thumb to rub against her clit. Baby girl was on fire! You'd a thought she was auditioning for porn by how quickly she moved her body and the way she screamed out again after she came. I was overly pleased with her performance and wasn't quite ready to call it a night. Neither was she, so she lowered herself and held my goods in her hands. She took a few licks around my thang, but when she took all of it into her mouth, she gagged. She attempted again, and that's when I realized it was time to call it a night. I moved aside as she placed her hand over her mouth.

"Baby, you ain't getting ready to throw up, are you?"

She nodded and hurried off to the bathroom. She didn't even have time to close the door, but I heard the puke hit the toilet. That just ruined the whole night for me. I stood up and walked to the bathroom where she sat on the floor, while holding her stomach.

"I am so embarrassed," she said covering her mouth again. She let loose in the toilet again, and I went to the tub and ran some water. I wet several towels in the sink and when she was finished, I flushed the toilet and picked her up from the floor. I sat down in the tub and laid her body on top of mine. I then placed the rags on her forehead and before I could shut the water off, Anna had passed completely out.

NO MORE LIES

By morning, I was the only one in the house who was up by eleven o'clock. Michelle and Gabrielle didn't leave until three in the morning and Antonio and Desmon had crashed out in the living room after playing a game of cards.

As for Anna, I didn't expect her to get up anytime soon. After I washed her up in the tub, I carried her to the bed and tucked her in. She was on hit last night. I hated to get her messed up like that, but I wanted to know how freaky she could get. I didn't expect her to consume as much alcohol as she did, and it messed me up how she was unable to keep herself under control.

Today, though, I had some serious decisions to make. My departure from St. Louis was coming soon, but I was feeling a bit uneasy about my plans with Rufus. I knew if I followed through with our plan, all of our lives would be in jeopardy. On top of that, there wasn't no guarantee that Desmon, Antonio or Anna would move to L.A. with me. I also knew I couldn't stay in St. Louis. Dominique's boys would definitely find out where I lived and Dwayne's crew might come after me too. Rufus underestimated all of them, but I knew what it meant to lose a partna. That's why a huge part of me didn't want to take the risk. It wasn't like I could call off the hit because if I did, I'd give them to opportunity to come after me before I got to them.

Either way, these were decisions I hated to make. Even though Rufus and my other partnas from L.A. were gonna take care of everything, it was gonna be hard to sit back and wait until it was all finished.

As for holding back on the love ones in my life, I wasn't going to. I planned to tell Anna my every move today, and I prepared to tell Desmon about us moving to L.A. soon as well. I knew neither of them would be excited, but I'd rather get it over with now, rather than later. That way, when the time came for us to jet, there wasn't gonna be any problems.

Desmon and Antonio woke up around two o'clock because of the vacuum cleaner I used to vacuum the carpet. They had popcorn and chips spread out on the floor and I knew if I didn't make it my business to clean it up, neither were they.

Desmon sat up first and stretched his arms, and then Antonio lifted his head from the arm of the chair. Desmon mouthed something, but I couldn't hear because the vacuum cleaner was too loud. I turned it off so I could hear him.

"What you'd say?" I asked.

"I said, why you trying to wake us up?"

"Because it's after two o'clock and it's time to get up."

"Is it that late?" Antonio asked. He looked at the clock on the wall to verify the time. He then stood up and stretched his arms. "I gotta go. I promised Michelle I'd be at her track meet today." He looked at Desmon. "Are you coming with me?"

"I guess, since I ain't got nothing else to do. I really need to go back to sleep, though."

"More sleep ain't what you need," I intervened.

"And why not?"

"Because you sleep too much as it is."

"Please. With all that action going on in your room last night, who could sleep through that?"

Now, I was beyond embarrassed. I looked at Antonio. "Man, I'm sorry. It had been a while and—

"Hey, no need to explain nothing to me. I know how it is."

"I don't," Desmon, said. "All that moaning and groaning, hollering and screaming didn't make no sense. Don't you know by now how to be quiet," he said, lowering his voice.

"I was quiet. You didn't hear me not one time. That was Anna."

"Man, please. She was out there, but you were out there too! You don't want me to repeat what you said, do you?"

I smiled. "Why don't y'all gone and get out of here. Y'all shouldn't even be in grown folks business like that."

"When you put us in it, we can't help it. Next time, if the p" Desmon cleared his throat, "if it's that good to you, just keep it to yourself."

Just then, Anna slowly walked into the living room, while holding her forehead. Her hair was in a mess and she had on my black Bob Marley t-shirt and some pink slippers with bunny ears. Desmon and Antonio turned to look at her.

"What?" she said in a grouchy voice. "What y'all looking at?"

211

We all just stared at her and smiled. Then, Desmon and Antonio giggled and left the room.

"What they laughing at?" she said, walking towards me. She stood on the tips of her toes and gave me a kiss.

"They just being silly, that's all."

"I feel miserable," she said cuddling up with herself and a pillow on the couch. "Why'd you let me drink that much?"

"I didn't let you do nothing. You did it yourself."

"Well, you didn't stop me."

"No, I didn't. But I'm glad that I didn't."

"Why?"

"Do you have any idea what you put on me last night?"

"We do," Antonio and Desmon said in synch as they walked to the door. They laughed and closed the door behind them. I looked out the window and saw that they were headed towards the bus stop to catch a ride.

Anna slowly sat up. "Did I do something I didn't have no business doing? I hope I didn't embarrass myself in front of Antonio and Desmon."

"Just put it like this, if you can't remember, then you missed out. And for the record, we both embarrassed ourselves in front of them."

She pulled her hair back and quickly turned around with a serious face. "Baby, what did we do?"

"You got sloppy drunk, got naked, and then, came over to me and dropped to your knees. You gave me some head, and then I leaned you over the couch and dug into you from behind. During the process, the boys came in and busted us."

Her eyes got wider as I spoke. "Uh-uh, quit lying," she said.

"Would I lie to you?"

"Yes. Especially, since I got a feeling you'd like for that encounter to take place now."

"It wouldn't hurt. Especially since you can't remember what took place last night."

Other than getting drunk, Anna got up and did just as I had implied. As I worked her from behind, I'll be damned if what I'd implied didn't become a reality. Anna and me quickly dropped to the floor and I slid the cover off the couch that Desmon used to cover up last night. I put the cover over our bodies and pretended to be talking to Anna as we lay on the floor.

Desmon stepped around to the back of the couch and cleared his throat.

"We missed the bus. I was wondering if I could use your car."

I turned my head slightly to the side. "The keys on my dresser. And, don't forget to put some gas in there."

"I ain't got no money. You wanna get up and give me some?" I looked down at Anna who had already covered her face from embarrassment. I knew if I got off the floor, Desmon would see that my shorts were down.

"Don't worry about the gas. I'll take care of it later."

He smiled and shook his head. "That's a shame. Y'all couldn't wait until we—

"Desmon, goodbye," I yelled.

He ran off and closed the door behind him. Anna and me broke off a quickie and called it quits.

By early evening, we got bored from being around the house so we caught the bus to the movies. Anna knew I'd attempted to keep her inside because I wanted to protect her as much as I could. She insisted whatever was going to happen, would happen, and said there was nothing either of us could do if it did. I agreed, but the memory of the last time we went out together stuck with me.

The movie was over about eight o'clock, so we stopped by *Outback Steakhouse* to get our grub on. After we ate, we headed back to the house. It was another beautiful evening, as the sun had gone down and the streets were filled with joggers, bikers and walkers. When we got inside the house, Desmon had left me a note on the table with my keys that said he and Antonio would be back later. He claimed they were going to a party and said he'd call me later if he didn't make it in tonight.

More than anything, I was glad that he was getting back to normal. Anna was right about him being strong, but a huge part of me already knew that.

I was ready to have my discussion with Anna, so I waited until she came out of the bedroom from changing her clothes. I did what I knew best and rolled up and joint, then took a few hits from it. I'd set the marijuana aside for a bit, as I tried to set a good example for Desmon. But, I couldn't resist the fact that it made me relax each and every time I felt under pressure.

By the time Anna came in, I was sucking in the last tip of the joint. She didn't say nothing to me, but just looked and rolled her eyes. I placed the tip in the ashtray, and then slid my hand down inside my pants and held my dick.

"I was just thinking," I said.

"Hell, no!" she responded. "I'm not going to have sex with you every day, Kiley. My body will not allow me to do it so, I'm sorry." She sat on the couch next to me.

"Did I ask you for some sex?"

"I assumed since you got your hand over your thing like that, you wanted—

"Your assumption was incorrect. My *thing* just jumped when you came into the room and I had to calm it down."

"You're so silly," she laughed, and then, laid her head on my chest. I wrapped my arm around her and squeezed her thigh.

"You got some small thighs," I said. I then swayed my hand back to her butt. "But, a nice butt."

She snickered. "Thanks. But, I thought you said earlier you wanted to talk to me about something. You wouldn't be beating around the bush, would you?"

"Just a lil bit. But, I'm getting to it."

Anna waited for me to get to it and shortly after, I did.

"Baby, I promised myself I wouldn't keep nothing else from you. I wanted to let you know that in a few more weeks, some shit gone go down that's gonna require me to move back to L.A."

Anna had already lifted her head off my chest before I could get another word out. "Kiley, don't put yourself in harms way if you don't have to. Just let what happened go. We'll be okay."

"I'm afraid not. There's some rumors circulating and I have to remain on top of things. If I don't, it's gonna bring hella trouble for me."

"What's about to go down?" I could tell she was getting angry.

"Look, don't go getting all upset. I got this all worked out, and trust me, everything is gonna be okay."

"You still haven't said what's gonna go down."

214

"Basically, some people gone get hurt. Now, I'm not gone pull the trigger myself, but—

Anna eased off the couch. "This is too much, Kiley. Do you realize how dangerous this game is that you're playing?"

"It's not a game. If I don't go after them, then they gone come after me. I can't let that happen."

"Who are you talking about—?

"Dominique and Dwayne."

"Who in the hell is Dwayne?"

"Jada's husband."

Anna really got mad. She gritted her teeth as she spoke. "You mean to tell me, that you are going to have Jada's husband killed? Why? So you can be with her? Are you that fucking jealous—

I grabbed her hand, as she stood in front of me. "Baby, calm down. It ain't even like that. Him and I had a disagreement—

"Over...let me guess, Jada? Right?"

She was right, but I really didn't want to tell her. "We got into a bit of a dispute because he saw Jada and me together. I broke his arm, and he's been looking for me."

Anna threw her hands up in the air. "Because you were with Jada, huh? Was this the day you fucked her, or have you been with her since then?"

"You know I haven't been with her since then. I thought you'd understand—

"Well, you were wrong! I don't understand none of this shit! You expect me to sit back and wait until you have your ex-freaking girlfriend's husband killed, and then fly off into the night with you like you're a damn prince charming! It doesn't work like that Kiley! What about us! Why can't we just live a normal and peaceful happy fucking life together!"

Knowing that she was upset, I stood up and tried to hold her. She snatched away. "We will be happy together, baby. Once all this mess is done with, we're moving to L.A. Rufus already go—

"Fuck a Rufus! He's an animal who doesn't give a damn about the human life! I can tell that just by looking at him!"

"You gone have to calm down," I said, getting angry myself. "Now, I was nice enough to tell you what's gonna go down. I didn't have to tell you shit, but I did! The choice is yours, baby. Either you gone roll with me, or get left behind!"

"What a stupid-ass ultimatum! I guess you're going to give Desmon the same alternative, huh?"

"Desmon ain't got no choice. He's coming with me no matter what."

"That's so damn sad! You're pathetic. I can't believe you would put his life at stake because you're too damn foolish to grow up!"

Before I knew it, I smacked the shit out of Anna. She fell to the floor and held her cheek in disbelief. I kneeled down next to her.

"I'm sorry. I didn't mean to do that."

She shoved me away. "Just get away from me. I hate what you're doing to us and I'm not going anywhere with you."

"Please don't make this hard for me. By asking me to stay, you're asking me to stay here and die. I can't do that, not even for you."

I stepped over Anna and headed towards my room.

"You'll be dead in less than a year," she said. "If you move back to L.A., you'll be dead in a year."

I turned to her. "It's a chance I'm willing to take."

I went into my room and closed the door. I sat on my love sack and propped up my feet on the footrest. I thought more than anything Anna would understand. I was sure Desmon would be the difficult one, but I guess I had my work cut out for me. I wasn't going to change my mind, and again, whoever didn't want to roll with me, then there wasn't shit I could do.

TIME TO GET THE SHOW ON THE ROAD

For the next few weeks, Rufus and me were on the phone twenty-four-seven. I hadn't talked to Desmon about my plans, but I prepared myself to do so when he got home from school. I felt as if he'd already been through enough with Ginger's death, so I wanted to wait for as long as I could to break the news to him about moving.

As for Anna, she remained pissed. She hadn't slept one night in bed with me since then and she'd been away from the house quite often. I was hurt, but she didn't realize that this was the nature of my business. She made me choose and I had to choose survival over her.

When Desmon got home from school, I let him get settled, and then, knocked on his bedroom door that was already open. He looked up and bounced his head to the music he had playing in his ear. He had a black stocking cap on his head and his baseball cap was backwards. His white ribbed oversized long t-shirt was sparkling clean and he looked quite like a gangsta with his baggy jeans that hung low on his hips. He made a knocking sound with his mouth as he continued to move his head to the music. When he saw that I wanted to talk, he turned the music down and took the earpiece out.

"I know you want to talk about something because I can tell it in your eyes. Can I do my sit-ups first, though?"

"Yeah, come on. I'll do 'em with you."

I got on the floor next to Desmon and we both lay on our backs. He looked over at me.

"Are you ready?" he said.

"Hold up," I said, and then pulled my shirt over my head. "Now I'm ready."

Desmon pulled his shirt over his head too and then laid flat on his back. "I'm ready too. How many we gone do?"

"Five hundred. First, we gone pull up to the right side, then to the middle, and then to the left side."

"Okay, cool," he said, looking over at me. "You ready?"

"Yep."

We started our sit-ups and did them at the same rhythm. I was amazed at how well Desmon was in shape and he was able to keep up with me until we reached two hundred and twenty-five. He slowed up a bit and I slowed down with him.

"Come on," I said. "Work them abs."

"How do you do this?" he strained. He slowed down even more and then laid flat on his back. "I can't do no more. That's it for me."

I laid back and we both took quick short breaths in and out. Sweat dripped from our bodies, and even though I felt good about being in better shape than he was, I kept the gloating to myself.

"So, what you want to talk about," he asked while still on his back.

"About moving."

He looked over at me. "Moving where?"

"Back to my hometown, L.A."

"Are you serious?"

"Yeah, man. Things getting kind of heated around here. I think it's time that I...we made a move."

"What you mean by heated? Everything been going cool, ain't it?"

"So far. But some things are gonna transpire soon. I had some issues with the brothas who jumped on me at the racetrack."

"How you got issues with them and they dead?"

"Well, one of them survived. Besides, your daddy ain't well liked in the Lou."

"What about school? What I'm gone do about school?"

"You can go to school in L.A. You only got a month left before the end of the year and I want you to see if you can take your finals a lil early."

"Umm...maybe. But, uh, what about Anna? Have you told her yet?"

"Yeah. If you haven't noticed, that's why she ain't been talking to me."

"So, what you gone do?"

"I ain't gone do nothing. If she don't want to go then I ain't got no choice but to leave her. I...we gotta get out of here."

"I'll talk to her."

"So, does that mean you don't have a problem with leaving?"

"Hell, naw. I would love to move to L.A. I just won't see my Gabrielle anymore, but too bad."

"What about Antonio?"

"If Anna go, he'll go. She'll change her mind."

"I wouldn't count on it. Something tells me that she's already made up her mind."

"Like I said, I'm going. I don't care who else go, but I'm going."

I held my hand out for Desmon's and he slammed his hand against mine. I was now more than relieved and my move was officially confirmed.

Anna had been listening closely in to my conversations with Rufus. She knew more than anybody that the big hit was expected to go down in less than 72 hours. Rufus and his connections were already at a hotel in the Lou setting shit up. We'd planned to stay as far away from each other as possible so I attempted not to see him and he made no attempts to see me.

I'd ended my call with him and was lying on the bed thinking about the long drive I had ahead of me. I'd already pretty much cleared out the house and gave most of my belongings to Michelle's mom who had asked for just about everything.

The other day, Desmon pleaded with Anna to go. He tried to explain to her how happy we'd all be together, but she just wouldn't listen. When she raised her voice at him, I got pissed and she got even more pissed at me for yelling at her again. She'd made many threats about leaving, but it wasn't until she stood in front of me with her bags packed that I actually believed her.

"I think I got everything," she said, as she leaned against the wall in my room. "In the meantime, if there is anything I can do to stop you from doing this, please let me know. I'm dying to stop this whole damn charade—

"Face it, baby, it's a done deal. Now, you need to stop getting upset and accept this situation for what it is. Time is running out and if you're going to leave me, then you need to go ahead and leave me now."

She walked up to me and looked so beautiful that I had to turn my head away. "Would you please just listen to me for one damn time in your life? Call whatever it is off with Rufus. Tell him you don't want no part of it, and let's just move further away from everybody."

"Have you not listened to anything I've said, Anna?"

"But, you're wrong, Kiley. You're going about this the wrong way. Don't you see?"

"Yes. I see that you need to get yourself together. I'm not gonna change my mind, au-ight!"

She turned my face to look at her. "Do you love me?" I didn't respond and she yelled it again.

"Yes, I love you. But, what does that have to do with anything?"

"Then you owe it to us to do the right thing."

I grabbed her shoulders. "I'm gone say this one more time. I'm not changing my mind! I love you and I'm gone do my best to protect you. If you don't want me to, then leave! I'll make it without you!"

She stepped backwards and took a hard swallow. She picked up her suitcase and made her way to the door. I made my way to the window and looked out. My eyes watered and I could clearly see her vision through the glass as she stopped and turned her head.

"If you won't change your mind for me, then how about for us?" she said.

I kept quiet for a bit and then responded. "No, baby. Not even for us."

After that, she left. I heard the front door slam hard and felt no need to go after her. To me, life was about making choices. Some good, some bad and some ugly. I hated more than anything that the relationship between us had to end the way it did.

Rufus called for the last time and all he said was for me to tune in to the news. I'd been on a drinking and smoking blunts binge since Anna left me, so I was a bit messed up by the time the news reporter came in with breaking news. There appeared to be two explosions. One on the city's Northside of St. Louis and the other on the Southside. According to the news reporter, the police said that both incidents were somehow related and more than eleven to fifteen people had been killed. Bottom line, when so many Black men were involved, it had to be drug related. The news reporter used words like: the worst crime ever, deadly attacks, never seen anything like it. Basically, you'd of thought St. Louis was at war. Then again, I guess we were. I knew if I didn't hurry up and get the fuck out of here, a war would surely follow.

As I continued to gaze at the TV, it was obvious that Rufus and his connections tore up some shit. Fires burned everywhere and when they started to show the faces of some of those who had been killed, the first face they showed was Dominique. The police referred to him as a long time drug lord that had corrupted the streets of the city for many many years. They talked about the large amounts of drugs and money found and showed faces of his many accomplices. When they showed Dwayne's face, they announced him as being deceased as well. I wasn't sure if they had the facts straight or not, but the news reporter made it out to be gang related, drug related, thug related, and anything else they could find to downgrade Black men even more. The people they interviewed on the TV didn't help the situation either. They couldn't even talk right and had no vital information to assist the police in determining who was responsible.

Desmon knew I was under a lot of pressure so he stayed in his room and watched the news from there. He'd watch me go through my hurt from Anna leaving me, and he knew that even though I didn't want to be a part of what went down, I was basically left with no choice. Especially since these fools had plotted against my life. He walked into the living room as I continued to flip through the channels.

"So, I see you've been tuned in already," he said.

"Yeah. I'm sorry that you gotta see—

"Don't even apologize, man. I just be glad when it's all over with."

I looked up at him. "You 'bout ready?"

"Naw, the question is, are you ready?"

"I'm as ready as I'm gone ever be."

"Au-ight then, let's go."

Since our bags were already packed and in the car, I got up and we left the house. We got into the car and just a slight bit paranoid; I hesitated to turn the ignition. When I did, everything was cool. I knew my days of paranoia would last for some time, but once my mind got settled, I expected to be back to normal soon.

Hungry from all the blunts I'd smoked, I asked Desmon if he wanted to stop for something to eat. He said that was cool with him so we stopped at a nearby Waffle joint to get our grub on.

At this point, I guess I was happy. I was happy to have my son with me for the rest of my life and it really couldn't get any better than that. I wished like hell Anna had changed her mind about coming with me because that would have made my life so much more complete. No doubt, she was one of the best things that ever happened to me. I hated to lose her the way I did, but I knew more than anything that nothing in life is ever promised.

Desmon and me quickly got our grub on. As we sat at the table to eat, my cell phone rang and unbelievably it was Jada. She'd called the house to distract Anna a few times after our incident, but when I threatened to fuck her up, that's when she stopped. I answered my phone and all I could hear were her cries coming through the phone.

"Hello," I said, pretending as if I didn't know it was her.

"Kiley," she screamed. "Did you have anything to do with what happened to my husband?"

"Calm down, baby." I tried to be polite. "Naw…wha…what happened to him?"

"He's dead! My husband is dead!"

"Your husband? I thought y'all got divorced?"

She sniffed. "We did. But, I still considered him my husband."

"Aw, I didn't know, but I'm sorry to hear that. I hope everything work out for you, though. As for me doing something to him, you know that's crazy. Why would I want to do something to that man? I ain't got no beef with him."

She sniffed again and I could tell she believed me. "Will you come see me soon? I'd really like to see you."

"When?"

"Maybe in a few days after all this stuff calms down."

"I might. I'm having dinner with my son right now, though, so can I call you in a few days? Maybe we can get together then."

"Alright. Don't forget."

"I promise I won't."

I hung up.

If Jada didn't already know one thing about me, she knew that many times my promises weren't worth a damn.

Desmon and me finished up and left. He complained about being chilly, so I tossed him my leather jacket to put on. He threw it over his back and we got inside of the car. He reached in my pockets to warm his hands, and when he pulled them out, he pulled out the picture I had of Myles Stein. He looked at it.

"Say, man," he said. "Who is this?"

I'd forgotten I put the picture in my pocket to hide it. I stuttered a bit and then asked Desmon if I could see it. I looked hard at the picture and passed it back to him.

"That's, uh, one of my boys from way back when. Myles."

"Aw," he said, continuing to study the picture. "He kind of look like family. Especially, all up in here." Desmon circled his hands around Myles upper face.

"Fool, don't nobody look like me but you."

"You mean...you look like me. I don't look like you, you look like me."

"I was born first so you look like me. So there."

"Okay, but even though I might look like you, I don't act like you."

"Good. I'm glad because I don't want you to be like me. I never wanted you to be like me."

"And, I don't want to be like you either," we both said and laughed together.

I hit the nearest highway to Los Angeles, California and told Desmon to blow the picture of Myles out of the window. He did just that, and my life as it was today, couldn't have been any better.

THE FINAL DESTINATION

DESMON

For at least the next five years, I'll sum up Kiley's and my life in three short words: OFF THE CHAIN! The moment we arrived in L.A. it was the bomb. Rufus had everything set out for us: houses, cars, money, money and mo money. We didn't want for a damn thing and I couldn't understand how or why Kiley wanted to stay away from so much love. For him, though, it wasn't so much of the money he enjoyed, but the thrill of being back at home with his partnas turned him into a completely different man. One would have thought that L.A. would've destroyed him, but it didn't. It gave him peace, and that allowed our relationship to get stronger and stronger each day.

At first, sometimes he seemed a lil homesick. I knew it was because of him missing Anna, but he soon made that an issue of his past. He'd hooked up with several drop dead, gorgeous ladies from time to time that I was sure he'd liked. Even ole Jada came to L.A. a few times to visit, but after realizing neither of them could feel Anna's shoes, he went back to the Lou to get her. He'd disappeared for two whole weeks and when he got back, she was with him. Eventually, she moved here with us and they became husband and wife. The day they got married, I think he was happier than I'd ever saw him in my entire lifetime. Antonio, though, he came for the wedding, but he made his way back to the Lou. He and Michelle got married right after high school, and sooner than later, had a baby on the way. We kept in touch all the time and he'd come down to visit on occasion.

Me, well, I sort of made a few mistakes. No doubt, my football career was on the rise, however, L.A. had so much going on that sometimes I didn't know whether I was coming or going. My downfalls were the clubs and the ladies. Kiley all ways said the Abrams men were weak when it came to women and he sure as hell didn't lie. I couldn't control my sexual appetite for them, and because I couldn't, I too had a baby my last year in high school. Kiley was furious with me because he wanted me to be different. He griped over and over about me not focusing on the important things in life and tried to encourage me to change my life around.

One day, though, his advice sunk in. That wasn't until the day he died. I'd been out for two days running the streets and when I walked into the house and called his name, Anna told me to be quiet because he was still in bed asleep. She was in the kitchen cooking and since I wanted to tease him about his long lecture, about my life, the night before, I went into his room to do just that. I'd noticed a grin on his face, so I hit him with a pillow to wake him. He didn't move. I'd panicked and thought about his choice of words the night before: life is too short, you reap what you sew, nothing in life is promised, live for today and not for tomorrow. Lastly, he told me he loved me. Not wanting my friends around me to hear me say, "I love you too" in return, I hesitated. He said it again, and embarrassed, I returned the love. They joked with me about it, but knowing that those words were the last words I'd spoken to him, I couldn't be mad. The funny thing about it all, was, I think he knew his day was coming. He'd complained about chest pains, but we all didn't think much of it. It was confirmed that a heart attack had taken him away during his sleep. I'm sure, he wouldn't have wanted to go any other way.

For his home going celebration to join Papa Abrams, Kareem, Quincy and Rufus, who had been gunned down a little over a year before Kiley died, Anna and me had his body cremated as he'd requested. His ashes stayed at his home in L.A. and remained in the urn he'd gotten from London, England while on his honeymoon.

Less than a week after he passed away, I continued to play football for *UCLA*. Even though I had scholarships lined up from the east to the west coast, Kiley encouraged me to stay in L.A. and take care of my son. At first, I was being selfish and thought only of myself. Then, he reminded me of what life could be like for a son without his father, or for that matter, without his mother. Thinking hard, I decided to accept *UCLA's* scholarship. And, as I sit in my chair thinking hard about my father, I wished like hell he could be here to share this moment with me. Moreso, I wanted him to see this new legacy he'd help me create for the future Abrams men.

I nervously twirled my thumbs together and sat with my elbows resting on my knees. I was suited up in a black *Gucci* suit and took a quick glance over at my wife, Alexandria, and my son who sat between her and Anna at the round elegantly decorated table. Alexandria could see the tears welling up in my eyes and she reached over and kissed my cheek. When they called my name to accept the Heisman Trophy Award, I stood up and the applause drowned out my ears. Every thing moved in slow motion as I made my way to the podium to give my speech. I waved at the crowd, and the flashing lights from all of the cameras, along with the tears pouring profusely down my face, made it difficult for me to see. For, nobody knew what I'd been through to get to this point, but me. I gradually shook the presenter's hand and he placed the trophy in mine so I could hold it. Before saying anything, I dropped to one knee, and placed my lips on the trophy. I looked up and held my arm up as high as it could go.

"This is for you!" I yelled out loudly. "I love you, Daddy, this...this is for you!"

Brenda M. Hampton

Printed in the United States
59721LVS00005B/41